W9-CKT-145

KATI, CARA, AND KT

KATI, CARA, AND KT

CHRONICLING A FAMILY'S LIVES

———◆———

G. W. Wayne

Jefferson Madison
Regional Library
Charlottesville, Virginia

WITHDRAWN

30858 0503

Greater soul has no one for another than that she should be her sister's voice.
Blessed be.

A reflection on John 15:13.

Although inspired by historical events and people, the characters and occurrences depicted in this novel are fictional. Any resemblances to actual persons and places are coincidental.

© 2017 G. W. Wayne
All rights reserved.

ISBN-13: 9780692982754
ISBN-10: 0692982752
Library of Congress Control Number: 2017917494
G. W. Wayne, Palmyra, VA

To I. and M.

Thanks to Helen for editorial eyes and Tony for encouragement. Thanks to Marilyn, first reader and keeper of the files. Thanks to Olivia for her web mastery.

KT to Margee 743-821-1922
OMG Momz makin me help clean attic. Durt n dust. Gonna take 4ever.
Txt u l8r. Luv u.
i no. i no. Liv home freebz.

Nov. 14.

KT to Margee 743-821-1922
Sorri. Took loooooong time clean'n. still sum 2 go. herd ur txtz hit.
W8td. til I wuz dun. 2 much grot. C u tmrw? Found old trunk. Keepn it.
Oold binder in it. Lookz like book. Wanna go NYC tmrw? Txt me plz.
Tird, tird, tird, napz! No skoolwork til tmrw. Get w8std? Plz say yes, k?

Nov. 14.

Excerpts from the Diary of Kati Krieger nee Scheu, with Commentary.
As translated from the German by her granddaughter, Cara Krieger
Maurer.
Introduction: September 1983.

One day, a long time ago, when I was about ten, I came downstairs to our
dining room in the old Brooklyn brownstone on Prospect Park West. It
must have been about 1928. The Crash had not occurred yet; we were
still living well, with the fluffy white lace curtains I liked to hide behind
rippling languidly against the green, tufted backs of the heavy mahog-
any dining-room chairs. Mom sat at the head of the table, a sheet over
the thick, polished wood.

I walked up quietly behind her. It must have been Saturday. Weekdays
I would have been in school. Sunday, the table would have been set for
dinner. I had been playing alone upstairs with the Raggedy Ann doll
Mom had sewn together for me the previous Christmas. Bored, I had
left her alone with her imaginary tea. Little could I have imagined we
would soon be a raggedy family, down to imagined tea and patched
pants and skirts like my doll. I still have that doll.

Anyhow, it was raining outside. It was late spring, or perhaps early
summer. Cars passed by out on the avenue, drifting along the edge

1

of Prospect Park, droning along in that muffled sound traffic makes through the moist haze of gentle rain. It was warm enough to open all the dining-room windows facing the street, but not so warm that I remember the air feeling uncomfortably humid, or that I was sweating. The chandelier overhead cast its light down onto the table, its many arms spreading gossamer shadows across the papers and photographs Mom had spread over the pale sheet on top of the heavy dark table.

My left foot hit a box as I approached Mom. She looked over at me and smiled; she then turned back to the many papers in front of her. They smelled old to me. They had the irritation of our attic: dusty and making my nose itch, just as the boxes of decorations did each late December when we decorated our Christmas tree, those boxes lying about the foot of the pungent, supple fir as we dangled gold and shiny scarlet balls from its many branches.

I looked down at my foot and saw a deep, wide wooden box, raw on the inside. I began to reach down to touch it.

"Careful, Cara," Mom said. "It's splintery."

I drew back and circled behind the chair to stand at Mom's other side, unaffronted by the intrusive box. "What is it?" I asked.

"It's Grandma Kati's," said Mom. "She told me to throw it out. She's not feeling well."

Grandma Kati had moved several years before to be with my Uncle Rudolph and Aunt Janine in Miami. She had begun to get forgetful, spending days sitting in our house, and then one day she was found out in the park and had been brought back by a policeman. Uncle Ru and Aunt Jan had no children and had taken her to be with them. She would live four more years. Occasionally, Mom would call Miami and speak to Grandma Kati, but I never saw her after she had left.

"Are you going to do that?" I asked.

"What, Carri?"

"Throw it all away?" I had spied a tinted photograph of an older woman in an oval frame. She faced right, gazing off calmly and proudly, with the hint of a smile, just a hint, keeping her face attractive. Her hair, auburn and stylishly set with a deep-yellow ribbon woven carefully through it behind her ears, had a modest forehead curl stopping about an inch above her eyebrows. A high-necked, ruffled blouse positioned itself staidly between the light-blue lapels of a coat of some sort. She wore no earrings. Her blue eyes focused far away contently but offered no hint as to what she was contemplating.

"No, of course not!" Mom said.

That photograph, reframed, hangs on the wall before me as I write.

"Is that Gramma Kati?" I asked.

"Yes," Mom said.

"I like it," I said.

"Someday you'll have it," Mom said.

An abrupt breeze from outside lifted the curtains suddenly and rustled some papers strewn across the sheet. One floated close to the edge of the table near me, and I put my hand on it to stop it.

"Careful, hon, they're old."

I looked down at the paper and saw a strange script on yellowed, lined paper. I tried to make out words but could not. Mom gently removed it from me and replaced it back on a pile before her.

"What language is that?" I asked.

"German," Mom said. "I think it's a diary. There are dates across the top. I'm trying to order them."

"What does it say?"

"I don't know."

I nodded. "Will you give me them too?" I asked.

"In time," Mom said and smiled at me. "In time."

It has taken time. Speaking German, being "German" in any way, was difficult and frowned upon in those years. Then Hitler arrived. Finally, in the 1970s, when I had some time, I began to study the language and do my best to understand the handwriting, and the strange, glyphic Fraktur print on many of the old maps and documents that had become mine after Mom had passed in 1968. I took to the old and yellowed, lined papers, now brittle and flaking, and carefully, slowly translated them. Here is what they told me.

Cara Maurer

KT to Margee 743-821-1922
R u awake? i jus got up. Izzit Sunday? soo w8std. OMFG woo wuz that hikkeyhed dweeb at Donalz? did he roofie me? I think my headz gonna xplod ☹ Red sum of that oold binder i txtd u abt sum kinda dairy, oops, diary txt me l8r no, tmrw <3 u

Nov. 16.

Thursday, August 13, 1896.

The newspaper boys along Forty-Ninth Street near the elevated called out today that the heat wave is expected to break tomorrow. I could take it no longer with Tessie and the Flogts in the tenement. It is like trying to sleep in an oven. All over New York people walk slow, work little. I sweat all day, all night. I have always been poor, my handout clothing faded, my dress patched. But until this heat, I had always been clean. Now, I smell like the goats in Misingen. I abhor myself. Head to toe I feel wrapped in a blanket of stink.

The newspaper boys say that many have died, over a thousand. It is likely true. The night before last, trying to sleep in Tessie's kitchen, in her top-floor apartment, the ceiling above me cracked and groaned as Tessie's neighbors rolled and shifted on the gritty tar-paper roof. I could hear them sigh and the children whimper. Many of the tenement went up there. I had tried it too. The air was just as thick. Cooler a bit, but loud and thick with hopeless people. Thicker than steerage.

So I went to the Pond last night. My favorite place in this merciless city during the day. The one just at the south end of Central Park. There were police walking about who had been stationed there to keep us out at night. But I sneaked in! Between two patrols. I felt back at home, back in Misingen, at farmer Gunder's watering pond just along the Castle Road near his wheat fields. There were more than a few others who had ducked in. I shuffled slowly down to the lip of the Pond. I was already barefoot, shoes in hand, having slipped them off where the street stops and this little paradise starts.

That we cannot enjoy the relief of the park! I guess we are too poor for its mercy. New York does not believe in the Bible. The police, the factorymen, even our own who have scratched out a little reward from this awful hell. They all think they can get through the eye of the needle.

I lay down there, at the water's edge. I let my feet slip into the water. It felt so good, tickling my ankles. My whole body seemed to cool. I looked up, but the sky was sullen and hazy. No stars. Still, I imagined them as I had seen them in Misingen, when Willi and I would lie summer evenings at Gunder's pond. Sometimes a few cows joining to lap the water.

I kicked my heels up lightly in the water, thinking of the sounds the cows made drinking. I giggled for the first time in weeks, no, months. I am sure.

Willi said he would marry me! Way back in Misingen. Way back in 1880.

A policeman came rattling the rushes and twisting his way through the small evergreens at the edge of the Pond. The silhouettes of tenement people rose and left bent and noiseless, crooked in despair, as he passed, coming closer to me.

I got up slowly, balancing my belly as best I could. The constable was close enough to see me in light passing weakly down from the street. He had passed from a stand of silver fir, and the aroma of their broken needles from his course! That full, sharp bliss of evergreen! It came with him. Lingered about him. He looked at me. I turned to struggle up the slight slope to the street.

"No," he said. "Stay," he said, in German. "Bleib mal; I'll go away. Ich gehe jetzt weg."

He disappeared up the slope, shaking his head.

"Thank you," I said. "Danke."

I lowered myself back down. Please let it be a girl, I thought. Still I smelled the comforting waft of the evergreen, and then I imagined the Christmas trees of Misingen. Rich in color. Spare in spotted apples.

I fell asleep. Lessia, if it's a girl, I remember last thinking. Lessia, if it's a girl, never Willi, if it's a boy.

KT to Margee 743-821-1922

No show? Lit boring. "Reformation novels." I spel tht rite? Boorrrrring! Kenni no show ☹ hey, red begning of oold binder. Diariz my grammiz grammi. Like from 1896! 1896!!!! Namz Kati Krieger. I spelt tht rite 2? Dunno. Momz sez Katiz my gr8t gr8t grammi. Kati, u no, KT! Like me! ☺

    No notes frm 2day. Zzzz'd in Lit.

    PS. KT wuz preggy!

Nov. 17.

The heat wave of August 1896 was one of the worst in New York City history. It is estimated over 1,500 citizens died, mostly young, immigrant laborers. This heat wave lasted from August 4 until August 14. It arrived after three years of economic depression. According to accounts of the time, temperatures reached ninety degrees at street level, with humidity at 90 percent and nighttime temperatures only dropping to about seventy. This may not seem so brutal to us today, but at the time, there was no air conditioning, and much of a tenement's air did not circulate. Also, tenements did not have running water, just a single pump in front of or behind the building, near the outhouses. It has been estimated that the temperatures in many of the older, dark tenements, the brick tenements, reached 120 in the top floors.

Many of the poor took to the rooftops at night. Or they lay out on the fire escapes, if a building had a fire escape! Anything to try to catch a puff of moving air. After nearly a week of this, some of the tenement dwellers, dazed and confused, would roll off a rooftop and fall to their deaths in the street or back courtyard. Even children would die this way! Some of the unfortunates would seek relief down at the piers along the East River, if they were close enough, and would roll into the river and drown.

If only the city authorities had allowed them to sleep in the parks, especially Central Park. But that was banned. It was only on the last day, on August 14, that the mayor, William L. Strong, called an emergency meeting. And it was only the police commissioner, Theodore Roosevelt, who led any effective relief efforts. He gave away ice to the tenement poor on the Lower East Side. So Kati would not have enjoyed that relief.

Many of the young men who died were, bluntly, worked to death. They were laborers who worked outdoors Monday through Saturday, in impossible living conditions, often four or more people to a room. They got no sympathy or relief from work; they had bad diets and struggled with dependence on alcohol and no medical care. They were the North's industrial slave labor. Worked to death.

Cara Maurer

KT to Margee 743-821-1922
OMG Nooooo! Im not pregnt! Kati in the bindr wuz! Sorri! Wth Lessia, or not-Willi.

Nov. 17.

Margee to KT 743-765-8040
Lessia? Not-Willi?

Nov. 17.

KT to Margee 743-821-1922
Namz KT, I mean Kati, wantd to name her kid.

Nov. 17.

Margee to KT 743-765-8040
LOL Not-Willi!

Nov. 17.

The type of tenement most common back then was called a "dumbbell" tenement, because of its shape. Kati likely lived in one of these. They were five to seven stories tall. The ground floor would usually have two small shops in the front, with small apartments behind them. There was one dark center hallway. The upper floors had four apartments per floor, four-room apartments in the front, three rooms in the back. Four families per floor, but families often took in boarders and were extended families, like with Kati, as you will read. Each apartment had only one window facing out on a street or a backyard. Windows in the rest of the rooms, if there were windows, opened into an airshaft. Dwellers often threw garbage into the shafts. These apartment rooms were very dark, and there was really no ventilation of which to speak.

Cara Maurer

Thursday, August 20, 1896.

It has been six days since the heat broke. Violently. Toward the evening it broke. Sudden, thick green clouds fell over us from across the North River. Heavy curtains of cooling rain in quick darkness! I did not care that lightning struck all about me and above me. Thunder rattled the cheap glass in the tenement store-fronts. I laughed and moved slowly down the sidewalk on Forty-Seventh Street from the el along Ninth Avenue. Cleansed in the rain, happy in the merciful release of the rain.

Then, Lessia moved in my belly. Moved fiercely. A small hand hard inside me, disturbed by the sound and the coolness abrupt and intrusive. So I moved deliberately to Cousin Tessie's, shuffled off my dripping clothes, toweled myself dry, and held my belly, stroking it slowly to calm her. Talking slowly and softly to her in Tessie's dark, insulated bedroom where the heat still lingered.

I forget now and then, I am two. I am a mother. I need to protect.

Willi had stroked my belly, when it was flat and slim, first after we had lazily ambled together out of Misingen on a Sunday afternoon toward our secret lily pond in a bend off Klingen Brook, over a hill and safely away from the road to Bechingen. He was fifteen; I was fourteen. He had promised to marry me then, and I had believed him.

He was a beautiful boy, then. Summer 1880. Playful breezes tickling his fine, thick auburn hair slowly losing its coif as we embraced and kissed at the pond. Kneeling down. Lying down. Opening my eyes to adore his, blue and looking into mine; running my fingers along his taut, nervous cheek, watching it redden slightly. He had compliant, gentle lips. A firm chin I cupped to bring him to kiss me. We would marry, we promised each other.

Tree pipits. As we moved into each other, they sang out clear and strong in extended loops of sharp, proud melody. No other sounds. Just the tree pipits, until I replaced their trills with my own, to Willi, and to myself. I was so full of love for us then.

A few more exhilarating trysts. Autumn intervened, and winter held us chaste. I did not become pregnant. We waited for spring with a touch here, and a kiss occasionally.

God, let this child be a girl.

I watched the constable lead away Willi to Ludlow Street Jail this afternoon. I had him arrested for breach of promise to marry. I do not think he can make bail. He will stay there. How long I do not know. I do not care.

His hair was dirty. Stringy. Weak and limp. His face was pockmarked and swollen, small veins, purple, twisting across his face. His mouth slanted unevenly across his face, hooking down on the left, lips thin and white. Eyes squeezed back deeply behind puffy mounds of sagging flesh. Did they even see me? Unshaven cheeks.

Sixteen years! He had left in 1881 for America, for New York; his brother was already there. Opportunity and prospects. I promised to wait for him, and he promised to send for me.

He did, finally, in 1887. But only enough for a steerage berth out of Bremerhaven.

And then seeing him in his brother's tenement. Already wearing down from the bondage of this city.

But I had faith in the Willi I had loved so long ago. The Willi who had stroked my belly, when it was flat and slim, first after we had lazily ambled together out of Misingen on a Sunday afternoon toward our secret lily pond in a bend off Klingen Brook, over a hill and safely away from the road to Bechingen. When he was fifteen; when I was fourteen. When he had promised to marry me, and I had believed him.

I held out for him to return to that young man. I thought I might help him. So I ignored the changes, his roughness, his anger, and the chains this ugly city wraps around its young immigrant men. The hours of work, the insulting pay. Bad water. Infested slop housing. Cholera. Dysentery.

God damn New York City. Damn you, Willi Rau!

I thought I could help him. Restore him. Nine years of patience. Alcohol wilts the man. But I persisted, blinded by self-doubt in my own fertility as much as the hubris that I could change anyone's character. Sharing squalor and a top floor, back apartment tenement. Fairy tales!

Only bruises and, now, a fatherless child. A mother a fool for thinking the promise of a family would resurrect the promise to marry.
Sixteen years!
Please, please let this child be Lessia.
I am thirty years old!

The date of promise to marry indicates Kati and Willi were enamored of each other within the bounds of German law regarding contractual obligation. The age of consent in Germany at the time was fourteen. I was able to find an article supporting Kati's assertion she had Rau arrested in the August 21 edition of the *New York American*, on page 41:

"Willi Rau, of 224 West 49th Street, was arrested yesterday on an order signed by Justice O'Dwyer in the City Court. The order was obtained by O'Malley and Wilson in behalf of Kati Scheu. Miss Scheu is about to sue Rau for breach of promise to marry. She says he promised to marry her repeatedly, beginning on August 24, 1880, and until several months ago, and that he failed to keep his promise. He was locked up in Ludlow Street Jail in default of $200 bail."

Kati took advantage of the law of the time. Breach of promise to marry is a civil tort in contract law. It has been abolished in many of the states. In New York, the tort per se was eliminated in 1935. The original intent of the tort involved the societal belief of a woman as vulnerable and inferior to a man. An 1818 Massachusetts decision read thus:

"When the female is the injured party, there is generally more reason for a resort to the laws, than when the man is the sufferer...a deserted female, whose prospects in life may be materially affected by the treachery of the man, to whom she has plighted her vows, will always receive from a jury the attention which her situation requires...It is also for the public interest that conduct tending to consign a virtuous woman to celibacy should meet with that punishment which may prevent it from becoming common."

Remedies of the era were called "heart balm." Evidence of sexual relations between the parties was sufficient to prove breach in most cases. The plaintiff's testimony would not need to be otherwise corroborated.

The incarceration of Rau at the Ludlow Street Jail was perhaps not as righteous a remedy as it appears on the surface. Opened in 1862 at Ludlow and Broome Streets, it stood near today's Williamsburg Bridge. It was meant for civil rather than criminal offenders. Many of those consigned there bought extra privileges. For fifteen to thirty dollars per week, crooked personnel allowed the "prisoners" the better accommodations with comfortable beds and curtains, visiting privileges, and access to a billiards room, a reading room, and a grocery store. These individuals could also leave the jail evenings to dine in local restaurants.

Ludlow Jail eventually became known as the "Alimony Club" in the early 1900s for men who preferred jail to paying alimony to their wives. A man who refused to pay alimony would be jailed for six months and then cleared of all debt.

Willi Rau, poor as he was, would probably have been shunted off to a dirty, cramped cell on the top floors: cold in winter and hot in summer. However, the records for city courts before the unification of the court system in 1962 are kept at several locations, including City Hall Library, the County Clerk, and New York City Municipal Archives. The disposition of Scheu v. Rau remains unknown. I have not been able to find it. We cannot say if Rau spent one day in jail. US Census records do show that he was living at 145 Columbus Avenue in 1900 along with his mother, Lorelei, and a brother, Wulpert. He lists his occupation as simply laborer. No further records of him seem to exist. Alcohol likely killed him.

Cara Maurer

KT to Margee 743-821-1922
HS. My gr8t gr8t grammi f-in' had balls! Sent SOB Willi who f-ed her n left her to f-ing jail! JAIL! Mabee. Hey! Iz there test in abnrml psych Fri?
Nov. 19.

Margee to KT 743-765-8040
Yes AbPsy test. Duz ol' KT abort?
Nov. 19.

KT to Margee 743-821-1922
Margee. Itz 1896! Dunno. Gotta read mor.

Nov. 19.

Margee to KT 743-765-8040
Dint uz condomz?

Nov. 19.

KT to Margee 743-821-1922
condomz? 1896? No Yaz 4 sur!

Nov. 19.

Margee to KT 743-765-8040
Nuthin, huh?

Nov. 19.

KT to Margee 743-821-1922
Gonna read mor. Cara keepz buttin in w/ lekturz.

Nov. 19.

Margee to KT 743-765-8040
????? R u ok? Lekturz????

Nov. 19.

KT to Margee 743-821-1922
My gramma, Cara! She wrot up this diary from gr8t gr8t grammi Kati.
Keepz buttin in w/ lecturz n commntz.

Nov. 19.

Margee to KT 743-765-8040
So, Cara wrot it, not ol' KT. Im cnfsed.

Nov. 19.

KT to Margee 743-821-1922
No. Kati wrot it. N German. Cara translatd it, and keepz buttin in w/
commentz. Did u no NYC had heat wave in 1896. Pple slept on roofs n
rolled off them. kerplunk. died. i need a party.
Googled NYC heat wave 1896. Wuz f-in' UFR.

Nov. 19.

Margee to KT 743-765-8040
K. watchu doin? gonna read mor?

Nov. 19.

KT to Margee 743-821-1922
L8r. watchin ol Law n Order on TV

Nov. 19.

Margee to KT 743-765-8040
like L&O SUV. kinky creepy ewwww.

Nov 19.

KT to Margee 743-821-1922
nah. Reeeel ol stuff. from 90s. then ill read mor. Txt me l8r?

Nov. 19.

Margee to KT 743-765-8040
K.

Nov. 19.

Friday, August 28, 1896.

I may give birth any day now. I am ready. I am sure Lessia is ready. Yesterday evening, Gus Krieger stopped by to talk with Cousin Tessie's husband, Sigmund.

Gus is not much of a talker. He smiles rarely but listens mostly to Sigmund talk about his solutions to our ills. Siggi is a socialist. Gus's full name is Gustav Adolph Krieger. His parents moved out of this city over ten years ago. They came from nearby Bechingen and knew Sigmund's parents, neighbors. Strange because they were Lutheran. According to Tessie, they were a grim, joyless sort. Named Gottlieb and Pauline. But Tessie says that Pauline bore twelve children, and only Gus, the eldest, and the youngest, a brother, Freddie, survived childhood.

What heartache for a mother! Just the thought. I have never asked Tessie about the details, especially now with little Lessia soon to be my first. I don't need to ask. Too often, the morning after a birth in the tenement, after the whole tenement has heard a mother bring her baby into these soiled rooms, too often a hearse appears, and the midwife helps load a tiny casket into its cavernous belly, leads the baby she could not deliver properly back out of these tenements, these dark, pestilent caves.

Ten of twelve buried before her! No other choice for Pauline other than to be joyless, and Gottlieb grim. And, perhaps, for Gus to be so quiet. Did he walk beside his parents for every trip out to the Lutheran Cemetery? Had he gotten to play with some of his younger brothers and sisters? Those that Pauline had been able to suckle through infancy? Before cholera claimed them, or typhus? Did Pauline have difficult births?

I have gotten so much advice. I have heard so many opinions on the pain. I wish I could talk with my mother, dear Mutti Lisbeth, but I can only speak to her in my prayers, and I get no answers. I do not remember her giving birth. Since I was second youngest, after my siblings Albert, Hermann, Ferdinand, and William, how would I? I'm sure Mutti was happy to have a girl. And then my little sister, Karolina. Mutti died only a few years after giving birth to her. I'm sure I must have been taken to a neighbor's when Mutti bore Lina. And then Lina died herself. I was only two when Lina was born. I was only four when she died. Were the two deaths somehow connected? I don't remember Lina walking at all. Will my baby be healthy?

I am so afraid. Tessie holds me when I cry. Siggi pats my head and drifts off into another room where their children, Amelia, Elizabeth, and little Leo, play. Leo is now one year old.

Yesterday, Gus played briefly with Leo. Such a sad smile as Gus tickled him.

I will not give birth with a midwife. I will go to the New York Infant Asylum. Tessie says she will go with me and attest as my friend that she will shelter me and provide for me.

I am blessed with my cousin. She is my guardian angel. Not even Mary had a friend such as her.

Damn New York City. Doctors should not only be for the rich.

Kati's choice to give birth at the New York Infant Asylum afforded her care 90 percent of the women of New York at the time did not get. Certainly, few immigrant women enjoyed such care. By the time Kati gave birth to Lessia (she would bear a girl), the institution had served over nine thousand women, who were referred to as inmates. The 1894 annual report for the asylum, titled *23rd Annual Report of the New York Infant Asylum*, lists several women among its attending physicians, a notable exception to the prejudice of the era.

Kati's decision may have revolved around the best care she felt she deserved, but the midwife-versus-physician controversy of the time involved deep conflicts of class and gender. From the class angle, not only did immigrant women with rare exception have little choice other than to bear a child at home with a midwife, but even a midwife's small fee might not be something that a truly impoverished woman would be able to pay, and therefore, she would have to depend on her family and other women in the tenement.

Gender politics, misogyny, and male dominance were also involved. Midwives were dangerous. They could, and did, give advice on birth control and abortion. Choice threatened the domination of the man of the house. How pathetic it is to read through rolls of US Census documents with the wife's occupation listed as "keeping house."

Doctors were almost invariably men, unsympathetic to a birthing woman. They were hardly more competent than midwives. Only a few had actually attended college. Most had simply trained as apprentices, just like midwives. Medical schools provided insufficient training in most cases. So even though there were means to mitigate the pain of childbirth, such as narcotics and scopolamine, they were often poorly administered. As a result, unable to push, women were subject to forceps deliveries, in an era that did not understand sepsis.

This movement to eliminate midwives was as misogynistic as the Comstock Laws.

Here are some of the rules for the New York Infant Asylum:

"1. Needy women in the City and County of New York, of previous good character, are received for confinement; the time of their reception being at the discretion of the Board of Managers; and they are required to remain in the Asylum at least three months after confinement. Applicants from any other county will be admitted to the Asylum only in accordance with the provisions of its charter concerning the maintenance of such applicants and their infants; and no applicant admitted from any other State other than New York can become in any manner a dependent on this City or State.

"2. No woman who has previously given birth to an illegitimate child shall be admitted to the Asylum.

"3. Mothers, when discharged, may leave their infants in the care of the Asylum, provided that they have remained in the Asylum for one year subsequent to their confinement. Should they leave the Asylum at an earlier period, they may be required to take their infants with them.

"5. As a general rule, the mother is expected to remain and nurse her infant for one year."

In addition to sheltering and providing for indigent, unmarried pregnant women and their babies, the asylum took care of abandoned infants and children. It also had a school. The children were either restored to their mothers or adopted.

Cara Maurer

KT to Margee 743-821-1922
i h8 AbPsy. Skizofrenya! tht byatch profz deluuuusnal! F'in whatz abnml sex anyway?
Do u now? i dont. im gonna faillllll!

Nov. 19.

Margee to KT 743-765-8040
Chilllllll! no1 failz AbPsy. Hey, read anymor tht diary?

Nov. 19.

KT to Margee 743-821-1922
yea. "Comstock lawz?" and "cholera?" I mean, howz cholera kill u?
Cara – my gr8t gr8t grammi's trnsl8r - kepz BSn abt Katiz entrees.
Katiz lifz f-in' hard. Ppl like crzy back thn. Lotza dmb rulz.

Nov. 19.

Margee to KT 743-765-8040
Dunno. Look m up.

Nov. 19.

KT to Margee 743-821-1922
L8tr. Letz go Psi prty 2nite. K?

Nov. 19.

Margee to KT 743-765-8040
K. meet u ur place abt. 8?

Nov. 19.

KT to Margee 743-821-1922
K.

Nov. 19.

We don't know why Kati Scheu immigrated to America. We have always been taught in school that America was the land of opportunity, but as Kati's diary shows, as well as the photographs of Jacob Riis, the works of the muckrakers such as Upton Sinclair's *The Jungle*, and documents from the day, such as the *New York World*, it was hardly that.

There were other factors, such as religious freedom. Kati was Catholic, baptized at Saint Anselm's Church in Misingen. We don't know how truly conservative or liberal they were. At the time in Germany, a fractious amalgam of independent and semi-independent royal states gradually being absorbed into Prussia, Otto von Bismarck was leading a culture war. Against the rising influence of secularism, the Catholic Church became quite reactionary, trying to maintain its hegemony in policy, public life, and education. Evidence of that strong move to the right was the promulgation of papal infallibility at the First Vatican Council in 1869-1870 during the term of Pope Pius IX. Misingen lay under the rule of the House of Hohenzollern, the Catholic Swabian branch. They had become part of Prussia back about mid-nineteenth century. The ultimate Unification in 1871 fiercely coalesced secular liberal versus reactionary Catholic voices into two feuding camps. Levels of discrimination were high in Kati's day, often unsoftened by olive branches such as the Mitigation and Peace Laws. Even some Catholics felt "yoked" by the ultraconservative environment in places such as Hohenzollern. In the United States, all could breathe much freer.

Maybe this is why Kati emigrated.

Cara Maurer

KT to Margee 743-821-1922
Lookd up summa Cara's wordz. "Comstock Laws" made "contraception obscene and illegal. It was a felony to disseminate birth control material

across state lines or in the mail!" Evn by a midwife! "Cholera" wuz "bacterial disease usually spread through contaminated water. Cholera causes severe diarrhea and dehydration. Left untreated, cholera can be fatal in a matter of hours, even in previously healthy people." Oh, n docz all guys.

Nov. 21.

Margee to KT 743-765-8040
U OK. i still got headake. u left Psi urlee. Rockin time. ☺☺☺. So, like h8in uz goz way back, huh? like, SOOLs. Midwifes wur felunz then? "Cholera" frm google?

Nov. 21.

KT to Margee 743-821-1922
"Cholera" frm Mayo Clinic googl. 2 bad. wood u want sum guy md stickn hiz fingrz up yur v?
Jus wuznt into parti. Guyz lookd lame.

Nov. 21.

Margee to KT 743-765-8040
oh, well. NBG. Whut did u do 2day?

Nov. 21.

KT to Margee 743-821-1922
read mor Kati diary. Yez. Guy md in ob/gyn iz like an oxymoron!

Nov. 21.

Margee to KT 743-765-8040
oxy what? izn't the wurd mentli chalngd? Ob/gyn = OB?

Nov. 21.

KT to Margee 743-821-1922
Grrrl!! Oxymoron, like "giant shrimp" or "meat salad." Ob/gyn, not OB-wan Kenobi, "Obstetrics and gynecology."

Nov. 21.

Margee to KT 743-765-8040
LOL. forget. witch deelz w/ yur repro stuff, witch w/ pregnanz? Slpt in sex ed. Rmbr last year parti kappi? gropin' gary up ur panteez?

Nov. 21.

KT to Margee 743-821-1922
WAL! felt like a slut nxt day. impotnt tode. Bad booz. Not funny. ☹
Obstetrics is "pregnancy, childbirth and postpartum care." Gynecology
is "female reproductive health."

Nov. 21.

Margee to KT 743-765-8040
ISS. Sorry, sorry. Luv u. Luv u. u bin spdng time w/ google!

Nov. 21.

KT to Margee 743-821-1922
Luv u 2. Whoz ur obi wan kenobi ? (OBGYN doc)

Nov. 21.

Margee to KT 743-765-8040
Dr. Samantha Woolenstone. Part of obi wan kenobi associates, Broadway,
TTown. Whoz urz?

Nov. 21.

KT to Margee 743-821-1922
Go 2 clnc on campus. Rot8s. obi wan kenobi of the day.

Nov. 21.

Margee to KT 743-765-8040
So, how do u no if u r on the rite Pill?

Nov. 21.

KT to Margee 743-821-1922
Gess I reelly don't

Nov. 21.

Margee to KT 743-765-8040
U shud get a stedy. How abt mine? U cn talk 2 her.

Nov. 21.

KT to Margee 743-821-1922
Mabbe. Ask Momz. Askd er if we r Catholic. She laffed. sed on Xmas n Easter.

Nov. 21.

Margee to KT 743-765-8040
???? wut?

Nov. 21.

KT to Margee 743-821-1922
NBD. Nevrmnd. C u l8r n class?

Nov. 21.

Margee to KT 743-765-8040
K.

Nov. 21.

Wednesday, September 9, 1896.

My water broke. I am in labor, not regularly yet. Siggi has gotten me a han-som. Pray for me, Mary. My child will be a Scheu. No father's name when there is no father worthy of such a gift.

Thursday, September 24, 1896.

There is so much to say. Lessia has just fallen sleep from nursing, and I write awkwardly, by the light of the single window in our apartment's front room. Tessie and Siggi have made a little nursery of it. Even though the noise from the street disturbs Lessia occasionally, she is a healthy child and falls back asleep quickly. Little Leo toddles in—he is an early walker—looks curiously at my little girl, Lessia Mary Scheu, and smiles. He likes to touch her hand.

I still feel weak, sometimes sad. I want to help my Tessie. Prepare a meal. Watch Leo. Shop for dinner. But Tessie and Siggi insist I rest and enjoy Lessia. I gave them all the small savings I had set aside since leaving Rau last April. My pittance from cleaning the halls of this building through July.

Labor was hard. It began right after I got into the cab, and Siggi had to half-carry me into the asylum. It was relentless, wave after wave of tightening pain. Small breaks, just enough time to give thanks for a pain-free body before another wave would start.

Then there was less time to rest, and less time. It felt like my body was trying to squeeze all of its insides out.

I remember looking up at the ceiling in the confinement room at the asy-lum, where I delivered. A young doctor, McCullen, was at my side. But a nurse was sponging my face and holding my hand. I remember, for some silly reason, thinking the ceiling looked like the ceiling of St. Anselm's. Indistinct and pale white, it seemed so far away, floating softly above me. Like clouds. I must have been at the edge of losing consciousness, because the words of the nurse became muffled, and the ceiling seemed to move gently, flow slightly. Like clouds.

Then, the nurse's words would bring me sharply back to my bed. "Breathe, Kati." And the contraction would squeeze me, and I would hiss a curse on Willi.

Then, back to the comfort of the ceiling of St. Anselm's, but calling out for Mary. I regretted cursing. Until the next wave.

It was late morning when I entered the asylum. After several hours, the pain changed to a burning. An impossible burning as the nurse urged me to push out my baby. How? I thought I would burst. I would die.

Then, Lessia was in my arms. My body still throbbed, but my baby was in my arms. The nurse smiled at me and gave me a long, cool sip of water. It was late afternoon. The light through the large, paned window in the confinement room was fading to gray. I must have been in labor for almost eight hours. I mumbled a small prayer to Mary and looked at Lessia, who lay sleepily on my breast.

Lessia Mary Scheu. She is stirring, and I must let her feed. My nipples are so sore! And I laugh when Lessia sucks hard on them!

Tessie says it gets easier after the first. I just smile and nod. I just want to be with my little girl now.

According to the records of the New York Infant Asylum, Kati Scheu was discharged in the care of a "friend," Mrs. Flogt, on September 21, 1896. The terse record indicates the child was officially named Lessia Scheu, with "Social Conditions" stated as both parents living, but the "Cause of Dependence" being illegitimacy. Lessia's physical condition was listed as fair, and mental condition as negative. That was it.

The most daring act Kati executed at the New York Infant Asylum was to have her daughter's name listed officially on her birth certificate as Lessia Scheu. Laws that had been passed in the middle of the nineteenth century made an immigrant woman's ability to become a naturalized alien, a citizen, dependent upon her marital status. The Act of

February 10, 1855, stated, "Any woman who is now or may hereafter be married to a citizen of the United States and who might herself be lawfully naturalized, shall be deemed a citizen."

Willi Rau himself became a citizen on August 15, 1891, in the Superior Court of New York County. He listed his occupation as a laborer and listed his residence as 321 West Forty-Sixth Street. Attesting to him as a witness was one Robert Jones, a teamster living on nearby West Forty-Fifth Street. Robert Jones? Given Rau's history, one wonders if fraud was committed. Tracking people via the US Census is difficult for 1890. Almost all records, paper at the time, were destroyed in a fire in January 1921 in the Commerce Department Building.

Thus, by not marrying Rau, and by giving Lessia her surname, Kati cut off an opportunity to become a United States citizen. Not that she would have had any evidence of her citizenship. The record of citizenship would only have mentioned her husband, not her, nor any of her children, already born or yet to be. She would need to produce a copy of her husband's record and the marriage certificate.

Some of the children of such a marriage, such as Gustav Adolph Krieger, would therefore go to a naturalization court upon the age of majority to again certify themselves as citizens.

Cara Maurer

Margee to KT 743-765-8040
Hey! U OK? missd u ystrdy n 2 day.

Nov. 23.

KT to Margee 743-821-1922
im ok. b n a womn wuz f-ing BRUTAL 4 Kati. No Yaz, no condomz(?), dctrz all men! Did u know, an immigrant woman wuz only a citizen if r huzbnd wuz! F-ing unreal!!!

Nov. 23.

Margee to KT 743-765-8040
? Wear u bn? Katiz got u gud.

Nov. 23.

KT to Margee 743-821-1922
Ken hom for Turkey Day.

Nov. 23.

Margee to KT 743-765-8040
Ur #1 FWB Ken? Will i c u b4 nxt Monday? Gvn him sum pie to celabr8e?
LOL

Nov. 23.

KT to Margee 743-821-1922
Cum ovr 2nite. Abt. 7? enuff Ken by then. ur my BFF, Ken …hmmmm.. not.

Nov. 23.

Margee to KT 743-765-8040
Cooollll! Want notez frm class?

Nov. 23.

KT to Margee 743-821-1922
2x coooollll! Email thm 2 me. Plz? PS Im gonna strt a diary.

Nov. 23.

Margee to KT 743-765-8040
3x coooollll!!! ☺☺ can i read it??

Nov. 23.

KT to Margee 743-821-1922
i dunno…. A diaryz privut. u shud rite ur own. ☺

Nov. 23.

Margee to KT 743-765-8040
Oooooooo. ill steel it!!! 4x coooollll!! Make it hot! C u l8r. K? Ken'll b gon?

Nov. 23.

KT to Margee 743-821-1922
K!!!! Yeah. No Ken.

Nov. 23.

KT to Margee 743-821-1922
PS U ever want kidz?

Nov. 23.

Margee to KT 743-765-8040
WTF? Like **children???** Nononononononononono. No. U?

Nov. 23.

KT to Margee 743-821-1922
Dunno. U? nevr?

Nov. 23.

Margee to KT 743-765-8040
U b trippin grl! Like fnd a guy whod b a reel dad. LOL

Nov. 23.

Sunday, September 27, 1896.

I finally slept through the night last night! When I awoke this morning, I was afraid at first. Lessia had been nursing about every three hours, and I was scared that something had happened to my baby. I got up from the old daybed that I was sleeping on in the front room, turned quickly to Lessia's tiny cradle, and pulled down her blanket. My hands were trembling. I picked her up, thinking of Pauline Krieger, her lost children, and the hearses that are wheeled up our street too frequently for their sad little cargoes.

Lessia squealed. And cried. I did too. I cradled her up to my breast, and she began to suckle almost immediately.

Lessia is quick to latch onto my nipples now. Tessie says to enjoy this time, because once Lessia begins to teethe, I will undoubtedly be bitten. To know my baby will be teething, is growing normally, will make that almost a joy, I think.

At the asylum, the nurse did not let my tiny baby lie against me long. "You must try to feed her; begin nursing now," she said. I was so exhausted, almost like I was outside myself, but obliging. "Touch baby's upper lip with your nipple," she said.

"Lessia," I said.

The nurse smiled. I was surprised. It had been a long day for her too. She had been with me my entire delivery. The doctor only came in occasionally, and at the end. He did not smile. But he was very young.

Lessia opened her mouth quite wide. The nurse guided Lessia fully onto my breast, making sure I was supporting her entire little body. "Make sure she covers as much as possible," she said.

I fed her almost every hour, it seemed, at first.

"Remember, your little girl has a very tiny stomach."

I never asked the nurse her name. Then again, I'm sure she will not remember mine. Six of us gave birth in that large room that day.

One baby was stillborn. The mother was in a bed on my left. Early in the afternoon. I was in too much pain to worry, or, sadly, to sympathize with her. I remember only that a nurse kept on saying to her, "I'm so sorry, Eliza. I'm so sorry. But you are young. You can have another."

Eliza kept sobbing, "I want this one. Not another. I want this one."

The fear of hearses on the streets of the tenements was not unfounded in New York City in the 1880s and 1890s. In addition to the heat wave of 1896, there was a particularly bad one in 1883. It killed a large number of children, especially poor ones, and led to Joseph Pulitzer publishing stories about its effects. Titles such as "Lines of Little Hearses" created a groundswell of outrage for reform, although it was slow in efficacy. Other terrors, such as cholera, dysentery, and whooping cough, cut down children at an alarming rate. A family of five children could expect to lose at least one child, and since those statistics were averaged including middle class, affluent, and rural populations, the experiences for tenement dwellers were grimmer.

The sentiment of the day, resigned but impassionate nonetheless, can be seen in a poem by Ella Wheeler Wilcox (1850–1919).

The Little White Hearse

Somebody's baby was buried to-day—
    The empty white hearse from the grave rumbled back,
And the morning somehow seemed less smiling and gay
    As I paused on the walk while it crossed on its way,
And a shadow seemed drawn o'er the sun's golden track.

Somebody's baby was laid out to rest,
    White as a snowdrop, and fair to behold,

And the soft little hands were crossed over the breast,
    And those hands and the lips and the eyelids were pressed
With kisses as hot as the eyelids were cold.

Somebody saw it go out of her sight,
    Under the coffin lid—out through the door;
Somebody finds only darkness and blight
    All through the glory of summer-sun light;
Somebody's baby will waken no more.

Somebody's sorrow is making me weep:
    I know not her name but I echo her cry,
For the dearly bought baby she longed so to keep,
    The baby that rode to its long-lasting sleep
In the little white hearse that went rumbling by.

I know not her name, but her sorrow I know;
    While I paused on the crossing I lived it once more.
And back to my heart surged that river of woe
    That but in the breast of a mother can flow;
For the little white hearse has been, too, at my door.

By my time, the little white hearses had disappeared. I only had to open the door to an undertaker idling a black one once at my curb.

Cara Maurer

Monday, September 28, 1896.

I want my Lessia to be baptized, but the church, the one near the corner of West Forty-Fourth Street and Tenth Avenue, Saint Michael's, next to the Cabinet Works, will not have it. Tessie asked. Those doddering old men called Lessia a bastard child! "Only if you marry Willi, before them," Tessie said Father Wolters said. The same man who touched my forehead at communion late in August, on the Sunday after the heat wave broke, and blessed Lessia in my belly, called her by name after I whispered it to him in response to his asking.

Now, she is not worthy of being saved. So he says.

Siggi said Tessie should have asked him if he would have denied Jesus baptism, considering Mary had not borne Joseph's child.

I will get this done. In the meantime, I have blessed her and drawn a small cross on her forehead from cool water in the kitchen pitcher. Now she is officially Lessia Mary. Lessia Mary Scheu. Siggi says that kitchen water is as holy as any.

Gus stopped by yesterday afternoon. Gustav Adolph Krieger. Such an imposing name for a wiry Lutheran man. He must weigh only about 130 or so. He works hard. He was startled when I asked him to hold Lessia. He was so hesitant and careful. He is, I think, about my age. Have I mentioned that earlier? Did I mention that he has a pale but healthy complexion, a full head of light, blond hair frozen in a wave above a long forehead? Intense blue eyes set somewhat close together. They dart around frequently. He is a very nervous man. High cheekbones. Large ears that protrude outward slightly.

Gus is always clean when he visits. He smells though of the eating house where he works as a waiter. He was trained as a weaver. The eating house is down on West Twenty-Eighth Street. Serves mostly workingmen from the neighborhood. Gus says there are lots of businesses in the area, and the eating house, I think it is called Delaney's, is guaranteed prosperity.

I saw Gus smile as he held Lessia. He said then, "She reminds me of Fridericka."

Then, he tried to keep smiling, but I could see it was difficult for him. His fluttering eyes tried to stay focused on Lessia. He rocked her gently back and forth, and then I took her back. I was anxious. Maybe I should have let him hold her longer.

Gus smiled briefly at me. He was blinking a lot and said, "I need to go now. I've left you some food. Eat well, Mutti. You still eat for two."

Later in the evening, Tessie prepared some cold beef for us, with green beans, bread, and boiled potatoes. I hope Gus did not take it from Delaney's, but clearly, I think he did. I asked Siggi to admonish him, gently, I insisted, but not to let him risk his job. Siggi works nearby.

It was only in the later nineteenth century that the word "restaurant" became commonplace in American English. In New York, the phrase was "eating house." In Boston, the locals would say "restorator." Other words used included dining room or dining hall.

Gus Krieger's eating house on West Twenty-Eighth Street was most likely the descendant of earlier "six penny" establishments, so called because that was the price of a main course. These eating houses were essentially a large, rectangular room. Tables for four or more were arranged in long aisles. Occasionally a counter ran the length of the room. Waiters would stand along the aisles, taking the orders of the hungry men, usually in a rush from their jobs. A chalkboard displayed the meal items and prices. These businesses cultivated the fast, sloppy eating habits that developed in New York City and the rest of the nation in that era.

About West Twenty-Eighth Street to West Twenty-Ninth Street, between Eighth and Seventh Avenues, on an 1885 New York City map, interspersed among tenements, lay George Keyes and Sons Dry Goods, T. Mayer's Livery Stable, a Mouldings Factory, a Transfer Stable, a Wire Manufacturer, Spaulding Provisions, Fr. Beck Paper Hangings, and T. M. Stewart Carpet Cleaning. Also nearby were an iron works, a sawmill, a brewery, and the New York Central and Hudson River Railroad yards, as well as its passenger depot at West Twenty-Ninth Street and Ninth Avenue. Plenty of patrons for an eating house, if not the immigrant laborers, then the managers, owners, and itinerant travelers.

The price for a dinner of roast meat with bread and vegetables was fifteen cents. Dessert could be had for a nickel, as could coffee.

It is highly likely Gus Krieger stole food for Kati. It would not have been uncommon, and it's also likely that waiters and other workers were fed by their employers. It is also the case that Gus would have been fired if caught, and jailed.

Cara Maurer

KT to Margee 743-821-1922
OMG OMG Margee. Ken condm broke. O FUCK.

Nov. 27.

Margee to KT 743-765-8040
Did u douche?

Nov. 27.

KT to Margee 743-821-1922
No.

Nov. 27.

Margee to KT 743-765-8040
Du it. Now.

Nov. 27.

KT to Margee 743-821-1922
Duz no gud. Went online. Duznt kleen, duznt stop infektshuns, STD, HIV. Duznt do shit.

Nov. 27.

Margee to KT 743-765-8040
Sez who?

Nov. 27.

KT to Margee 743-821-1922
ACOG. American College of Obstricians and Gyncologsts. MarG, can i c ur obi-wan doc?

Nov. 27.

Margee to KT 743-765-8040
u gonna hav tell momz?

Nov. 27.

KT to Margee 743-821-1922
No prob. Jus say i wanna reg obi-wab doc, not doc-of-day @ skool.

Nov. 27.

Margee to KT 743-765-8040
Whutz ken sayin?

Nov. 27.

KT to Margee 743-821-1922
FUCK KEN!! Wont answr fone. i left like riteaway.

Nov. 27.

Margee to KT 743-765-8040
gess Ken got othr FWBz?

Nov. 27.

KT to Margee 743-821-1922
NS sherlock. dunt we all??? Fuuccckkkkkk!

Nov. 27.

Margee to KT 743-765-8040
hey grl im ur BFF, huh??? wear r u?

Nov. 27.

KT to Margee 743-821-1922
Train. MTNorth. neer Ynkrs.

Nov. 27.

Margee to KT 743-765-8040
Stp @ irvngtn. ill cum get u. we can talk. U can stay ovr if u want. Plz
say u will.

Nov. 27.

KT to Margee 743-821-1922
thx. yes yes yes.

Nov. 27.

Margee to KT 743-765-8040
On my way. Call momz n let er no.

Nov. 27.

KT to Margee 743-821-1922
ur the best.

Nov. 27.

Monday, October 5, 1896.

Funny, it is less than two months after that terrible August heat wave, and we are having our first cool day. Lessia sleeps longer now. I have just fed her and spent some moments watching the sights and listening to the sounds on Forty-Seventh Street below with her sleeping bundled on my chest. The window rattles lightly. When I put my hand against the pane, I can feel how the breezes off the North River have cooled all the city off.

At first I was afraid to look long out the window, for fear of seeing Willi, or worse, of him looking up to see me. But he has made no appearance, and I do not believe he will. He does live several blocks east, and I suppose he has no reason other than me to venture out toward the river. And, I guess, I am no reason at all, and my child even less so. We could have shared her.

Soon, I think I will try to get my old job back as house janitor. I am feeling much stronger, and I need to help out Tessie and Siggi. They have been so loving to me. I can stop to nurse Lessia occasionally, and she will find a curious little guard in Leo, and a fine aunt in Tessie as she keeps house.

So many men walk this street to work early in the day. Packs of men. Scarcely a woman to be seen. Loud talk. Tobacco smoke occasionally reaches the window and pushes its stale, choking odor into the room. If I were down among them, I suppose I would smell alcohol as well, or stale sweat locked into faded, patched work pants and yellowed, worn shirts.

Sometimes, if the wind blows right, the smell from the stockyards rolls up from the river, along with the bellows and complaints of driven cattle. The acrid stench of festering manure and some faint tinge of something else, something primitive and repulsive, from the slaughterhouses, adds its character.

The men herd themselves to work, driven as the cattle. But at least they return in the evening. Most of them. Along with the men, I see children out to work. Some accompanied by their fathers, some alone, some in small packs seeking space on the sidewalks among the vast, drifting clots of men.

Lessia will go to school.

Gus comes over weekly, if not more frequently. He always plays with Leo and holds Lessia and talks to her. Siggi cautioned him about the food he brings, and Gus assures him he has brought it from home, although I doubt it. It is already cooked. He is taking a big risk.

I went to school. I graduated. And she will not depend on a man for her life. I must help her with that. As I can.

It is difficult to absorb the environment that assaulted the immigrants of the 1870s and 1880s on the west side of Manhattan between Thirty-Fourth and Fifty-Ninth Streets from Eighth Avenue to the Hudson—or North—River: Hell's Kitchen. Just saying that development and construction were scattershot, there being no zoning, does not convey the proper image for the consequences. Today, for example, a grammar school would not be erected flush to an iron foundry. But that was the case then. Perhaps the best way to imagine it is how the neighborhood enwombed its residents in sounds and smells, in sights and feelings.

Just a few blocks down and over from Kati loomed the Manhattan Gas Works. Stretching from Eleventh Avenue to the Hudson between Forty-Fifth and Forty-Sixth Streets, by 1861 it had become fourth in gas production in the entire world. Although it would switch to water gas production from coal around 1900, a devil in its own right, the plant during Kati's experience was coal gas, the means of lighting through-out Manhattan, and for that matter the world. Edison and the lightbulb were still decades away from general usage.

The process converting coal to gas produced a highly flammable product that included hydrogen, carbon monoxide, methane, and other VOCs, volatile organic compounds. Byproducts included coke, coal tar, sulfur, and ammonia. These were environmentally destructive, and some were carcinogenic. Spills and waste were flushed directly into the Hudson. The acrid, stinging odors drifting from this plant, especially on a hot, humid day, would have affected breathing and left eyes burning.

During the gaslight era, six major companies served NYC. The streets were constantly being torn up by one company or another install-ing or repairing their mains, or removing those of a rival. If work crews from rival companies met on the same street, fights would break out, hence the term "gas house gangs."

Just beyond Eleventh Avenue on Forty-Sixth Street lay a slaugh-terhouse. Although not the major cattle slaughtering center located between Thirty-Ninth and Fortieth Streets along the Hudson, it none-theless provided the full range of sounds and smells that accompanied the mass killing of animals. Since large-scale refrigeration and freez-ing did not exist, meat was supplied to butcher shops daily, with cattle trained in to Jersey City, ferried across the Hudson—in this case to the ferry terminal at the western end of Forty-Second Street—and then driven north along Eleventh Avenue to the abattoir.

Many of these operations were, at best, poorly regulated if regulated at all. The odor of rotting manure left behind by the animals added to that of horses that plied the Tenth Avenue horsecar line. Offal was dumped into the river; blood flowed out into drains that sometimes led to the Hudson, or at other times just to the gutter. Also, the cattle did not go quietly.

The IRT Ninth Avenue Line, often called the Ninth Avenue el, was the first elevated railway in New York City. It opened on July 1, 1868, as the West Side and Yonkers Patent Railway. Although at first a downtown phenomenon, by January 18, 1876, its noise and smoke pollution with residual soot from clanking steam locomotives had reached Sixty-First Street. Another charming feature of the el was to blot out sunlight to street-level activity.

Along Eleventh Avenue ran a street-level railroad, hence the nickname it acquired of Death Avenue. Steam locomotives of the New York Central Line once chugged down the center of the avenue, hence its unusual width. Cowboys on horseback would often precede the trains to warn traffic and pedestrians, obviously often to no avail.

The large influx of German immigrants in the nineteenth century prompted the building of many breweries within the city. They were often small, identified with a particular style of beer, especially lager or pilsner, and lent their own particular aroma of fermenting grains and hops to the neighborhoods they served. Of course, they also often drew their water from wells or the Hudson, into which much local industrial pollution had seeped or flowed. Despite contamination, beer by virtue of the alcohol did not pose the risk of cholera that drinking local water or even milk did. Croton River water did not come to the tenements until later, or there was simply one hallway faucet to serve an entire floor.

A gasworks, a slaughterhouse, a horsecar line, the Ninth Avenue el, a railroad running down Eleventh Avenue, and a brewery. Quite a mélange of acrid coal gas, ammonia, and sulfur intertwined with the sour stink of blood and offal masked every ten minutes or so by the floating remnants of a cloud of choking train smoke. Reprieve occasionally afforded by the fermentation drifting out from the brewery. Cattle protesting and crying out at slaughter. Screeching complaint of metal wheel against rail as trains braked to station. Horse manure corrupting in the gutter, only occasionally swept away.

These were some of the daily experiences of Kati and her tenement life in Hell's Kitchen.

The area gained notoriety as being gang-infested after the Civil War. Oddly, Kati rarely mentions them in her diary. One of the original gangs was organized by Dutch Heinrichs about 1868. It started out specializing in raids on the Hudson River Railroad yards along Thirtieth Street but soon branched out into extortion (protection racket), breaking and entering, professional mayhem, and highway robbery. It merged with the Tenth Avenue Gang and for decades terrorized the neighborhoods, spawning the eventual leaders of the Hudson Dusters and Gopher Gangs.

The grammar school Lessia would have attended, had Kati remained in the neighborhood, was Grammar School 51, located on West Forty-Fourth Street midblock between Tenth and Eleventh Avenues, and—as noted previously—smack flush against an iron foundry. Despite all, it provided at least a sixth-grade education for the children of the newly arrived.

Cara Maurer

Margee to KT 743-765-8040
How r u?

Nov. 29.

KT to Margee 743-821-1922
OK i gess. Scared. Sooo much 2 get my head arownd.

Nov. 29.

Margee to KT 743-765-8040
u did c obi wan, plz say yes?

Nov. 29.

KT to Margee 743-821-1922
Oh, yez. Thnk u thnk u. shez gr8t. saw me l8 ystrdy. Like 7ish. i jus mean like i had 2 tell her sooo much abt me, n took a kwik test, n mor l8r i gotta b more careful. im sooo wureed.

Nov. 29.

Margee to KT 743-765-8040
ull b ok. wanna studee w/me @ libs tmrw eve?? Mdwk parti l8r @ Sig? Get lttl bit looooz?? Get ur head 2 stp wurreez.

Nov. 29.

KT to Margee 743-821-1922
Stdee yez, parti no. Gotta get gr8z up. U now, like gradu8!!

Nov. 29.

Margee to KT 743-765-8040
K. u herd frm ken?

Nov. 29.

KT to Margee 743-821-1922
Keep leavn mssgz no answrs. F him plz dunt menshun him evr agin!

Nov. 29.

Margee to KT 743-765-8040
K K. u evr wanna talk call. Anytime. C u tmrw 5 @ libs grab snackz n studee jus studee

Nov. 29.

KT to Margee 743-821-1922
K. ☺

Nov. 29.

November 29, 2010.

I have decided to keep a diary just like Kati did and like because doctor woolinstone said it may help me. She told me to call her doctor sam. I like her. She is friendly, an spent time with me, even though it was reaallly late for her. I'm not sure I like this spellcheck thing. It corrects me a lot, but then again I can read what im writing better. Usuallee. (Ha ha, didn't correct me there.)

Lotz to discuss with her, and she wants to c me again in a week. I told her abt FWB Ken, and also Greggi, and Steweee. She seemed concerned, but no wrinkly forehead or eye flttr lik Momz. Jus put her hand on my wrist an sed mabbe I shud b sure to write down there addresses and phone nmbers, in case we need to talk to them.

Thatz all she said abt that part, but I new whT she meant. HIV/AIDS. Shittttt! Shit. Shit. She said if I write down my thoughts, and read them l8r, it may help me. Like get it off my chest. She also said whatvr I write and wanna share with her, please do so.

Shrink stuff. But, OK. im so nrvs. I know therz drugz n stuff 4 HIV, an I wont die, I hope, but still. An why do I go rite to deth n stuff lik that? Momz said I worri 2 much.

Woodnt know it from my gradz!

If I could write this in another language I would. Keep it so private. I never told anyone so much about my private life as I did Dr. Woolenstone. (P.S. Can you tell my writing is getting better. Stopped for a sec and read what I had written. Ugh! Like hard to understand. I'll still make mistakes, but Im gonna try to do better.)

Im NO Slut. Hell, boyz r ALWAYZ counting. Doc Sam asked me if I counted too. I said, not really, I mean not exactly, but then yes I guess I do. She asked me to think abt that an we'd talk about it nxt time. Like maybe I'm tryin to act like a guy??? Me???? No LGBTQ whatever with me. (How many letters are they gonna add to that anagram anyway?)

I may go off sex. For a while. Mabbe.

Doc Sam gave me a rapid antibody screening test. Took my blood. For that and a general STD screen. I called her for results this afternoon. Negative. TGFT. But, that's mostly for old stuff. She told me to be really sure, I'll need to take another series of tests. Like through the end of February. Next year! Even if that's negative too I need another test three months after that 2 b, I mean to bee, be sure.

I really can do better than this!

Doc Sam talked about antibodies, antigens, nucleic acid tests (NAT) and so much more! I've gotta lot to read. She gave me stuff to read. (Ha! Got that all spelled rite!)

TG its winter. Had a sweater on. Momz didn't see the band-aid on my forearm. Its off now.

No parties, at least this weekend.

PS Doc also gave me a brochure about the effects of HIV/AIDS. I gotta be honest, Im too scared yet to look at it. One thing I do remember from sex ed in high school was those skeleton people on death beds from AIDS that we were shown. As bad as the podcasts from exsmokers washing out their throat plugs and dying too. But, ewww, who wants to smoke??

Yellows teeth and makes you smell like a brush fire.

At least she thinks Im on the right Pill. For now.

KT

Sunday, October 11, 1896.

I have gotten my old job back as the tenement's housekeeper. Not janitor though I asked. It's half the wages of a janitor, and the only difference the tenement's owner, Mr. Lausberg, could give me was that I could not fix a broken pipe. No pipe has ever broken in this tenement, and if it did, I'm sure Mr. Lausberg would not let old Eddie O'Reilly, the janitor, near it. He can hardly stand up straight! But Mr. Lausberg has Eddie busy with four tenements he owns on this street alone. So he's saving there too. I'm sure I could learn to repair a pipe. It just would not look good for me to show up a man.

Still, at half the wages of a janitor, it means that Siggi and Tessie again pay half the rent for our apartment, because I live there! That's five dollars a month!

Mr. Lausberg was very happy to have me back. Siggi said I should have "struck" for more! Tessie elbowed him and scolded, "Just say thank you! Besides, then someone else would probably have taken the job for less, and where would we be?" All Siggi said was something about "scabs." I asked him about that word. He said it meant someone who was willing to work for less, to defy his union and be a traitor to his class.

I wonder, if Lessia's health depended on it, would I become a "scab"? I asked Siggi, if Tessie and the children were going hungry and he could stop it by being a "scab," would he. He grumbled and then said just, "Maybe." Tessie smiled.

Anyway, the tenement was not as clean when I was not being the housekeeper, and Mr. Lausberg knew it. Also, my replacement at that time, Hilda downstairs, got her brother into a vacant apartment in the building, and he did not last long. Did not pay the rent for the first month after he moved in!

I have not seen Hilda since I returned from the asylum. She had to have been working, at least until recently, or the building would really have begun to smell. Although maybe not so much with the cooler weather.

Am I already a "scab"?

I'll know better about the shape of the tenement tomorrow, when I start working.

Life has gotten better for Siggi and Tessie. My woe has been their benefit. Gus's food and a rent reduction. What is the old saying of Jesus in the Bible, "Come unto me all ye that travail and are heavy laden, and I will refresh you"? Like the church really practices that! And it looks like I, the heavy laden, wound up refreshing Siggi and Tessie and the children.

Leo got another cold. He is getting better though. It was a scare for all of us, and I worried about Lessia, because he had been playing together with her nearby. But Lessia seems fine.

Tessie is happy to watch my baby while I work. I will stop to nurse her.

The duties of a tenement housekeeper in Kati's day in New York City would have included cleaning the public areas of the building, collecting ash and garbage, and collecting rent for the landlord. A valued housekeeper would also help maintain occupancy in the building, seeking out reliable tenants. Most housekeepers would have received a bonus for this. Often, the housekeeper also oversaw local children, maintained moral standards, policed public cleanliness, and kept an eye out for alcohol abuse.

Kati was, in practice if not title, the local "sheriff."

For that, she indeed would have received only half the wages of a janitor, who would have also had the duties of maintaining plumbing and drainage.

Some of Kati's other duties could have included cleaning the roof and cleaning out the shafts of dumbbell tenements. Since Kati's tenement had four floors for tenants, with four families per floor, and a shop on the ground floor, her work was arduous and kept her busy at least ten to twelve hours a day. Remember also, there was no air conditioning in summer or heating in winter, apart from small apartment stoves. The tenements were all walk-ups.

Kati's stamina would make "Rosie the Riveter" look weak by comparison!

Also, I have it on good report from family stories that Kati took breaks during the day to nurse Lessia.

The following is an interesting excerpt from *Practical Real Estate Methods, For Broker, Operator and Owner*, published by Doubleday, Page and Company, for the West Side Young Men's Christian Association, New York, 1910. Page 61:

"The janitor is a very important matter in a tenement house. The tenants should like him and use him well. The janitor joke, like the mother-in-law joke, is badly overworked. It is possible to get painstaking men and women in these positions. In a cheap tenement, where the rents are, say, $10 to $15, your janitor will sometimes be the best man or woman in the house, economically and socially. It is a good thing if it is so. If he has some executive ability, it will be of value to you. He ought to have some mechanical sense, and be handy at repairs. If you can get work done by employees paid by the month, and thus save mechanics' day wages, it will be of considerable advantage to the property."

The paragraph above only parrots what a practical landlord already knew. Mr. Lausberg saw Kati as a valued asset to his property by virtue of her work, not her belly or circumstance, and also saw fit simultaneously to exploit that belly and circumstance to his financial advantage.

Cara Maurer

KT to Margee 743-821-1922
Thnx. im gonna help Momz w/xmas decor l8r. zup n attik lotza boxz thn stdee wanna ace AbPsy. Dealin w/Ken enuf "abbi nrml psyk" 2 help me do well!! LOL

Dec. 1.

Margee to KT 743-765-8040
u find him?? whutd sob say?

Dec 1.

KT to Margee 743-821-1922
Yak yak yak bs bs waz bizi thn got reeel btchee w/me. Tol him GFY u MF dckhd.

Dec. 1.

Margee to KT 743-765-8040
Sooo no more FWB?

Dec. 1.

KT to Margee 743-821-1922
No more B. wuz nvr a F, gess, jus B. wutz a F 4 u? wut duz that mean?

Dec. 1.

Margee to KT 743-765-8040
U wanna ace filozfee 2? Goin deep grl! i dunno? How abt u?

Dec. 1.

KT to Margee 743-821-1922
Pizzas heer!! Gotta go. Yum yum. Txt u l8r! K?

Dec. 1.

Margee to KT 743-765-8040
K. Pepperoni??

Dec. 1.

December 1, 2010.

Wow! I forgot how many xmas decorations Momz had. Its been awhile since I helped her pull all that stuff down from the attic. Its early I know, but its her way of getting thanksgiving out of the way. Her dad, my granpa eddie, died in the Korean war. Momz was only 4 years old, and she says she and the whole family were having thanksgiving dinner when the news arrived. It came by way of a telegram. He died somewhere around a place called triangle ill.

Momz is very anti-war. She's better now. Says she was very bitter when younger. She says she remembers only that her mom, my granma sam, threw a turkey leg at the TV because the president, somebody named

40

Truman, was speaking on it about "the abundance of gods gifts." Momz says granma cara and granpa irv, then only neighbors to her, were big helpz to them.

I was born the year granma cara died! I think. Hmm. Why did Momz go back to her unmarried name?

So, anyway, thanksgiving is never really a holiday at our house, but Momz does make sure we go out for a fancy meal on the Saturday after. Momz cant get into the xmas spirit, meaning buying us all neat gifts, until that weekend is gone.

I understand, I think. Its nice to write about this stuff. Margee just doesn't have the time. She gets bored quick, and starts playing with her necklace, and suggesting something to do, or asks a question about something totally off the wall. Silly Margee.

Wow, Im tired. Really tired. Those boxes were heavy, and then Momz and I got into ptting all the wreaths and garlands up on the doors and bannisters, and Momz began to ask me if I thought maybe we should have the hallway repapered, its been about five years anyway, to match the garlands better, and flow more into the great room and around the fireplace. She's thinking of a pale green, more yellowish than harsh.

I said, "I dunno, how about pepperoni pink?" We laughed and stopped for some cold pizza.

Well, all that's done now. Ooops, how many contractions have I butchered. I really want to try to write better. It's not easy.

Out of nowhere, Momz stops and looks at me over the last slice of cold, dead, shrivelly pizza with funny, little warty pepperoni slices on it as we sit on the floor near the fireplace and says, "Everything alright, Kati?"

"Sure," I said. "Finals coming up."

"Well, okay," she said. "Remember, if you want, you can talk to me. I'm never too busy."

"Sure," I said. Geez, Momz sense. Like, spidisense x 1000! Maybe because I told her about my new obi wan? Maybe because I'm actually studying?

I'm really tired. Worked hard today! Well, need to go online and study.

KT

P.S. Ken lame excuses for not getting back to me pissed me off. And then, when I asked him about other girls, his MYOB was the last straw. It is my business, dickhead. I guess I'll never know how many other women I was "in the pool" with. Dumb fuck!

Sorry, diary.

Sunday, October 18, 1896.

It has been a busy week, but I am so glad to have been able to get back to work. I am most happy that I can still nurse Lessia. Siggi was worried that all that housekeeping might upset my system and make me dry. I'm not sure if he was more worried about me, or the extra expense of milk if I did fail to lactate.

I did not tell them about my confrontation with the Reichmans. Siggi would get agitated and might have tried to go up and pick a fight with them. Siggi one day will have words with someone who would rather land a fist in his face than argue back. I can see it happening. But anyway, it all turned out well, because Mr. Lausberg was very impressed with my insistence, and now the Reichmans are gone.

On my first day back this week, I decided to attack the work Hilda had obviously neglected, such as cleaning out the airshafts. What a mass of stinking refuse and junk lay in them. I don't think she had cleaned them once since I left the job. It took me most of the morning, and five ash carts, five!, to get back down to the floors. And then to scrub out the hollow spaces, that took another hour!

While I was attacking all that filth, I heard a few times windows on the shafts opening up. I knew what was coming, so I shouted out, "Don't you dare, I'll bring it back up to you!" So no garbage showed up. Among all the garbage, I found a few dirty diapers, old ones getting too holed from endless washing to provide much help, and I knew only the Reichmans, with a baby boy, Carl, I think, had an apartment with a window on that airshaft.

That evening, after I had finished and washed up, I knocked on their door to ask them not to throw garbage down their shaft. I was so hungry, and the smell of

42

their bratwurst and sauerkraut dinner still held thick in the air that wafted out of their rooms when Mr. Reichman opened the door.

I tried to be polite at first. "Excuse me, Mr. Reichman, but I just cleaned out the airshafts. I know Hilda just let it go, but that's bad air for all here, so I try to do my best now that I'm back working."

He didn't even give me a chance. "Well, now that you're working again, little whore, maybe you won't have time to open your legs so easily." He laughed and just closed the door in my face.

That was that. So I told Mr. Lausberg the next morning when he made his rounds of his tenements about the diapers, and only that Mr. Reichman refused to hear me out about his garbage dumping. He nodded, looked at me, and seemed lost in a bit of thought.

"Maybe he was just tired," Mr. Lausberg said. "They do have a new baby. Been late on the rent for a couple of months now."

"Late on the rent," I said, acting surprised. "They can waste money by throwing dirty diapers down the airshaft, and the rich smell of sauerkraut and bratwurst that came out of their apartment! Seems like they have money enough!"

"Mmm," said Mr. Lausberg.

The city health inspectors are getting tough on new sanitary regulations. There is a push to clean up the worst of the tenements, especially the rookeries. The fines are heavy. They look for things such as polluted airshafts, and you either bribe them or pay the fines. Either way, it is money lost to the landlord.

The Reichmans were out by this past Friday.

Now, at the end of the week, I can say that the airshafts have remained free of garbage, and the roof has been swept. I have pulled someone's old mattress, probably left from the heat wave, down onto the street for the refuse wagon, whenever it gets here, and all the hallways are scrubbed and smelling fresh from soap and bleach. The sidewalk outside is scrubbed clean, and any manure and dog refuse is swept into the gutter. I can only do so much.

"So, Miss Scheu," Mr. Lausberg said as he visited our tenement on Friday, "now that you've gotten everything so clean, what will you do next week?"

"Well, sir," I answered quickly, "the school sink and privies out back will be cleaned thoroughly."

He laughed and pulled a dollar out from his wallet. "This is for you. I'm glad you're back. Be careful with yourself!"

I smiled, curtsied slightly, and took his money. "Thank you," I said. "I will work hard."

"You always have," he said. "You deserve better. I made a few remarks to my friend who owns Willi's tenement. He's gone now."

I almost wanted to give him the money back, but I put it in my pocket. I know Mr. Lausberg is only protecting his wallet, and having Willi farther away works toward that.

Having done a considerable amount of family research, I can almost with certainty aver that Gottlieb and Pauline, for part of their early life in New York City, rented rooms at a rookery. The address listed on the death certificate for one of their children, Lina, is 449 West Forty-Fifth Street. At least on an 1885 ward map, that address, next to the Second German Baptist Church, shows a small, brick structure set back from the street, much as rookeries were. They were crowded, converted former single-family homes whose advantages had been lost as large tenement buildings sprang up around them as the city pushed northward toward the farming community of Harlem in the nineteenth century. These miserable structures, occupied by the very poor, were often referred to as "dens of death." The particular one likely occupied by Gottlieb and Pauline lay close to an infamous tenement known as "the House of Blazes." It was called that because arson was apparently the profession of a number of its residents. A more grisly explanation for its designation, perhaps an urban legend, claims that residents would lure derelicts to the spot, ply them with liquor, then douse them with more and set them on fire.

Jacob Riis once commented on these God-forsaken structures, "It is of no exaggeration to say that the money paid to the owners as rent is literally 'the price of blood.'" On these miserable conditions, Riis also noted in *Battling with the Slum*, "I have known drunkards to wreck homes a plenty in my time; but I have known homes, too, that made drunkards by the shortest cut. I know a dozen now—yes, ten dozen—from which, if

I had to live there, I should certainly escape to the saloon with its brightness and cheer as often and as long as I could to brood there perhaps over the fate which sowed desolation in one man's path that another might reap wealth and luxury. That last might not be my way, but it is a human way, and it breeds hatred which is not good mortar for us to build with. It does not bind."

One thinks of Willi Rau and pauses in condemnation. He was perhaps simply a weak, one might say sensitive, man, who buckled and collapsed, as poorly built tenements sometimes did.

What is certain about Hell's Kitchen where Kati, Willi, the Flogts, and the Kriegers lived is that police would never venture alone into its corners, usually intervening only in groups of three or more, as the situation dictated.

There but for fortune!

Cara Maurer

KT to Margee 743-821-1922
Na. gonna stick in. tired. Thnk i aced AbPsy. mabbe talk w/momz. jus wanna talk w/momz. read alot ths wk.

Dec. 3.

Margee to KT 743-765-8040
u shur??? Lammi prti gonna go. u not getting deprssed??? Cmon w/me get bck into thngz. TGIF!!

Dec. 3.

KT to Margee 743-821-1922
No im OK! ☺ jus wanna chill Txt me l8r?

Dec. 3.

Margee to KT 743-765-8040
K. dont nerd out on me ☹ b well txt if i can. K?

Dec. 3.

KT to Margee 743-821-1922
K. jus glued to toob now. Fav TV L&O. jack, lenny n curtis.

Dec. 3.

Margee to KT 743-765-8040
ooooo. Career men! lol. sugar daddies?? ☺

Dec. 3.

KT to Margee 743 821-1922
ewwww! ☹ jowls n guts. Ugh ugh ugh nasty girl!!!!

Dec. 3.

Margee to KT 743-765-8040
Hahahahahaha

Dec. 3.

December 3, 2010.

Kati really had it tough. I can't imagine ever being able to be a housekeeper the way she described it, even without having just popped a baby outta my vajayjay, oh hell, out of my vagina. Pulling garbage and stinking diapers out of some shaft? Kati never even talks about washing diapers. Cloth diapers! Like did you wash each one as the baby pooped it, or wait and do a whole bunch at once? Momz said when she was a baby, granma sam had a hamper for dirty diapers, and washed a "load" of them at once. Ewwww! But at least you could dump the poop in the toilet, I said. Well, sometimes, momz told me. Baby poop can be very runny!

Ahhhh! Noooo! Kinda like mustard, she said.

That's it for mustard.

Great great granma Kati was a fighter, and a weasel, at least with one tenant in the building where she house kept. Is that a term? Getting some asshole named Reichman thrown out. Hmm. That's redundant, no? She knew her employer was using her, so she used him. Tit for tat.

I wonder if Kati had any close family here in the US with her. Like mother, or sister, brother, or even father? She doesn't say.

I thought if Kati had been more practical earlier on with Willi, she could have done something to prevent getting pregnant, if she wanted to. She must have felt that somehow, if she had a baby, it would bring back the old Willi. Would bring back love. Love by Willi, for Willi, for Kati, by Kati, and Lessia. Love all around.

That was a tough lesson for her, I suppose. Sacrifice just gets you contempt.

For Willi it was just sex. Like Ken. But then again, that's what it was for me. Lesson learned?

So I was curious, and googled birth control in the 1890s. Oh my God! They didn't even understand the rhythm method back then. They thought a woman was most fertile when she was menstruating! Unbelievable! And so abstained from sex during a period. Jesus! And had sex when she was most likely to conceive.

This was medicine then???

They used withdrawal. Yeah, good luck with that! Getting some grunting Romeo off your ass when he's going to cum?? Douching, which didn't work anyway. They used vinegar! Later on, Lysol! Good God, why not just set yourself on fire? Cervical cancer. Pelvic inflammatory disease, endometriosis. In a weird way, the Comstock Laws of the 1890s may have helped a bit by outlawing this shit.

Then again, they outlawed suppositories, diaphragms, and abortion. Momz says abortion was illegal until she was twenty-five! That's like 1973. Back in Kati's time, surgical abortion brought infection (and death), and either they used some "home remedies" or actually struck a woman's abdomen to induce labor, or stuck something up her vagina to irritate it.

Kati! Kati!

Doctor Wollenstone will see me this Monday, December 6. I think this more of a "how are you doing" type of meeting, a chat, maybe to see if I'm still active. I go back for a three week or so antibody test on December 20. This is part of what doc calls the "window period." It may take my body that long to make antibodies that a blood test can detect. I know what antibodies are, it's the antigen I'm afraid of now. Doc's going to give me a combination test for antigens as well as antibodies at the same time. Then, another combo test on January 20. Then, I get another antibody test in late February. Then one final time three months later.

I'm afraid. Am I going to hate Christmas, the way Momz hates Thanksgiving? I'll have to tell her if it's positive, and that'll ruin Christmas for her too!

I don't want that to happen! But what can I do now, except wait it out.

KT

Sunday, October 25, 1896.

Gus was over this afternoon. We had quite a conversation. He is looking to find a new family to board with. The one he is with now has just had another baby, and he hardly gets any sleep. He says he knows it will be rough to leave them, but he has to be awake at his job, especially since the manager is training him to be head waiter, at an extra two dollars a week. And he helps out the cooks before the doors open for lunch.

He seemed very happy when I told him there is a fine family downstairs that would probably take a boarder, and that he could use me as a reference, at least for Mrs. Lambert. But they are English, I told him. Would that be difficult for him?

"No," he said, "maybe here we talk English too. It will do us good, both of us."

"I am agreeing with you," I said.

"Oh," said Gus, smiling, "you mean you agree with me."

"Ah, so," I said.

"That is very German, saying 'ah, so,'" said Gus.

We went on with our "English," and I realize I will be able to learn more from him than he from me. He must work every day with many languages, but mostly English, because nearly everybody who goes to his eating house can talk to one another that way, no matter where they are from. That would be very good for me, and Lessia. She should start in English,

So I took him downstairs, right then and there, and introduced him to Mrs. Lambert. Thank God she came to the door. It was a gamble, but worth it. Gus was in his Sunday clothes, a used set, but clean.

He will be moving here in a week! And the rent will be less.

Gus smiled at me, ear to ear. And he said, "Thank you."

I have been in this country since 1887. I need to stand up for myself now, and for Lessia, and learning English well, or better than I now try to garble it, is very important. We have agreed to speak every day, and Gus suggests that if Mrs. Lambert will help out, he will pay her a dollar a week as a teacher.

He says he has money saved. In a bank!

I am happy in this moment.

Kati Scheu arrived in New York City aboard the MV *Leerdam* on October 17, 1887, after a trip from Amsterdam in steerage. That was quite a journey from the small village in today's southern Germany, about fifty miles north of the Swiss border. She arrived alone, twenty-one years old, listed on the ship's passenger manifest as a servant.

The *Leerdam* was about as long as a football field, built in 1881, and had begun the Amsterdam–New York route in 1883. Kati was one of her 392 "third class" passengers.

Immigrants traveling steerage were packed in like cattle would be in a boxcar. These passengers were often denied space on the open deck, despite the foul and cramped conditions in the former cargo holds. In addition to the bad air and possibility of the spread of illness such as tuberculosis arising from the close quarters, there was little deference given to single women or men traveling to the States, and certainly no privacy. Ships such as the *Kaiser Wilhelm II* in the early 1900s carried as many as nine hundred steerage passengers. Emma Lazarus, in her 1883 poem, "The New Colossus," spoke from the heart when she composed the lines, "Give me your tired, your poor, your huddled masses yearning to breathe free. The wretched refuse from your teeming shore."

The food at mealtime was slopped out of huge kettles begrudgingly into dinner pails. Water was foul. As many as several hundred would sleep in one hold in bunks, if that, and toilets were spare, perhaps one to a hold. It was told that the bread on one passenger ship was so molded that the steerage unfortunates just threw it into the ocean.

Kati was fortunate in one aspect of her voyage. She arrived in 1887. On December 16, 1889, the *Leerdam* sank after colliding with a British steamer, the *Gaw-Quan-Sin*, in the North Sea.

Kati immigrated to the United States in the last of three great waves of German immigrants. The last wave began in 1880 and eventually totaled nearly two million souls. Many of the immigrants settled in New York City, and most of those settled among their fellow countrymen. Many settled in the Lower East Side between 1840 and 1890 in an area called "Kleindeutschland," little Germany. Its territory ran from Third Avenue and the Bowery in the west to the East River, and from Division Street to the south up to about Fourteenth Street. And within that realm, families dispersed themselves into separate Catholic and Protestant neighborhoods, and further divided blocks according to the parts of Germany from which they had come. In 1875, one-third of New York City's population was of German origin.

Avenue B became known as "German Broadway." It was the Main and Market Streets of the community. Much like the pictures and movies we see today of old immigrant neighborhoods, the avenue was lined with small shops and factories, many in basements. Sidewalks were the hawkers' realm. Nearby Avenue A boasted lager beer halls, groceries, and oyster saloons.

The insular community reflected a broad cross section of society. Some toiled in the damp cellars and unventilated workshops. Some toiled out of their tenement apartments, making cigars or tailoring in a piecework system. Others worked long hours as bakers or independent artisans. However, many did have an advantage over other nationalities: a least a rudimentary education. Many Germans prided themselves on obtaining a high skill level in whatever work they plied, in the old guild tradition.

I have Kati's diploma from her school in Misingen. It is clear she was an excellent student, which is also reflected in the expressiveness of her diary.

Diploma number 72.

Kati Mary Scheu, daughter of the factory worker Oskar Scheu, born March 1, 1866, attended the [word unclear] school since the first of April, 1872, and has received upon graduation the following grades:

Moral behavior:	exemplary
Efficient use of abilities:	praiseworthy
Attendance:	regular
1. Religion and Bible study:	good
2. German language and style:	very good
3. Reading:	very good
4. Arithmetic and Geometry:	good
5. Geography and History:	good
6. Nature studies:	good
7. Writing:	very good
8. Drawing:	good
9. Singing:	somewhat satisfactory
10. Feminine crafts:	good

Misingen, March 31, 1880.

Vogelsang, lead teacher

There would eventually be shop managers and factory owners, landlords and beer hall owners within the new German American community. And a strong socialist tradition after Marx and Engels, mirrored in such as Siggi Flogt, which led to many forming a good portion of the labor movement agitating for better pay and fewer hours in the strife of the late nineteenth and early to mid-twentieth centuries. This brought them into direct conflict with their fellow expatriate capitalists.

By 1890, many Germans had begun to move toward today's Yorkville, and quite a few others interspersed themselves with the Irish of Hell's Kitchen. An immigrant of Kati's era could comfortably live an entire "new life" without having to learn a word of English.

For some, there was opportunity. For others, they simply became the wretched refuse on a new, foreign shore, still grasping for the most rudimentary space, the meanest crumb.

There but for fortune.

Cara Maurer

Ken to KT 743-8765-8040
Hi, KT how r u?

Dec. 3.

KT to Ken 914-521-6700
Im bz no time 4 u

Dec. 3.

Ken to KT 743-765-8040
K. wuz ldring f u'd wanna c me.

Dec. 3.

KT to Ken 914-521-6700
No. f u iz rite!

Dec. 3.

Ken to KT 743-765-8040
im sorry KT. ☹ got scared. sorry how abt i c u 2nite?

Dec. 3.

KT to Ken 914-521-6700
spose u gonna say u got betr condomz. ??? FU

Dec. 3.

Ken to KT 743-765-8040
well, I did. But, if u jus wanna talk n hav dinnr.

Dec. 3.

KT to Ken 914-521-6700
K. talk. spose I got preg??

Dec. 3.

Ken to KT 743-765-8040
Whaaaaat? r u ? k. u wanna abortion?

Dec. 3.

KT to Ken 914-521-6700
spose yes, and no, i no wanna abort??

Dec. 3.

Ken to KT 743-765-8040
U r preg? r u f'in nutz??? 2 erlee 2 tell????

Dec. 3.

KT to Ken 914-521-6700
Mabbe 4 u. no txt, call, rite, c me agin. Final notice. I will go to lawyer.

Dec. 3.

Ken to KT 743-765-8040
U sure? Letz talk. Plse???

Dec. 3.

KT to Ken 914-521-6700
No txt, call, rite, c me agin. Final notice. I will go to lawyer. U understand?? Yes or no?

Dec. 3.

Ken to KT 743-765-8040
Fine. Same 4 me, momma ho. U r f'in nutz!!!

Dec. 3.

KT to Ken 914-521-6700
G8 good bye Ken. Lawyer will luv ur final wordz.

Dec. 3.

Margee to KT 743-765-8040
KT u ther?

Dec. 3.

KT to Margee 743-821-1922
Sup?

Dec. 3.

Margee to KT 743-765-8040
Pls plse com pck me up!

Dec. 3.

KT to Margee 743-821-1922
Whatz rong??? Wher r u ??

Dec. 3.

Margee to KT 743-765-8040
Lammi feel lik sht thnk ben roofied.

Dec. 3.

KT to Margee 743-821-1922
Call 911. Gonna 911 u 2 now!

Dec. 3.

December 5, 2010.

I'm writing this up in my diary not so much because I want to, but because I can't sleep. It's dawn. Sunday. Momz fell asleep a few hours ago after we talked about what happened. Margee is still in the hospital and probably won't be released until Monday, or maybe later.

After I called 911 on Margee at Lammi, I went shrieking downstairs and grabbed the BMer keys off the kitchen hook. I was yelling to Momz that I had to get to Margee, that she'd been roofied at Lammi and that I had called 911 and was going there.

All I can remember after that and until we got to the frat house was that Momz wound up driving, and I was trying to text Margee, then call her, again and again, until we pulled up as close as we could get. Never got my seat belt on.

What fucking disaster. Fire, police, ambulances. Red lights bouncing off cars, frat boys and cops pinning frat boys against the Lammi wall. Radios blasting out static and voices. Momz had to park a block down, and I flew out of the car before she even started parking.

I thought Margee had died. Fucking died. Like when you watch those paramedic shows on TV. Some EMTs were rolling her down the lawn on a stretcher to a fucking helicopter across the street on the commons. A goddamn helicopter like ready to fly! They were talking, no, shouting to her. "Stay with us, Margee." "You'll be all right, Margee." And "Breathe, Margee."

Her head was all loose and raggedy. She had a tube stuck down her throat, and one girl was squeezing some black bag at the other end of the tube. There was vomit on the sheet over her, and there was an IV in her arm. She looked real blue, even in just the searchlights from the fire truck. Blue and dead.

Some big machine, like an EKG, on one side of the stretcher, beeping. A green tank near her feet, hissing.

One of the EMTs suddenly pulled down the sheet. No blouse or bra. Her boobs were bouncing as they rolled closer to the helicopter. He put the palm of his hand between her boobs and rubbed it against her chest.

"Marggeeee," I screamed. But some cop caught me around the waist before I got to her.

"Who are you?" he asked, like cold and annoyed.

"I'm Margee's friend," I shouted at him. I tried to pry myself loose, putting one arm underneath his, and went for his balls with my leg, like we practiced in gym class. That pissed him off. He got behind me with an armlock, I think.

"I'm the 911 caller," I said. "That's my friend, Margee. Is she dead?"

It was like a scrum. There must have been three or four cops. Then, Momz got involved too, and finally a lady cop came and held me. Real close and harder than any of the others.

"Listen to me, honey," she said, with me kinda spread-out against some fence and Momz behind the cop, crying and begging, "Calm down, KT. Please?"

I guess I must have kinda got run outta strength, what with first fighting four cops, and then this woman.

"Listen to me, honey," she said, pressing the side of her face against mine and talking sharply into my ear. "The paramedics are working to save her now. You can't do anything here."

"Is she alive?" I cried.

The cop hesitated, then said, "Yes."

"No, she isn't, is she?" I said.

"Yes, she is. You're the 911 caller?"

"Yes," I said.

"Okay, so you come with me. I'll take you to the hospital for her. But you gotta stop this."

"Okay," I said. I think Momz had gotten her hand in somehow and was stroking my forehead. "Calm down, KT. Calm down. Please!" Momz was sobbing.

"Let's take you to your girl," the cop said.

"Okay," I said again. The cop let me go slowly. I almost fell down.

All I remember was Momz and me in the back of a patrol car. Sirens and horns. Buildings popping up in blue and red lights and flying by. The hospital. A cold waiting room. And then some guy detective approaching me and asking me questions and questions and more questions.

Most of my answers were "No" and "I don't know."

The cops took my cell phone for evidence. They said I could probably have it back Monday, after they download the texts.

I'm gonna look like some freak. Some party ho.

I hope Momz doesn't get to read all that.

By the time we left, somebody, I think it was a doctor, but she looked almost as young as me, said that Margee had made it, but that she was in ICU, and it would be best if I went home and came back tomorrow, late tomorrow to see her. Call first.

That didn't sound good, and I wanted to stay.

"You saved her life," the maybe-a-doctor said. "Margee had ingested GHB, a lot."

Momz hugged me.

"But now Margee needs to rest," said maybe-a-doc.

Yeah, date rape shit. She got roofied.

Damn, that coulda been me!

That lady cop was still there. She was kind enough to drive us back to our BMer. I thanked her and cried a bit on her shoulder. I think I left some snot gobs there.

KT

Sunday, November 15, 1896.

It has been nearly two weeks since little Leo died. We have all been sad and bitter. Tessie lies around the apartment, mostly trying to cook, clean, and look as though she is coming along, but really she gets very little done. I do whatever I can on breaks from housekeeping, but I am still nursing Lessia, and I get tired by ten o'clock evenings.

I was surprised by Gus, who not only spent most late evenings helping Tessie, but stayed most of last Sunday doing laundry. He says he does his own anyway, so why not a bit more. Siggi was not much help at first, ranting on about oppression of the workingman and such. Finally, Gus took him into the hallway. They had words, and I was worried, but when they came back inside, Siggi went over to Tessie and asked her to forgive him for being cold.

She did, and they hugged.

Amelia and Elizabeth have both done much in getting groceries together and putting food on the table. They even missed school for one week, but then Tessie said they must not miss any more. She is right.

Tessie and Siggi had been very fortunate with Amelia and Elizabeth, and even Leo too. Hardly ever even a cough, bad cold, or a runny nose.

Until nearly three weeks ago, in the middle of the last week of October. It was so sudden. In the middle of the night, Leo woke up crying and held his throat. Tessie picked him up, walked him about the apartment and then the hallway. Leo had developed a fever, and I could hear Tessie pumping water from the sink onto cloths and wringing them out to place on Leo's forehead.

I slept in fits and starts, worrying that Leo might pass his infection on to Lessia. In the morning, Tessie suddenly woke me, shook me, and said, "Get the doctor, Kati; he has the patch."

I said nothing, only dressed quickly and ran out toward Sixth Avenue, to Doctor Montrose's house. It was already too late. No child survives diphtheria. At least no child in the tenements.

By then, little Leo had the croup cough. His neck had swollen, and he shook. Tessie kept calling to him, cradling him, and pacing slowly through the apartment, but he was listless and did not even look at her. Siggi paced up and down behind them, until I took Leo from exhausted Tessie and placed him in Siggi's arms.

"Walk with your son, Siggi; Tessie is dead tired."

"But I—"

"Work can wait; work will be here tomorrow," I said. I stared at him, hoping he would understand my words.

He did, and took Leo to comfort.

The doctor arrived. Siggi placed Leo down on his cradle bed. We moved the bed into the front room for light. I held Lessia at the back of the room, while Tessie and Siggi huddled behind Doctor Montrose.

When Amelia and Elizabeth wandered in sluggish from bad sleep, I shepherded them back and got them ready for school. Stale bread and a little cold wurst was all I could offer them for breakfast.

Doctor Montrose tried to give Leo a tablet of some sort to ease his pain, but he was so limp, and his throat so swollen, that he could not get it to pass to his stomach. He left after a somewhat cold diagnosis of diphtheria, and a remark to keep Leo as comfortable as they could. He had other such cases to attend to. Apparently, there was an epidemic forming. Bad water, he observed. He would be back in the evening.

So where would he be going? Hustling from tenement to tenement to proffer his impotent advice? Handing out laudanum to children, as though they could be cured by numbness? Collecting his fees nonetheless.

If we had called him from Fifth Avenue, from a fine stone palace, Leo would have gone to the hospital, and at least there would have been an effort to save him.

By evening, little Leo had died. I fetched the undertaker. Then I checked on Lessia, felt her forehead, and listened to her breathe.

She was fine. I sighed. I don't know if I did wrong, but I whispered a small thanks to Mary.

A note from *Harper's Weekly* in 1879:

> "One-half of the deaths of the city are of children under the age of five years. Since 1872 the deaths in New York have been 32,647 of whom 16,188 were under the age

of five years. The mortality is not the sum total of the damage. Where there is one death there are seventy-five cases of sickness."

Cara Maurer

December 6, 2010.

Did not do much yesterday. I did call the hospital on Momz's land-line to see when I could visit Margee, but they told me she was still not able to see anyone, and that I should call back tomorrow. Well, that's today, and they said the same thing.

I'm worried. I don't want to bother Margee's mom, because I'm sure she's got enough to do and's probably at the hospital almost all the time. I keep waiting for Margee to text me. Keep trying to pull out my phone to see if I missed a buzz. Like every ten minutes this morning. Keep for-getting, it's at the police station.

I didn't want to go to classes, but I did anyway. Momz drove me over on her lunch break. I think she stayed in the parking lot the whole after-noon until I was done. There were several empty coffee cups in the cup holders, and some crumpled chip and snack wrappers on the floor. That means she missed work.

I was afraid the other students would be talking about it. The usual bullshit, maybe dissing me for 911'ing on the frat. Buzzkill KT. I assumed my name would be out there. But it wasn't. At least it isn't, yet. The vibe's different this time. I don't know why. Not much being said. Actually, I heard nothing.

I was surprised not to see lots of media on campus. There was the local News 10 truck, but no ABC, NBC, CNN, like the time last year when that freshman Liz said she had been raped at Pi. So far very quiet.

If my name gets out as the 911er, and the media get hold of it, are there going to be satellite dish trucks camped on Momz's front lawn?

Shit, my life'll be over!

Or maybe not. Damn, if Kati can woman on after getting dumped eight months pregnant in stone-age New York, I can too. And I did a good thing. A good thing. Writing about Kati, I reread her entry about

59

Lausberg getting Willi off the block. That was only October. So Willi didn't stay long in jail. And Kati didn't even mention it. I guess it was what she expected back then.

When I got back into Momz car, I caught myself looking in my bag for my phone to see if Margee had texted me. Wanted to take it off vibrate.

Rescheduled my obi-wan appointment for Wednesday.

I did get a call from the police at home. I can pick up my phone this evening. Can't wait! Hope Margee isn't angry at me for not answering her. I'll explain.

KT

December 6, 2010. Evening. Late.

So, I don't know where to start. I guess I'll just go through things as they happened, though I want to talk about Margee first. Momz caught me crying as I came back from the police station, and I told her I wanted to find the dumb fuck who spiked her. I wanted to see him go to jail. I don't care if everybody knows I'm the one who called the cops on Lammi. I kept talking about lots of stuff. Then, about Ken, too.

Momz was great. We walked and talked all around the neighborhood for like over an hour. I told her everything I'm writing down now. And more.

So I guess this isn't much of a private diary! At least this entry. Most of it, anyway.

I got down to the station about seven. There was this unhappy cop at the front desk, behind this thick plexiglass. He asked me what I wanted, and when I told him I had been told to come pick up my phone, all he said was, "Oh, you're the one," and called back into the station. He didn't even look up after that, just kept typing something into his laptop.

A door behind him opened, and it was the same lady cop from Lammi. Next thing I know, she's in the little reception area with me and invites me back to her "ready room." I hesitated, but she insisted, so I went.

It was no big deal room, painted light green, no windows, just a messy bunch of desks with laptops, in bins, and the smell of burned coffee, or stale coffee, I hate that odor. When I was ten, and at the wake for my father, I sat in a small side room, with a forgotten pot of slowly evaporating coffee thickening on a far table.

Nobody else was there with us. I felt really uncomfortable and embarrassed.

"I'm sorry I sobbed all over your uniform," I said.

'No big deal," laughed the lady cop. "I've had much worse, believe me."

"Like Mr. Magoo last week," said somebody behind me. I jumped. I had thought the room was empty.

A young cop peered out from a door at the far end of the ready room. The lady cop laughed. "Yeah, like him."

"What happened?" I heard myself ask.

"Too much booze. Tried to step down from a curb, missed, and did a face-plant into a fire hydrant, right, Officer Bozel?"

"Yeah, Georgie, boys, booze, and boobs. Bad mix. Got his blood on my shirt."

"Lucky it wasn't his eye, Marsi," said Georgie.

I must have looked really upset, because the lady cop, Officer Bozel, stopped snickering.

"Hey, Georgie," she said. "Give us some space."

"Sure," said the other cop, and he disappeared.

"Sit down, hon," Officer Bozel said, slapping her hand against the back of an old metal chair.

"You have my phone?" I asked as I sat. Officer Bozel was shorter than me but distinctly wider, without being fat, like many of the local cops are. She had long, blond hair pulled back tight in a ponytail, no makeup, and sharp blue eyes that were staring right at me. She was looking at me from the edge of her desk, I guess it was hers, with her arms holding her up, as though she was going to start doing some type of lean-in push-up. She could have been forty, or more.

"Sure do," she said.

I didn't know what to say next. She kept on looking at me, for a long time, then pulled open a drawer, reached into it, pulled out my phone, and plunked it down on top of the desk, forcefully.

"Can I take it?" I asked.

"Yes." She just kept looking at me. She sighed. "Look, hon, you know nothing you send out into the ether ever goes away, right?"

I was afraid I was going to get a lecture. I reached for my phone and said, "I just want to see if Margee's texted me. The hospital won't let me see her yet."

"You two close?"

"Yes. We're BFFs."

"I don't know what that means," said Officer Bozel. "I can see it means for you that you have her back, no questions asked. Would she do the same thing for you?"

"I guess so," I said. "I hope so."

"You're not so sure, are you?"

I tried to look at the lady cop while I fumbled to see if Margee had left me some messages. "Nothing," I said.

I was not going to cry on her again, but I wanted to.

"Do you know how she is?" I asked. And then, suddenly, for some reason, I asked, "When the medics were taking her to the helicopter, why did they pull down her blouse like that?"

"Sternum rub," said Officer Bozel.

I must have given her some "huh?" look, and angry, too, because she leaned over and held my shoulder.

"When a victim isn't breathing, h—KT—some paramedics and EMTs use it to try and induce a response. It's misapplied a lot. It was there, but the intentions were good."

"Is Margee gonna die?" I just blurted out and started sobbing, even though I didn't want to.

"She's going to take some time to recover, KT. I'm also concerned about you."

"You read all my messages!?" I said real loud. "Everything?"

"The lawyers read what they needed to decide what they needed to download."

"Lawyers? And who else? You, and who else?" I was getting angry. I stopped sobbing, feeling angry at myself, too, for being such a *girl*.

"Frankly, KT, I only downloaded the 911 part for our records, but I had to scan through some other stuff to get to it."

Officer Bozel dropped her hand from my shoulder and tried a new approach. "Take some pride in yourself, young woman. Be careful what you say and what you do!" She really put down the hammer on the word "do." "Protect yourself."

Silence again. Then she said, "A court order of protection is really of use only after it's been violated. Small comfort, KT."

"You mean Ken," I said. I got weak. I was angry at her for having read that. But I also felt thankful for what she had just told me. I sort of knew that, but, nonetheless.

"You are seeing a doctor?"

"Yes. Already have. Series of tests lined up."

"Good. You gonna get a COP?"

"A what?"

"Court order of protection."

"Oh, yeah. I don't know."

"Never bluff with scumbags, hon."

She must have read the Ken stuff thoroughly. "So, what can I do?" I said.

"Make better choices."

"It's kinda too late now," I said. "Once this stuff gets out, I'm dead."

"It probably won't get out," said Officer Bozel. "Everyone's lawyering up, and nobody, not the school, not the frat, nobody, wants this out there." She paused. "And," she said, putting her hand back on my shoulder and looking me dead-on with those eyes, "trust your mom."

I nodded, got up slowly to leave, and said, "Thank you."

"You're welcome, KT," she said. "Here's my card. If you ever want to, or need to talk, call me."

"Sure," I said, not sure.

"Oh, and get a new phone and start over," she said.

"Yeah," I answered, a little hesitantly.

"Put in all your contacts one by one yourself," she said. "And think about them as you do, maybe you'll want to leave a few out. Put in one labeled ICE, and put in your mom's number."

I nodded, thinking, damn, this lady cop's really scoped out my life!

"Maybe you'll put my number in there," she said.

I looked over at her. She meant it in a good way. I could tell. I'm not sure about the new phone thing, at least until I know about Margee. I keep hoping I'll see a text from her. Just one. A "Hi!" That's all.

And now that I've read this over, I sound like a guy, what with "lady cop" and "girl."

KT

Sunday, November 29, 1896.

Today, many of the families on the block celebrated the American Thanksgiving holiday as best they could. The holiday itself is supposed to be celebrated on the last Thursday of the month, set by the great President Lincoln, but we the poor cannot dare to miss work for our meager recognition of the event. So we do our best on the only day, Sunday, given to us, begrudgingly, because it is set so as a matter of faith, to which our employers give forced honor.

For the Flogts and me, the holiday was mutely ignored. An affront to little Leo's memory. It was just as well. What could we have added to the table? One extra sausage? A fresher loaf of bread? Perhaps a raisin pie might have been appropriate, in honor of Leo but still a treat to the palate?

Tessie has lost some of her somnolence as she works through her day. The work itself, and the help of Amelia and Elizabeth, their presence alone, turns Tessie's thoughts from little Leo. The colder weather has also helped her in a way. Tessie at first forgot occasionally about the fire in the stove, letting it go out. But now, it is cold, and she has been paying it the mind it demands. She is also back to keeping the floors scrubbed and the curtains washed against the constant soot. The chamber pots no longer go unemptied.

So, in this way, little Leo's memory is softened by household chores and the presence of daughters. Work numbs, yet it forces the heart to beat harder and dissipates the malaise of mourning. Love for children quickens the heart, if the work to support them tires it. One escapes to the present.

What would I do? I only have a tenement to care for, hardly a family. And if Lessia would contract cholera, or diphtheria, or any of the ills that haunt us in the tenements, to whom would I turn? Who would lift me?

Yesterday evening, Tessie did muse that she had not gone to Calvary to lay a flower on Leo's grave last week, and that once it snowed, there would be no finding his place among the many until spring, and even then, it might be difficult to find that small, troubled spot in the large field of our destitute, unmarked graves. There are so very many of them, apart from the fine monuments of the rich lying off to the east.

Gus, interrupting his talk with Siggi, offered to go for her and bring a flower. Then, he turned to me and asked if I would go with him. "But Lessia," I protested.

"I will see to her feeding," said Tessie. "I will offer her some of my milk. I am still able to feed. Would you please?"

I nodded willingly, hoping my hesitation was not offending and my reluctance was masked behind a wan smile. "Sure," I answered briefly.

Gus smiled. "I will be up after breakfast. We can take along a few cold sandwiches."

I was angry at him briefly for making his offer. Then, I thought him a good man for supporting Tessie and felt annoyed at myself. But it is the water. It is the milk from the dairy. It must be, for seldom does a child solely nursing die of these plaguing diseases. I wanted to emphasize this to Tessie lest she offer Lessia a small spoon of either, but I said nothing.

The day was cold. Damp. The sky was low and gray. It took time for us to get to the horse trolley on Seventh Avenue, then to the ferry at Twenty-Third Street and the East River to Queens, and finally to endure the slow, jarring ride in another trolley to the cemetery.

Gus grasped two small paper flowers, imitation white roses, in his hand the entire trip. It meant that everyone knew where we were headed, and generally gave us a bit more space in the packed cars. I tried to pay my fare, but Gus would not hear of it.

"You are my guest," he said.

We spoke only English, stammering and laughing at times at our incompetence, but carrying on nonetheless in our American tongue.

"I have been here too long to speak German," he observed as we approached Calvary. "But I have out of laziness, and perhaps a bit of fear. And you?"

The question caught me off guard. "Perhaps on both counts," I said.

"Well, now we can challenge each other, help each other," he said.

It took a while to find Leo's grave. It was simply a disturbed mound of piled dirt, now sinking back to the level of the frozen brown grass around it, as were many other small mounds about Leo's. We had both accompanied Tessie, Siggi, Amelia, and Elizabeth to Leo's burial, and we were certain we had arrived at the right spot. I had huddled Lessia close under my coat. By spring, however, it might be another matter.

There were other small groups of quiet, hunched mourners leaving tattered flowers or paper imitations on the tiny brown hillocks roiling the damp field. The wind and weather of past days had scattered prior offerings about the flat, dreary ground. Some of the visitors mumbled prayers and stood stock-still in a chill breeze shivering through them across the open land, suffering in memoried sympathy to the pain of their now departed beloveds. Others plucked the best of the detritus of last week's meager offerings and placed them on the graves of those they honored. I heard German, French, Italian, Spanish, and other languages. In the tenements we carefully carve out our national spaces. The dead unite us here.

I noticed Gus had dropped both flowers on Leo's grave.

"Why two?" I asked.

"One for Leo," he said. "And one for my dead brothers and sisters: Lina, Gottlieb, Mary, Fridericka, Rudolph, Adolph, Charles, Karl, Paulina, and Sofia."

"Where do they lie?" I asked.

"*Some at the Lutheran Cemetery here in Queens, some in a small field in Bechingen.*"

He looked at me and wiped away a tear.

I had been thinking of Lessia while we paid respects to Leo, wanting to return to her, nurse her, and protect her, assure myself she would not join those tiny tragedies interred about us. I wanted to ask him to leave but hesitated. He sensed my need, however.

"*We have been here long enough,*" *he said.* "*You need to return to Lessia.*"

We were silent to the ferry. As we stood to its back as it slowly pitched to Manhattan, Gus looked me close in the eye and took my hands softly. He spoke in German.

"*Kati, we are alike in having been deeply disappointed in our lives. I think we have an understanding of hope in the face of sorrow and pain not many have, even among our wretched immigrant troop. I would like to be your friend, and perhaps later, well, more. Would you let me see you Sundays, a walk in Central Park with Lessia? A concert? Perhaps lunch in a respectable beer garden?*"

I did not speak for several minutes, in fact until the ferry jolted to a stop against the pier at Twenty-Third Street.

"*Yes,*" *I said.* "*We can visit and enjoy some of New York.*" *That was all I could manage.*

"*That would be a fine start,*" *said Gus.*

"*Yes,*" *I said.*

So now, as I look at sleeping Lessia after having nursed her, I write my diary and wonder what would be best for her. Eventually she will ask after her father. Do I lie? Do I tell her she is, in this society, a bastard child and worthless?

If I were to find Gus fit for a husband, Lessia would become a citizen, as Gus is naturalized.

Do I think I could love Gus? Does he love me? Or, as he said, are we like victims of fate? And will that suffice?

I do not know. And I wonder, do Tessie and Siggi have a part in this? For my benefit, or to make room in their apartment, despite the benefits my job gives them? Does Lessia's presence tear at Tessie's heart? Is it envy? She was able to nurse her today.

Will Gus respect me if I insist on working on? I find respect for myself in working. I need it. He must. I guess it is worth exploring.

It is hard to conceive of the labor keeping house required late in the last century. To begin, there was no central heating in winter and no air conditioning in summer. Of course, there were also none of the current appliances we rely on today. No vacuum cleaners, no self-regulating stoves, no washing machines. None of that. No electricity. Buildings had no elevators. There was no indoor plumbing. It is estimated the average American consumed close to four thousand calories a day, without the fear of weight gain. One need only look at pictures of immigrants and immigrant children, especially, to note the thinness and occasional swell of a belly to mark life on the edge of hunger and malnutrition.

Each tenement had a wood-burning or coal-burning stove usually of cast iron. That meant it had to be constantly replenished with fuel, often over thirty to forty pounds daily, hauled up stairs. Ash accumulated constantly below in an ash box, which needed emptying, and then the ash was removed from the building. The flue would need tending to keep steady heat.

A consequence of this stove was also soot, which layered itself on curtains, floors, and whatever furniture or rugs there were in the apartment. Floors would have to be scrubbed, rugs beaten, curtains and tablecloths washed. The water for this chore would be hauled up from a pump in front of the tenement. If it was a newer building, there might be a pump and a sink in each apartment, but no drain. Once gotten to the kitchen, the housekeeper, inevitably the wife, would need to heat it up to wash clothing and all, and then haul the dirty water back downstairs to the gutter.

Washing clothing was a daunting task. The steps were as follows:

1. Soak the clothes overnight in warm water.
2. Scrub the clothes the next day on a washboard using lye soap.
3. Place the clothes in boiling water and stir them with a pole.

4. Rinse them twice, once in plain water and once with bluing. Bluing was in fact a blue dye used to offset the accumulated dinginess of older white clothing.
5. Ring them out.
6. Set them out to dry.
7. Press them with a flatiron reheated from the stove and starch any collars.

Chamber pots had to be emptied and cleaned every morning.

There were no refrigerators or freezers. Meals were shopped for and were prepared daily. All food came as whole items. Potatoes had to be peeled and boiled, as all vegetables needed to be prepared. Meat, when a part of the meal, often—as in the case of a chicken—was sold live to the housewife and needed to be killed and then plucked. Fish would need to be scaled.

Through all of this, infants were nursed and children tended to.

This was "women's work" for the fairer and more delicate sex!

Kati mentions raisin pie. Raisin pie was also a German tradition called funeral pie. It was generally prepared for family and friends during the days of a wake or funeral. It was especially popular among Old Order Mennonites and Amish. It was popular because it kept well, and the ingredients were generally available. It did not need to be refrigerated and could last several days. This allowed the family to lend hands to other tasks during the bereavement. It was also believed that the sweetness of the pie allowed mourners to forget their sorrow, if only for a moment.

I have a recipe from Kati Scheu Krieger's recipe box, a later variation in the 1920s, when the baker's labor was less arduous.

Ingredients:

1 cup packed brown sugar
2 tbsp cornstarch
2 cups raisins

½ tsp finely shredded orange peel
½ cup orange juice
½ tsp finely shredded lemon peel
2 tbsp lemon juice
½ cup chopped walnuts
Pastry for a lattice-top pie

The older versions would preclude the zests and juices, possibly the walnuts. Hence the overwhelming sweetness.

In a saucepan, combine brown sugar and cornstarch. Stir in raisins, orange peel and juice, lemon peel and juice, and 1⅓ cups cold water. Cook and stir over medium heat until thickened and bubbling. Cook and stir one minute more. Remove from heat; stir in walnuts. Fill a pastry-lined nine-inch pie plate with raisin mixture. Adjust a lattice crust and flute the edges. Cover edge of pie with foil. Bake in 375-degree oven for twenty minutes. Remove foil and bake twenty minutes more, or until crust is golden.

In Kati's day, the raisins would need to be pitted.

Cara Maurer

December 7, 2010.

I walked into ICU bed one, right in front of the nurses' station, where Margee is. Her mom was there, and her dad too. I was told not to touch Margee, to stand back and just talk, but softly. Well, what could I say with her parents standing there that might not have gotten them angry or made them cry? All the time I stood close as I could, at the side of her bed, with the nurses looking hard at me, and her parents talking to her like she was awake or something. I could tell they were also watching me.

What were they afraid I would do? Maybe my behavior at the frat house got down to them, somehow. Maybe they were afraid I was going to suddenly start acting up hysterical and all. Well, I did there, and so what? She was, she is my best friend.

I know. I wrote "was," and I'm really worried that might happen.

Oh, Margee! There were all these machines and monitors beeping, pinging, and whooshing. They are keeping her alive, but I wonder if she really is? Did she even know I was there? Her eyes were almost closed, just a little white and the shadows of her pupils visible in the middle of those slits. She had a tube sticking out of the middle of her neck, soft bandages all around it. It was a breathing tube. I followed it to a pale white machine whooshing away regularly at her bedside. A tube ran from that to a green outlet labeled "oxygen."

All I said when I entered the cubicle was, "Hi, Margee, it's KT."

Mrs. O. immediately grabbed my hand and squeezed it hard, pumped it several times, and kept on holding it, hard. I had to hold hers tight as well. Especially when she said in a quaver to Margee, "Hon, KT's here. She's your hero." Mr. O. leaned around Mrs. O. and patted me on the shoulder. He said, "Thank you, KT." I nodded at him. Said, "All for Margee." Loud enough for Margee to hear me. "She's my best friend." He was all red-eyed. Mrs. O.'s hand holding mine lightened a little when I said that, then tightened up again. Really hard.

Margee's EKG beeped pretty regular, every now and then it looked shaky on the monitor when her breathing machine gave her a deeper breath, like every several minutes.

There was a pad underneath her. It swelled and relaxed once while I was there. It startled me. I flinched a bit. What is that thing doing?

The light was low in the room. So the machines added a weird greenish glow. They had IVs dripping into Margee's left arm. A big one and two small ones with their tubes going into the big one that disappeared into Margee's arm under some gauze.

Margee just lay there. Flat like. Flat. Mr. and Mrs. O. kept talking to Margee about dumb stuff like the weather and how they were having the chalet fixed up so when Margee left the hospital they could all go skiing. It would be after Christmas. And what would she like for her first meal at home. Mindless crap like that. Not, oh, Margee, we love you, and we can't wait to see you open your eyes.

But then I thought, maybe they have, and maybe they will if I go, and maybe I should. So I squeezed Mrs. O.'s hand, hugged her again, and said, "I'm gonna leave now. I'll be back tomorrow."

I remember Mr. O. saying, "We'll see you then."

Are they on a vigil?

I smiled and nodded briefly at the all-seeing nurses as I left. One nodded back. I guess I passed the test of "adult behavior." I kept it all in until I got to the lobby, where Momz waited, and then, on the way out, I broke down.

Mrs. O. is old, maybe close to sixty or more. She must have had Margee late. She's one of those older moms who tries to look like her kid. Skinny jeans. Clog heels. Sweatshirt top and long necklaces hanging over it. But way too color coordinated. Way, way too new. Washed and ironed. All shades of blue for Margee's mom. Powder-blue clogs, deep-blue jeans, powder-blue sweat top matching the shoes and "yellow metal" bangled necklace. Way too much metal and fake.

Eyeliner. Powder blue. Hair too blond and obvious roots. Mrs. O.'s had some "nip 'n' tuck" done too. Her forehead looks like if she cut it, her skin would snap back to the back of her head.

I like Momz better, turkey neck, no makeup and all.

Mr. O. Surprised he was there. He's some CEO type for Agram Foods. Always on some other continent or out in the Midwest. Works hard. Looks it. Baggy eyes. Baggy belly. A few strands of hair on top. Hair in his ears. Maybe what Popz would have looked like if he had survived his heart attack.

Why do these "good dads" all think they have to work themselves to death? I'd drive a used Civic if I could have Popz back.

If I write this all up, maybe I can sleep tonight without thinking about that hospital and Margee lying there. Maybe.

Damn, I just keep writing!

Googled Court Order of Protection. It doesn't look like I qualify either in Family Court or Criminal Court. It says basically I have to be a victim, and I guess I'm not here. I mean, we were FWBs. Ken didn't assault or rape me, it's just that the condom broke and he disappeared. He wasn't arrested for anything. So Criminal Court is out. Family Court says I had to be in an intimate relationship with him, which would be the only situation where I would qualify.

What does that mean? The website says more than just buddies, but not necessarily sex. Huh? It says the situation could involve dating. Who dates? But it also says I'd have to have a case pending in court.

I guess I could lie and make stuff up against Ken, but not even my phone has evidence of any threats or stuff. "Momma ho" scarcely qualifies. And then it would turn into a "she said, he said," like on *Dr. Phil* or *Judge Judy*. And we'd need lawyers. Course I could out-lawyer him easily. He's pretty moneyless. But that would involve Momz's money. And her heart. We've already been over Ken.

Let it slide. Momz sometimes says, "The more you stir it, the more it smells." I know that would mean Ken, but what exactly does that mean. Got to ask?

Why did Officer Bozel ask me about a COP?

Well, I see Dr. Woolenstone tomorrow. For what, exactly?

And I am going to get a new phone, and a new number. Momz thinks it would be a good idea.

KT

December 8, 2010. Early morning.

I just gotta write this down. Its like 3 am and I'm cold and sweaty. I hadda dream.

I'm in a hospital room. Alone, I think. Pale, bright, and white. Its a typical semi-private. Curtain between beds. And then Im walking to the bed near the window. Im picking up a body from the bed. All wrapped up in wide bandages, sorta lik a mummy.

And next Im wheeling this mummy body on a cart down a hallway. Nobodies there. Its real quiet. I cant remember how long it takes, but Im now at big doors and I open them.

Its an auditorium, or a theater. Its dimly lit. There is no stage I can see, only a thick, heavy curtain like a deep green. But I can see in the theater. I see rows of these mummies all seated and facing the stage. I bring the cart to the next empty row, and then Im seating my mummy in the next open seat.

All the mummies, all these wrapped, like invisible bodies have a divers mask, tinted black, over there eyes. Theyre all motionless, quiet, staring at the stage curtain. And its dimly lit, and I seem to float away.

And now Im here, writing this up. And I wonder if I can go back to sleep.

Is Margee dead?

KT

Tuesday, December 1, 1896.

Siggi came home today early at noon with his head bandaged in a dirty, bloody rag. Tessie called very upset down the stairwell to me, where I was scrubbing the back second-floor landing. All she said was, "Siggi's hurt, Kati; please come help!"

I wiped and dried the landing clean as quickly as I could. I could not leave it wet and steaming, slippery for any child or tenant to fall on and blame me. Tessie called several times before I was able to leave my work.

Siggi was sitting on the edge of a bed in the back bedroom. In the weak light, I could still see that he had taken quite a hit to the top of his head. Blood had scabbed through the makeshift dressing, which looked like a strip of cloth ripped from an old shirt, and glued the fabric against his skin. He was shaking, and Tessie was holding him against her. She had not done anything but that. We would need to better attend to his injury, so I told Siggi we needed to move him to the front room, close to the window, to dress his injury.

Siggi said nothing, only nodded, and Tessie was half beside herself, mumbling only "Poor Siggi," and repeating occasionally, "How could they let you leave work like this?"

He is not a large man, but it took determination and patience for Tessie and me to maneuver the wobbly Siggi the few feet to the front of the apartment and prop him against the wall next to the window.

I would not know how badly he was injured until I could remove the bandage and check his scalp. I remembered back in Misingen how occasionally a horse would kick a farm boy in the head. A glancing blow was survivable. Those instances when the force of the hoof caught the startled lad square were inevitably fatal. The skull would be cracked. Infection would set in, the head swell, and delirium precede a slow death.

"Get some water to boil, Tessie," I said. "Find me a cake of soap. Do you have an old shirt or towel to spare?"

Tessie tossed me one of Siggi's shirts from a pile of clean laundry near the door. It was a still wearable one, but I did not reject it, just let Tessie go on nervously and shakily hauling and heating water. I could see her fumbling about and called to her to hold Siggi. I would see to the water and soap.

Tessie had just finished stoking the fire in the stove, so we soon had good, hot water after I hauled a bucket from the pump downstairs and set it on a front burner. I kept looking out the window, hopeful we could get Siggi mended and to bed before Amelia and Elizabeth returned home from school. I noticed Tessie was holding Siggi steadier than she had been, and her face seemed to show more anger than hurt or fear.

"He was at the protest in Tompkins Square Park," she said to me when I approached them with a small pan of steaming water.

"I see," I said. "Tenth Ward Workingmen's Association?"

"Yes," said Tessie, in a voice edged between anger and love. "And we live in the Twenty-Second Ward."

I suppressed a smile at Tessie's illogical comment and began slowly to drip some water onto the edge of the caked and glued-on bandage and peel it away as the blood softened into a dark, poisonous-looking ooze. I wiped away the runoff and continued, ever so slowly, to disengage the makeshift dressing from Siggi's scalp. Fortunately, Siggi kept his hair short, and I did not need to cut it away from the wound.

Siggi was lucky. Whatever hit him had not struck directly down onto the top of his head but had come at him from the side, oblique to the top of his head. It had lacerated his skin and caused quite a bit of blood flow, but that is typical of head injuries.

Siggi only stiffened and grunted occasionally as I cleansed his scalp, dried it, and then applied some light pressure to staunch the added blood flow that resumed from the cleansed injury. I let enough out to wash away dirt and any contagion from the old wrapping.

I applied a new bandage about and atop his head made from strips of the shirt.

"Take him back to the bedroom, Tess," I said. "Prop him up. Best to help start healing. You might want to clean his face. I'll tidy up here and then get back to work. Good the children did not see this."

"Yes, very good indeed," responded Tessie. She by now was glaring at Siggi, his head hung down as she very forcefully led him out of the front room. Although she had taken to my practice of speaking only English, she was now spitting German out at Siggi as she moved him. All to do with his ignorant, self-appointed role as the righteous Christ of labor. In less savory terms.

I returned to scrubbing the hallway, and the chore lasted until nearly eight in the evening. By then, word had passed quickly up from Tompkins Square Park to us near the North River about the labor riot this day there, the police charge, and resulting casualties.

Times are difficult. There is greater unemployment here, and much discontent. The papers call it the Panic of 1896. We in the tenements only know it as an excuse by factory owners to increase hours, look for the slightest opportunity to fire workers, and increase workloads on the remaining "serfs." They do not seem, themselves, to have gotten any less fat.

It may be bad for Siggi. He will not be able to work tomorrow or likely this week. I am not sure how Tessie will respond; she had tended to be meek in the acceptance of her husband's ways, perhaps too accepting. But now?

This means my work is all the more valuable to them. I must stay until matters mend themselves.

But how? Especially if Siggi is blacklisted as a troublemaking socialist. Why must so many men feel the need to crusade? It never ends well.

Tompkins Square Park was laid out in 1850, named after Daniel D. Tompkins, the vice president of the United States under James Monroe, and a governor of New York for ten years until 1817. It is bordered by East Tenth Street on the north, Avenue B on the east, East Seventh Street on the south, and Avenue A on the west.

The park had been a focal point for a number of social protests prior to the riot, including a protest by immigrants against lack of jobs and food in 1857, and one scene of the New York Draft Riots of 1863.

Siggi's socialist views were common among the German immigrants of the day, as previously noted. It resulted in part from the Panic of 1896, which was actually an extension of the Panic of 1893. Many labor groups, including over one thousand men from the Tenth Ward (Kleindeutschland) Workingmen's Association, had assembled in the park. They and socialist and Marxist groups were demanding public-works programs to relieve joblessness among the immigrant masses. The demonstration that Siggi attended that day was to be a stepping-off point for a march on City Hall.

Although initially a permit had been granted for the assembly, it had been revoked the day before, but no mention of this was made to the gathering crowds. Over seven thousand demonstrators soon filled the park, the largest such throng to date in New York for an event of this type. However, over fifteen hundred police were also on the scene, including many on horseback.

Midmorning, the police entered the park to disperse the crowd, using their billy clubs to do so. Many of the mounted police cleared the nearby streets of the workers driven from the park. The protestors, at least those from the Tenth Ward Workingmen's Association, did not go without fighting back against the police.

Later in his life, Samuel Gompers, in his book *Seventy Years of Life and Labor*, would remark about the incident, which he had attended: "Mounted police charged the crowd on Eighth Street, riding them down and attacking men, women and children without discrimination. It was an orgy of brutality. I was caught in the crowd on the street and barely saved my head from being cracked by jumping down a cellarway."

The Panic of 1896 was caused by a drop in American gold reserves, which precipitated a period of deflation, making it especially difficult for debtors, especially agrarians such as farmers, to repay debts with the lower prices that they were getting for their products. It was difficult for anyone, however, who owed money, such as capitalists, to repay outstanding loans when prices for their output were falling, and thus their resultant attempts to cut costs, such as by lowering wages and demanding more of a smaller workforce, hit immigrants especially hard.

Cara Maurer

Grggi to KT 743-765-8040
Hey, KT!

Dec. 8.

KT to Grggi 875-922-6045
Sup?

Dec. 8.

Grggi to KT 743-765-8040
Finlz over. n u?

Dec. 8.

KT to Grggi 875-922-6045
No.

Dec.8.

Grggi to KT 743-765-8040
U wanna meet?

Dec. 8.

KT to Grggi 875-922-6045
No. herd abt Margee?

Dec. 8.

Grggi to KT 743-765-8040
Ben tryn 2 txt her. Like fry day. No answr.

Dec. 8.

KT to Grggi 875-922-6045
In ICU. Got roofied bad.

Dec. 8.

Grggi to KT 743-765-8040
Ow! U OK?

Dec. 8.

Grggi to KT 743-765-8040
U 2 r like thing 1 n thing 2. BFFs, no?

Dec. 8.

KT to Grggi 875-922-6045
Yup.

Dec. 8.

Grggi to KT 743-765-8040
Sorri. Mabbe wanna go out? 4get abt it?

Dec. 8.

KT to Grggi 875-922-6045
No. No. No.

Dec. 8.

Grggi to KT 743-765-8040
k. well, if you do, txt me

Dec. 8.

KT to Grggi 875-922-6045
Don't think so, evr agin.

Dec. 8.

Grggi to KT 743-765-8040
?

Dec. 8.

KT to Grggi 875-922-6045
Evr agin. Ciao! Good-bye. Auf widderscene. Aw revor. Basta!

Dec. 8.

Grggi to KT 743-765-8040
WHAAAAAT?

Dec. 8.

Grggi to KT 743-765-8040
Y? U OK? u don't mean it??

Dec. 8.

Grggi to KT 743-765-8040
????

Dec. 8.

December 8, 2010. Late evening.

I was right about my appointment with Doc Sam. It was more of a talk session, and I was happy to have it. I think I zombied through my classes today. I came home and took a nap before going over to her office for the six o'clock meeting.

We discussed a lot of stuff. It was interesting to be part of a session experiencing practical application of some of the stuff we studied in psych. Doc Sam may be an obi-wan, but she is really versed in person-centered psychotherapy! So many reflective questions!

I started out telling her all about my visit to Margee in ICU, and my fear for her death and the dream I had earlier today. I don't remember how we got there, but she helped me realize much of my worry was that it could have been me in that bed, roofied and unconscious, or worse. And that I really would not want to do that to Momz.

I asked her how I could help Margee. She said just being there, as difficult as it might be, just being there, talking to her, holding her hand, would be a great help. Apparently, some people who are believed to be comatose can actually hear what is going on around them.

I asked her if there was anything else I could do.

"You won't know until the opportunity comes," she said. "Then, take it. Be kind to others around her. This has got to be hard on them as well. You know, parents never think of their children as vulnerable to this kind of thing."

I nodded. Mr. and Mrs. O.

"Just be yourself," Doc Sam said. "You're a good person."

I'm going to see Margee tomorrow, and every day I can.

Kati is a strong woman. Helping out Tessie like that with Siggi. I just wish Cara would stop with all the "facts." I wonder what else Kati might have written about that Cara did not translate. After all, it does say "Excerpts" on the title page. Does Momz still have the other stuff? I'm going to ask her.

Duh! I don't speak German! I guess I could take up the language. Not now. Guess I better stick to "Professor Maurer's" selections.

It's odd though, I did google up the Tompkins Square Park Riots, and it says 1874, but the diary was written in 1896. Let's do the time warp again? There must have been another one later.

And what is a recipe for raisin pie, really?, doing in there?

Kissed off Greggi. OMG, was he FWB w/ Margee 2? Oops. Text speak! No, not possible. Margee would have asked first! Like, if he was worth it.

Officer Bozel called. They have been unable to find Margee's cell phone. Never found it? She asked if I had it, by any chance. I'm not sure I would want it, now.

KT

December 9, 2010. Early morning.

Got my period. I'm a few days late. But lots of stress. Never so happy to wash sheets. (Later, of course.) That just means throwing them into the permanent press cycle after a little stain remover. No hauling water from a pump. No boiling and stirring. No bluing. And, my god, no ironing! I wonder if it's still done that way in like Buttfuckistan, by women, of course.

KT

Grggi to KT 743-765-8040
KT, how r u 2day?

Dec. 9.

KT to Grggi 875-922-6045
Stp txtng me.

Dec. 9.

Thursday, December 3, 1896.

Siggi is going to see if his job is still available. He is going back to Strober's Silk House early tomorrow.

Gus has told him to say he was robbed on the street by a couple of gang thugs. He even gave him a story: That he was walking alone up Tenth Avenue, when he was attacked from behind, his coat pulled down off his shoulders to pin back his arms, and then his pocket picked. Gus told Siggi to say he tried to turn around, and that was when he got punched and hit on the head.

Poor Gus. It must have happened to him.

Gus laid out a very reasonable story for Siggi.

"Tell old Strober you had stopped at the Second German Baptist Church late Monday, on the way home from work, and you were set upon after that."

"But they know I'm an atheist," Siggi protested.

"You've had a change of heart," countered Gus.

"Why should I?" scowled Siggi. "Priests and ministers, all they do is kneel to the capitalists. Our glory in heaven? Damn them."

"Because you damn us with this socialism," said Tessie suddenly from behind Gus. "You and the glorious revolution of the workingman! For what? For strangers? What about us? Our money is nearly gone. What about Amelia? Elizabeth? Me?" Tessie had never given Siggi her opinion before, never. Only sighs, shakes of the head and crisp silence to his lectures and quotes from Marx.

"Be quiet. What do you know about the struggles of the workingman? What do you know about my work?"

"And what do you know about mine?" answered Tessie.

Siggi started to rise from his chair in the front room. I picked up Lessia from her cradle and backed off to the kitchen should there be a fight. Gus, soft-spoken, gentle Gus, pushed Siggi right back down onto his seat, his arm firm on Siggi's shoulder, and leaned down and stared at him, face to face, with a sudden taut mask of cold anger and a clenched jaw that broke harshly into the flickering candlelight that bathed the room.

"She is right. You are wrong. She has listened to your stupidity, tolerated your lectures, and held her opinion long enough. She is right. You are wrong. Where are your brothers-in-arms now? Where is their money to help you? Who cleaned you? Kati. Who bandaged you? Tessie and Kati. Who has fed you and cared for you, stretching your meager pennies for you? Tessie."

Gus let Siggi go, and he wobbled in his chair, holding his head.

"Almost Christmas," Tessie said softly, "and not even a penny to spare for a small marzipan treat."

"And why are you an atheist?" asked Gus. "Because you know so much about the world and the universe, or because you cannot tolerate any opinion except your own?"

Siggi stayed silent.

"You stubborn fool," hissed Gus. "You go back tomorrow and tell them the story I gave you. You beg for your job back."

Gus rose and backed away from Siggi, moving slowly to the door. He stopped in the doorframe before entering the hallway.

"I am going to bed. If I hear any noise, any shouts or screams, I will be back, and you will wish that cop had broken your skull on Tuesday."

Then Gus was gone. Siggi stayed seated for hours and moved off silently toward the rear of the apartment as I nestled in uncomfortably next to Lessia's cradle.

There was no conversation or sound from the back rooms, only an occasional, muffled sob. I could not tell if it was Tessie or Siggi. Perhaps both. I asked Mary for a reconciliation. I rose, lighted a candle, and wrote this down.

Friday, December 4, 1896.

Siggi was betrayed. He has lost his job, and probably will not be able to find any work as a weaver in all Manhattan. The owners keep lists. Siggi is certainly on it.

When he came back to the tenement, I had just finished sweeping the sidewalk and sprinkling it with some coal ash. There had been an early-morning dusting of snow, perhaps an inch, and I was out whisking it away as soon as it had stopped. I heard footsteps crunching down on the cinders as I strewed a few last handfuls near the stoop. Looking up, I saw Siggi, and my heart sank. No good news could come from him reappearing so soon.

I followed him back into the apartment, and helped him with his coat. He sat down in the same chair where Gus had lectured him so sternly the night before. He looked down at his worn work boots, toes turning up slightly from an ill fit, and the sides pasted with coal ash and a few patches of snow melting to glistening blotches on the black leather.

"What happened?" I asked.

Tessie came forward from the kitchen, where she was boiling up potatoes for dinner later. She said nothing, and Siggi only looked up briefly to her before looking back down at his shoes.

"I was betrayed," he said.

"How so?" I asked. "Did you present Gus's story? It was reasonable."

"I never got the chance," Siggi sighed. "I was betrayed."

Tessie and I waited. Siggi did not want to speak further.

"How so?" I asked.

Siggi just waved his hand in front of his face, as if to dismiss any explanation, and us from its knowledge.

"We have a right to know," said Tessie resignedly. "We suffer from this"—she hesitated—"betrayal as much as you. You must tell us."

"Fine!" sighed Siggi. He just kept looking at his shoes. "When I entered the factory, I walked to the back and stood at the office door of old Strober and asked his secretary if I could see him. On the way back to the office, I noticed there was someone working my looms.

"Strober was out directly, and grinning ear to ear. He led me by the arm to the edge of the factory floor. Then, he did something I had never experienced before. He called for work to cease!

"In the sudden quiet of the room, with nothing to do, the workers all stared at us.

"'Brother Flogt,' he said. 'You have had quite a knock on the head. Is that why you have missed work?'

"'Yes,' I said. 'I was fallen upon and robbed Monday evening on the way home from work. On Tenth Avenue, near Forty-Fifth Street. I had—'

"'Really,' cut in Strober. 'Really, I had heard otherwise. I heard—'

"'I was just leaving—'

"'Tompkins Square Park,' laughed Strober. 'Isn't that where you were? Tompkins Square Park. Seems you got off lucky from a bull's billy club.'

"There was some nervous laughter from the work floor.

"'Where were you Tuesday? Not at work where you should have been. I could fire you just for that. Tell me, truthfully, where were you?'

"'I was at the rally,' I said.

"'*You mean the riot,*' *Strober spit out.* '*The socialists, Marxists, atheists and other rabble-rousers. The riot.*'

"'*The riot, sir,*' *I said.* '*Can I have my job back?*'

"'*Here?*' *said Strober.* '*I see only honest workingmen here. No anarchists, shirkers, and rioters. Honest workingmen.*'

"*I looked out into the room, to my friends, to Wolthers, to Gunders, to Bachmeister, and the others. Friends with whom I had spoken and shared jokes for years. They just turned away, or looked beyond me, to Strober. And there, at my looms, was Lindherr, who had been with me at Tompkins Square. When I looked at him, he glared back at me. Strober noticed.*

"'*I can accept one prodigal,*' *he said.* '*Like in the Bible, one repentant son. But not two. There is no work for you here.*'

"*I know that Lindherr had to have informed on me. That was undoubtedly the price he paid to get his job back.*

"'*Let this be a lesson,*' *said Strober in a booming voice that echoed off the factory back wall.* '*Anyone who wants to be a malicious anarchist will never find work here. Now go, Flogt. Leave.*'

"*So I left. As I reached the door, Strober commanded the machines be restarted. That was all.*"

"*Would you have turned in Lindherr if the situation were in reverse?*" *asked Tessie.*

Siggi shook his head and stayed cemented on his chair, looking downward.

Tessie huffed and returned to her boiling potatoes. "*Still a fool,*" *she hissed.*

I returned to work as well.

"*There is no difference for weavers, either in Prussia or here. America, bah!*" *said Siggi as I turned away.*

Friday, December 4, 1896. Late evening.

All is not lost. Gus says he can get Siggi a job as a waiter. At Delaney's. But he says Siggi will need to hold his tongue. Gus's reputation is on the line.

"*Of course he will prove that you have fine judgement, won't you, Siggi?*" *said Tessie immediately.* "*Can he start tomorrow?*"

"*Yes,*" *said Gus.* "*I think so.*"

For Amelia and Elizabeth, the story of the robbery holds. Same for the neighbors.

Being a weaver in one of the small principalities or duchies in the preunified German lands was a life of misery in the nineteenth century. Prussian trade policies did nothing to help improve the plight of the trade. Unrest and revolution were trademarks of working-class weavers. This was picked up thematically first by Heinrich Heine. He wrote a poem called "The Poor Weavers." It first appeared in 1844 in the Marx paper *Forward*. Much of its distribution occurred in Silesia, which was a hotbed of weaver labor protest. Later, the Nobel Prize–winning playwright Gerhardt Hauptmann would write a play, *The Weavers*. Many weavers immigrated to the United States, hopeful for better lives. Many had their aspirations dashed, not only in the sweatshops in New York City, but also in outlying industrial hubs such as Paterson, New Jersey, as Kati and Gus would later experience. I have roughly translated Heine's poem below. It reflects the bitterness and cynicism of the trade.

In their dry, dark eyes there are no tears,
They sit on their weaving stools and gnash their teeth:
Germany, we're weaving your burial shroud.
We're weaving a triple curse into it—
We are weaving, we are weaving!

We curse God, to whom we prayed
In the cold of winter and in hunger's grip.
We have hoped and sobbed in vain,
He aped us and mocked us and abandoned us—
We are weaving, we are weaving!

We curse the king, the king of the rich,
Unmoved by our misery,
Who squeezed the last penny from us,
And shot us like dogs—
We are weaving, we are weaving!

We curse our betraying fatherland,
A land of shame and destitution,
Where every flower is plucked in the bud,
And decay and mold encourage the worms—
We are weaving, we are weaving.

The shuttle flies, the loom groans,
We are weaving industriously day and night—
Old Germany, we are weaving your burial shroud,
We are weaving into it this triple curse,
We are weaving, we are weaving.

Cara Maurer

Grggi to KT 743-765-8040
Hey KT how abt we go shop NYC? N go to village?

Dec. 10.

KT to Grggi 875-922-6045
Iz Englsh tuff 4 u?

Dec. 10.

December 10, 2010.

I went to see Margee earlier today, after classes but before dinner, though I wasn't able to eat much. I told Momz about the visit. On one hand, I was happy to see that Margee was out of ICU, even if it was only to a "critical care" wing that still looks a lot like ICU, lots of nurses and doctors, and Margee still had her IVs all hooked up and EKG beeping, but at least she was breathing on her own. Even if it was through the traech tube. I learned about that by googling it. She's getting oxygen in it as well, a long, skinny green tube hissing softly into the plastic hole in her neck, all protected by bandages.

She was sitting up. I don't know if she recognized me, but I talked to her as if she did. She looked at me, I think, and blinked a few times. One time, she seemed to smile, but I wasn't sure if it was a smile or just a muscle twitch.

87

I remembered when Momz told me about Aunt Hanna's newborn. I told her it had smiled at me and looked at me when I held her right after Aunt H. came home, but Momz said she really couldn't see me yet, and the smile was just a sucking reflex.

Oh god, oh god, I hope Margee's brain hasn't been fried by the GHB. That's what one of the nurse-docs-whoever told me she had taken. In any case, I told Margee I would come to see her, see her every day, and I held her hand, even when she was just staring straight ahead, and told her I would give her my class notes and help her study and make up her finals when she was feeling better. I lied and lied and lied about getting her back to class. Then, I just talked about the weather with her, and what was going on in town, the new clock up at the intersection with Beekman Avenue, snowflake decorations on all the lampposts, and snow we might have coming up.

I felt like I had been there an hour, but when Mr. and Mrs. O. came in, I told Margee I was sure she'd like to be alone with her parents and touched her hand lightly. It felt cold. I looked down at it, and her veins were visible and purple.

I had only been there fifteen minutes. Except for family, visiting hours are only an hour or so late mornings and late afternoons / early evenings.

My finals are over. I just have one paper to submit, and I'm going to finish it up this weekend. I'm also going to see the dean about rescheduling my courses for spring so I have time in the afternoons to visit Margee. Funny how I want to believe she will be better fairly soon, but I'm fixing my schedule through May realizing the opposite is probably the case.

Margee probably has suffered HAI, or hypoxic-anoxic injury. I researched it when I got home. Downloaded a bunch of information from some reputable medical websites, like only. edu or. gov sites like from university hospitals or such. If Margee's oxygen level to her brain was low for about four minutes or longer, either hypoxic (low oxygen) or anoxic (no oxygen), her brain is most likely injured. All the sites emphasized the longer the lack and lower the oxygen level, the worse the injuries to the brain might be.

I so want to see the fucking assholes who did this to her in jail. I used to think I was against the death penalty, but I'm not so sure now. Seeing Margee like I have, I think I could pull the switch on the jerk who did this. Maybe.

Margee may have suffered toxic anoxia, but I'm not sure. That's when toxins in the blood keep its oxygen from being used well.

I also looked up what the problems are that result from HAI. Not good. Not good at all.

1. Short-term memory loss. Margee won't be able to remember new information or recent events. Does that mean she won't remember my seeing her today? That's because her hippocampus has been injured. It looks like it's deep in the top part of the brain. (I can only remember so much medspeak.)

2. Inability to focus on more than one task or think deep, not able to form opinions or reason well. When I was in high school, we had a kid in our freshman English class out of special ed who I think had that problem, now that I know what it is. At the time, we were all just annoyed at him for taking up so much of the class time repeating things for him. Poor Gabe! I wonder what caused his HAI.

3. Effectively blind. Without going through all the medical stuff, Margee may not be able to see, even if she thinks she can.

4. Anomia, which sounds really scary, like trying to talk, but not being able to find the right word, using the opposite word, or even not understanding basic language.

There are lots of other effects from HAI. Like ataxia, or a lack of coordination, like you were drunk. Weakness in your arms and legs, that's called quadriparesis. Spazzing out. I mean, like jerky movements and trembling that they cannot control. It's called myoclonus. Finally, an inability to do common tasks, like brushing your teeth or feeding yourself.

It sounds bad. Real bad, like Margee may never be Margee again, at least to me, and Mr. and Mrs. O. But I wonder what she might be thinking? If she is thinking, and hoping we keep treating her like the Margee we knew?

I read about what doctors need to do to treat HAI, and it looks like it's all being done. At least the first interventive steps. I hope they think she's capable of some of the others, like therapies. All types of therapies: recreational, occupational, physical, speech, and others. It sounds difficult. The websites say it is. It's like Margee is going to have to try, or be told, to relearn living again.

And I want to help her with some of this therapy, however I can.

I'm writing just like Cara Maurer! Such a lecture! But it helps me understand what's going on. Writing it down. Maybe that's why Cara wrote the way she did. She was trying to understand Kati's diary. And maybe helping other readers understand it too.

But I don't want or expect my diary ever to be read. I don't think.

KT

Sunday, December 20, 1896.

Gus stopped in after Sunday dinner. It has been two weeks since Siggi started as a waiter at Delaney's. Every time he starts to complain, Gus stops him and says he should he happy he got a second chance. He reminds him to be responsible to Tessie, Amelia, and Elizabeth. And himself. Gus speaks only English, and Siggi grumbles on in German.

Gus brought a photograph with him. It is a picture of his parents' home. They bought a house in Paterson and have tenants! It is located at 67 Garrison Street, in a place called Ward Two, near someplace called Temple Hill. It is small and does not have all the fancy appointments of a middle-class home, said Gus, but it is a start.

The home is fairly new, only ten years old, and Gottlieb and Pauline bought it new. It has three bedrooms, a kitchen with a pump and a sink, a parlor, and an indoor toilet! No chamber pots!

It is close to a new town forming on Paterson's edge, called Haledon. It is still sparsely populated, but Gus thinks there will be opportunity there soon in new construction. He says the factory owners are behind the building, trying to encourage their workers to buy into the middle-class way of life.

"Not a lot of factories in the neighborhood," he said. "No slaughterhouses, els, belching steam locomotives. But there is a park on nearby Oxford Street, where many children play. A school too several blocks over."

He went on about Paterson, on and on. Good water, lower crime, more space to breathe, looking at sunsets from Temple Hill, and trolleying down to a small beer garden near the Great Paterson Falls. On and on. I nodded and smiled.

He asked me how Lessia is doing. "She is a plump, happy three-month-old," I told him. "She recognizes her mother," I added.

"Does she recognize me?" Gus asked. Then he tickled her chin lightly. Lessia looked directly at him and laughed. "She does," he said.

I know what Gus is trying to do. He wants me to be attracted to Paterson. He forgets, but I did hear him talk about moving there back in August. I think he wants me to join him. Is it because, as he said, we both have had disappointment and sorrow? Because we both have been kicked about by fate? If it is fate.

Or is he, turning thirty, in need of a wife to be respectable? To "take the next step"?

As I sat looking at the photo and listening to him sing the praises of Paterson, I weighed the good and bad about this man, Gustav Adolph Krieger.

On the good side, he is patient and kind. He seems to care for me and Lessia. He has never tried to push himself on me or taken advantage of me when we are alone in Tessie and Siggi's apartment. He saves his money. He does not smoke or drink. He is clean and only swears when I would. I do not think he gambles.

He also listens when I speak. When he passes me working, he stands aside to let me pass or compliments me on the cleanliness of the tenement. He does not try to do my work, or assist me, or say what a shame it is I must work.

He thanked me for finding him the downstairs boarding opportunity with a marzipan treat. He is modest.

But Willi was patient and kind once. He seemed to care for me. I was as eager to know him as he was to know me, and we went together hand in hand to our little pond in Misingen. He saved enough money to bring me to New York. He did *not smoke or drink. He was clean. Then, he found alcohol, or it found him. My belly then gave him an excuse. Or had I been a deluded optimist?*

Will Gus want children? And even if he does, how will he treat Lessia? As well as his "own"? Men change. Then, so do women. I will insist he adopt her or say she is his. And that cannot be too far off in the future. Within the year, I want to hear Lessia's "Mama" and a "Papa."

Being away from Willi Rau, away from any claim he may make on Lessia, would be good.

Then there is the Gus who lectured Siggi. The good-hearted Gus who found Siggi work and helped support Tessie, Amelia, and Elizabeth that way. But also the Gus who said he would beat Siggi up.

Could he behave like that to me? He seems to be steadfastly Lutheran, while I pray to Mary, not the old, stiff Trinity.

Slowly, go slowly, I thought to myself, as Gus talked about Public School 14.

"On a Sunday in spring," I said. "I'd like to visit Paterson, with Lessia, and visit with your parents."

I was surprised when he said, "Fine. I have already told them what a good friend you have been to the Flogts, and how hard you work. My mother respects that."

I was startled. How far ahead is Gus in his planning for me in his life?

I need to test him about children. I want a few more, not the overbearing crowd many of our tenement families bring thoughtlessly into these hovels, but some. That means Gus will need to control his urges. Does he do so now? How?

And I want to work. And I will never stop being Kati Scheu.

Sometime in the late 1870s and early 1880s, according to Kati's diary about 1886, Gottlieb, Pauline, Gustav, and Frederick Krieger left New York City and settled in Paterson, New Jersey, in that area of the city that was or would become the Second Ward, bounded on the south by Totowa, on the east by the Passaic River, on the north by the First Ward, and on the west by Haledon, formerly Manchester. Gustav would eventually return to work in Manhattan. The exact reasons are unclear.

Paterson, like most of the industrial East Coast of the United States, had grown quickly in a very short period of time. It was the Great Falls of the Passaic River that gave birth to an industrial city powered by its natural energy through a series of intricate canals channeling millions of gallons of water to mills and factories, the "cradle of American industry." The impetus had been given by Alexander Hamilton, who in 1791 helped found the Society for the Establishment of Useful Manufactures (SUM) as a means of reducing the country's reliance on foreign manufactured goods. William Paterson, the second governor of New Jersey and a signer of the Declaration of Independence, granted the charter to Hamilton and his investors for SUM; his generosity led to the naming of the new city after him. By the time the Kriegers arrived in Paterson, the municipality had burgeoned into a major manufacturing center, producing guns, locomotives, and most importantly for Gottlieb the weaver, silk and silk ribbon, garnering its nickname, the "Silk City."

Most attractive to immigrants such as the Kriegers was the ability to escape from the hard tenement lifestyle to a more ordered urban environment with better-regulated water and sewer systems, public schools, safety, and above all, the ability to own one's own home. Paterson was no elysian field. Sewage emptied into the Passaic River, as did effluent from the various factories. Working conditions were still draconian by modern standards, with labor expected six days a week for twelve hours a day. Occupational hazards in the silk mills ranged from working with carcinogenic aniline dyes to working in unheated and uncooled, poorly ventilated rooms and being exposed to dangerous machinery. Child labor was rampant. There were no effective unions to prevent dismissal for any one of many reasons. One worked as long as one could, since social security consisted of the mercy of one's own family housing one as one became elderly and infirm. Infirmity came earlier in life, due to the grueling work environment.

Gottlieb was listed as a weaver in the directories of the era, and life would have become harder as he aged, considering the demands of work, although certainly the amenities of a compact, bustling, and prospering community such as Paterson would have provided a comfortable vitality that Hell's Kitchen lacked. Trollies ran into the heart of a vibrant commercial district. There was a stop for the line to Main and Market Streets only two blocks away from Garrison Street. Public School Number 14 also stood only several blocks away from Gottlieb and Pauline's home on the corner of Union Avenue and Coral Street. A branch of the free public library lay close by at the intersection of Hamburgh Avenue and Belmont.

Although we do not know where Gottlieb worked after he arrived in Paterson, there were many mills and factories working silk within walking distance of his home, such as Donohugh Dyeing Company one block away on Jane Street, or others in the Second Ward: Crescent Mills, Pelgram and Myer, Reinhardt, National Silk Dyeing Company, and Goldy Ribbon Company. Others lay concentrated on the east side of the Passaic River, closer to the Great Falls.

For Pauline, downtown Paterson along Main and Market Streets offered the same wide varieties for shopping as New York City had done, with greater ease and safety. Local farmers would travel to the city late in the evening, their carts loaded with local produce, waiting off Main Street until midnight, when they would then secure locations along the avenue to sell their fruits and vegetables on market days: Tuesdays, Thursdays, and Saturdays. Meyer Brothers Department Store, at 179 Main, rose five floors, had eighty departments, and employed close to one thousand people come holiday seasons.

One can imagine Gottlieb and Pauline later in life affording themselves a few of those amenities, and a slice of strawberry-rhubarb pie. One hopes Pauline, during her shopping, would have occasionally purchased some small item from Meyer Brothers, if only a lace curtain for the living room of the Krieger home, bought by the hard work and strict money management of the immigrant couple.

Cara Maurer

Grggi to KT 743-765-8040
Hey! KT wear r u? bz?

Dec. 11.

KT to Grggi 875-922-6045
Uranus

Dec. 11.

Friday, December 25, 1896.

So, today was Christmas. Gifts are wanting here. It just means for all of us to take a small pause and remember our faiths.

Siggi has none and is getting bitterer by the day. He complains that the younger waiters are able to serve faster and make him look bad. He dropped a plate a few days ago, he says, and the others laughed at him. He had it taken out of his pay. The customer was annoyed and asked for another waiter, even if the table he was sitting at was assigned to Siggi.

We are growing tired of Siggi's complaints. He doesn't seem to see how hard Tessie is working with less money to still keep food on the table. He has not asked about how Amelia and Elizabeth are doing at school. He sits and sulks in the bedroom, now ignoring Gus when he drops in evenings to say hello. I realized this evening we don't really talk with him anymore; we just let him talk on and on when he emerges from his lair and hope he will disappear soon back inside.

Amelia and Elizabeth have been a great help to Tessie and to me as well, tending little Lessia if she is awake evenings and needs comforting while I finish my tenement chores. I thanked them with a small marzipan treat from the money I saved from Mr. Lausberg's "generosity." However, they smile less now and talk openly about graduating soon and going to work for the family. Elizabeth mentioned quitting school for the piano factory several blocks away that had a "help wanted" sign posted asking for a clerk, but Tessie said, "No, stay in school." Softly. Siggi was pouting in the bedroom. If he heard, he didn't seem to care, one way or the other.

Tessie and the girls often go to Mass Sunday mornings at the Assumption Church on West Forty-Ninth Street. Last week, Amelia stayed home with Lessia, who was fast asleep, and I joined them. I don't ask them what, exactly, they believe. I do not think either Amelia or Elizabeth takes communion, yet. Or has been confirmed, yet. I don't know if Tessie is hesitant to school them formally in the Catholic faith because of Siggi's turn to atheism, and how that may change as time passes. He may become more intolerable as the girls become young women.

I do not ask Tessie about her opinion about a state of grace. Do I or anyone else need to spill my soul to some anonymous priest behind a grate? Isn't contrition in one's own soul enough? Mortal sins! Often defined by men, for men. I have never, though not having outwardly said this to anyone, grasped or really put much credence in transubstantiation. Isn't the belief of sharing bread and wine, a meal, with others, especially the poor, enough to connect one to Jesus? Or Mary and Joseph, especially Mary, my source of faith and strength? Or an apostle, if you are disposed to one of them? Or any like soul in the world?

And as though we, the masses in the tenements, would need to be admonished to fast!

Who is more divine, God, or the Mother of God?

Yes, I do attend communion. I am part of the table, no less deserving to be there than any other tested soul wending her way through life!

But it is getting late. Saturday I still must work, and I must write about Gus. It is cold here near the window, and the candle is fluttering from a draft. He surprised me on Thursday evening with a small, brightly wrapped box, saying it was my Christmas present. I felt embarrassed, as I had no gift for him.

"You are my gift this Christmas," he said, smiling. "Just as you are a gift for all the Flogts."

That flattered me and made me think more about him later, with hopes and doubts. When I opened the box, I found an elegantly needle-tatted silk handkerchief inside, one I scooped out gently and unfolded very carefully. White silk with blue tatting that ebbed and flowed from a light powder hue to a deep, proud navy as it ran along the fine fabric's border. Just inside one edge were embroidered my initials, KS.

Impulsively, I leaned forward and kissed him lightly on his cheek. Gus accepted my kiss but did not kiss back.

"It's so beautiful, so fine. I love it," I said. No one had ever given me anything so impractical and immediately precious. "It's so light and lovely," I added.

"My mother made it," he said. "I picked out the fabric and thread. Silk for your skin and blue for your eyes."

That made me start. I looked away from him and was not sure what to say, or to think about his motives, or next step. Was he moving too fast for me, or I too slow for him, or even myself, considering Lessia's needs?

"I'm glad you like it," Gus said. And then he did lean in, and kissed me so very gently on my temple I could scarcely feel it. Just a soft, lingering touch that caused me to turn back to him, to offer up a firmer sign of affection, lips to lips, but he had backed away already.

"You have work tomorrow," he said. "It's time for me to go. Merry Christmas, Kati Scheu. Merry Christmas!"

His eyes were happy and relaxed, kind and soft, as he pulled himself up from his chair. He nodded to me as he backed to the door and then moved off into the dark hallway, the sound of the latch on opening and closing a very weak click under his steady, slow direction.

What am I to think? He is unlike the men of this tenement, this block, this neighborhood. Some of them surely do not smoke or drink, as he does not. Some certainly do not gamble, as he does not. A few refrain from cursing as he refrains. Perhaps a handful actually save money as he does. Many respect their mothers, but how many take time to visit them, or fathers, too, on the one day off they get per week in this outer circle of hell?

How many are as calm and deliberate as he? I know of no other.

He can act so comfortably in my presence now. So easy. I have never seen him angry, except for that brief outburst with Siggi, and even that was so controlled.

I worry. He is thirty years old, and I do not know if he has ever been with or courted a woman, not that we here clogged in creaking shacks and penniless have the time, privacy, money, or instruction in that.

Yes, he has been tried by life in the loss of his brothers and sisters. I remember our trip to the cemetery. Graveside by Leo. The small groups of quiet, hunched mourners. Tattered flowers on brown hillocks. Mumbled prayers. The dead united us there.

But can they unite Gus and me in life?

I remembered how Gus had dropped both flowers on Leo's grave.

"Why two?" I asked.

"One for Leo," he said. And, as I remember it, "And one for my dead brothers and sisters: Lina, Gottlieb, Mary, Fridericka, Rudolph, Adolph, Charles, Karl, Paulina, and Sofia."

Is my disappointment in Willi enough to unite Gus and me in life? Especially when he seems so good. Too good. And too passive? Is he a "Nancy"?

That's unfair.

I need comfort and companionship, in bed as well as anywhere else. I so miss my early days with Willi! That time in paradise. He was a beautiful boy.

I was so full of love then.

And I am still, waiting. Is Gus the one? Or a one, and is that enough?

I look at sleeping Lessia, as I did when these questions first arose. I write my diary, again, and wonder, again, what would be best for her?

If I were to find Gus fit for a husband, Lessia would become a citizen, as Gus is naturalized. And she would not need to ask after her father. She would not be isolated as a bastard child.

Do I think I could love Gus? Does he love me? Or, as he said, are we like victims of fate? And will that suffice? Is Gus a man for a woman?

So often, like in the country, the landscape, like life, looks so enchanting and easy on the horizon. Then one approaches what was the horizon and finds weeds and thorns among the swaying elms, and the sun, having backed further into the sky, replaces an earlier soft morning, an enchanting distant glade, with heat and uneven, treacherous terrain that makes one sweat and wish one had stayed home in familiar circumstances.

If I do go with Gus, and he respects me, my work, and my child, I can train Tessie in my housekeeper's job, so she can earn money too. Amelia and Elizabeth are old enough to help in the apartment. As Siggi sinks, Tessie will need to rise.

So that is one more reason in favor of Gus, if a secondary one.

Homosexuality was a crime, a felony in Kati's day. No longer punishable by death, as it had been earlier, but nonetheless condemned as sodomy, which included any sexual act not involving the male-female standard coital position. So, oral sex, anal sex, whether homosexual or hetero-sexual, and bestiality all fell under the same offense.

In America, sodomy laws are still enforced in many states, although the penalties have been reduced in those states that have adopted the Model Penal Code and eliminated the act as a crime per se, while pun-ishing its solicitation. Homosexuality is still reason for a dishonorable discharge from the US military or a 4F classification by a draft board.

It was only in 1974 that the American Psychiatric Association declassi-fied homosexuality as a disorder, followed by the American Psychological Association Council in 1975. The World Health Association still views it as an abnormality.

The most immediate challenge to the homosexual community today is the emergence of AIDS, or acquired immune deficiency syndrome. This disease may be caused by an infectious agent, according to the Centers for Disease Control. Earlier this year, they noted that it seems especially predominant among homosexual men with multiple sex part-ners, drug addicts who inject, Haitians, and hemophiliacs. Apparently, it is transmitted sexually or through blood or blood products, and it can be passed on to female partners of bisexual men.

The signs and symptoms of the disease include unusual, debilitating lung infections, extensive skin lesions, and an aggressive cancer, called Kaposi's sarcoma, now being labeled "gay cancer." Tumors form often on the skin or in the mouth. Those on the skin evidence themselves as purple, red, or brown blotches. Other tumors form in the lungs, liver, or digestive system, where they bleed.

Cara Maurer

Sunday, December 12, 2010.

Read a good chunk of Kati's diary...and Commentator Cara, unfor-tunately this time. Cara questions Gus's sexual orientation.

Thanks for the lecture on AIDS, Cara! Just what I needed! Damn! "Nancy," huh, Kati? How about negative Nancy, honey?

G. W. Wayne

Okay, got that out! I suppose you can't expect people to be all you want them to be. I was so liking Kati, and I guess I still do, compared with Cara. I mean, she's in a tough spot. And, wow, she does like sex. And she wants a man who can please her and still be a dad to Lessia. Okay. Not easy, especially since guys like to mark their territory and make their own babies with a woman. Her diary is really moving. In spots. And she had, what, a grammar-school education? Bright girl, I mean, woman.

But, Cara! Really! Of all the things in Kati's entries there you could "observe" on, you had to go there? Not even use the word "gay"—until the end? Then again, I recall Gramma Cara was born during the First World War. So I guess she was trying to be objective. I need to find out when that CDC article was written. Probably when Cara was putting together Kati's diary and writing up her remarks. Hell, Grams, I learned more about gay life in the day from English Lit and Oscar Wilde. I guess Cara never read about Bosie, or learned "The Ballad of Reading Gaol."

Oral sex a crime! It's only a crime I haven't gotten any, at least anything good, you know, to come, though boys expect it for them.

Enough. Need to talk about Margee.

Was at the hospital later this afternoon. Margee is still not out of her coma, well, not a coma, but being Margee, oh, hell, just being! When I entered her room, she was in a chair facing the window. We were having lighter snow flurries then, and I could tell from Margee's faint reflection in the window that her eyes were open. She blinked when I said hello; that made me happy. So I pulled up a chair from the corner of the room and started to talk to her about the weather and the outside world we could see. Beyond the parking lot, there was a low rise of trees, and on the other side of it, the village ran up the side of Beekman Hill. Margee and I really didn't go into the village much, just stopped occasionally on weekends late after parties to coffee up before wobbling home. However, the lights, the snowflake decorations on Main Street, twinkled up warm and yellow along with the streetlights, so I started out talking about these and how they had changed them from the candles and Noel ornaments that used to hang up there when we were younger, and still stealing out from the high school, cutting some boring phys ed class to grab a sandwich and soda at Camalerie's Deli up on the hill. One riff about high school led to another, and I found I was asking her about that day in Mrs. Natalli's Italian class, when we scoped a spare cow's eyeball we had been dissecting in advanced bio and placed it on her desk between some books. She was always late to class.

What a piercing scream from such a tiny lady! No one ever told, even though the vice principal had us all in after school in her room and humphed and snorted his way up and down the aisles promising apocalypse if no one told. He dismissed it, and nothing ever came of it, except Mrs. Natalli began showing up on time to her classes.

I paused. I was still laughing when I looked over at Margee's reflection in the window. Her eyes were closed, and she was sleeping. I caught my laughter and turned my chair to her. It scraped along the tiled floor and squealed scratchily, almost like nails on a blackboard, back in the day when we had blackboards.

Margee didn't respond. Was she even breathing? I felt anxious, really almost light-headed suddenly, and swallowed hard, then said, "Margee? Margee?" I started softly, but my voice was getting louder when she suddenly took a really deep breath.

But her eyes remained shut.

"It's okay, she sleeps a lot, hon."

I turned. It was a nurse, I think, although it could have been an aide. I still don't have the color codes down, and even then, sometimes somebody "breaks code" and I'm calling an aide a nurse, a nurse a doctor! Everybody carries stethoscopes!

"Oh," I said.

I guess it was an aide, 'cause she was carrying a tray with some gelatin cubes on it, and what looked like consommé.

"I need to feed her," said what must be an aide. I don't think a nurse could take that much time for one patient. Pink, pink means aide, I said to myself.

"Can I help?" I said, without thinking about what I was saying.

The aide hesitated. "Well—for now, you can watch." She smiled. "Watch how it's done. Then, I'll have to ask the head nurse at the station, maybe the doctor. Liability, you know."

"Okay," I said.

That was when I noticed Margee's tracheotomy had a cap on it. It wobbled on her throat as she breathed. It seemed so vulnerable, she seemed so vulnerable, and for a second, I wondered how it would feel to have some tube like that penetrating my neck, stuck in my windpipe. I felt a little weak. Margee had a green tube, oxygen, flowing from the wall and draped in front of her with two little prongs just below her nose hissing into her nostrils. I looked at the wall gauge. A small ball inside it floated behind the number two.

I wanted to hold Margee, at least touch her cheek or stroke her hair. Tell her I was there. I cared.

When I looked back up to her face, her eyes were open. They were staring at me. Blankly.

I rose from my chair and pushed it back to the corner. The aide pushed in one of those adjust-a-trays that you normally see beside hospital beds. She had set the gelatin and broth down on Margee's bed, and now she placed it on the tray next to Margee. She unwrapped the gelatin first and took a tiny portion, almost nothing, and slowly touched Margee's lips with it.

"Margee, it's Della, your aide. Your friend's here."

She turned back to me and asked, "What's your name, hon?"

"KT," I said. "KT."

"KT's here to see how you can eat. Can you open your mouth, Margee? Open a little for some food?" The aide patiently slid the spoon along Margee's lips. I noticed they were chapped and had been coated with some type of balm. "Open, please, Margee? Food's here! Time for dinner."

"How about a spoonful for me," I said.

Abruptly, Margee's mouth opened. Well, actually, her lips just quivered slightly apart, and Della slipped the tiny slice of gelatin between them. Margee clumsily stuck her tongue out between her lips, and the gelatin dropped onto her chin and began to slide down it. Della expertly scooped it up with the spoon and plopped it onto Margee's fluttering tongue. It disappeared into her mouth, and then Margee swallowed, forcefully.

I felt so sad. Margee was being fed like an infant. Like a baby being weaned from a bottle!

It went on and on. Close to an hour. I think Margee ate maybe a quarter of the gelatin cup. Della never even tried with the consommé. "It's okay," she said to me as she wiped Margee's mouth after she had finished, "Margee still gets her IV."

But, I noticed, Margee was looking pale, and thinner, at least in her cheeks.

"What if she doesn't start eating?" I asked.

Della paused, then said, "We'll have to use a feeding tube." She then asked me immediately, "Do you still want to train to feed her?"

"Yes," I said. "Yes, definitely."

Della patted me on the shoulder. "Good, hon, I'll get the ball rolling." I guess it would be a relief to her. What with everything else she needs to do, this has got to be a chore. "You are KT, right?"

"Yes," I said. I spelled my name out. "K-a-i-t-l-y-n C-a-n-t-o-r-i." For some reason, I added, "Like my great-great-grandmother, Kati Krieger." But how would you know, all different last names. That sucks. Della asked for my cell number. I told her she could text me too.

No Mr. or Mrs. O. the entire time I was there.

I didn't want to go, but I knew visiting hours were over, and I didn't want to get on the bad side of anybody.

Margee had fallen back asleep. I got my chance to brush my hand slowly and softly along her cheek, then leaned over slowly and kissed it, lightly. She seemed cold and kept sleeping.

I've looked back and reread my diary entries. So much has happened in so little time. No wonder I only got to Christmas shop a little bit earlier today down in White Plains at the mall. Didn't want to neglect Christmas, but it wasn't much fun. Too many people, like vultures picking over stuff.

I looked at a few scarves and capes for Momz. She loves to wear them; she looks good in them, real flowing and artsy. She especially likes mute purples, lilacs, and earth browns. I saw a gorgeous cape in Neiman, but the same vultures were there, picking, picking, picking. Just that their nails were spectacularly manicured, unlike Macy's, or Walmart, where those fingers are lucky to have nail polish. Walmart's good for novelty items you don't expect to last. Like rabbit's feet slippers. I was gonna get those for Margee, but that would be cruel now, like dressing a baby in funny clothes and laughing at her.

Besides, I'd buy that cape with Momz credit card, so it'd be like her gifting herself.

It was dull, boring, and no fun. But I did settle on a cape from Macy's. Momz kinda unique, all the classy clothes, but a direct, unmadeup face. She does have her nails done. Quirky.

I guess, for Margee, the best I can do is be there for her. On the day. Help feed her. I wonder if they'd allow me to bring in a tiny light-up tree for her room? Would she even know it was there?

When does Chanukah start this year? We kinda celebrate that too. Sometimes. A little menorah. We're really confused!

KT

Friday, January 1, 1897.

Another useless holiday for us. Toast to what? Prosperity and health? Prosperity is meeting the rent and affording enough potatoes and a piece of wurst for dinner. Health is not having died from cholera, diphtheria, phthisis, or some horrible wound from work. We toast to the past, to survival, a year survived, and one more uncertain one upon us. New Year's! Useless to us!

But how Lessia laughs at me now! How she looks at me, sees me, recognizes me, and coos at me. When she is uncomfortable, just looking at her helps soften crying. I giggle at her, and she smiles back. She reaches out with a tiny hand and holds my finger so tight. Just yesterday, she put her little hand on my cheek.

Even when I am exhausted from the day, she gives me comfort and purpose. She is so my little light and miracle.

And I want her to grow and thrive. So that means I must compromise, accept Gus, as little as I really know him. So much of my life has been others. When I read my diary, so much of it is about others, and little, though some, about my own needs and thoughts.

I am as others have formed me. A simple farm girl charmed by a farm boy and brought by him to America. Believing in him, serving him too patiently. A brief burst of independence for Lessia, but, again, for my daughter, not for me. Not for my independence, but for her protection, I suppose. Anger. Grateful for Tessie and Siggi, but having to live under another's roof, unable to do anything else, although my work, as mean as it is, I am proud of.

Now, to continue for Lessia's sake, I accede to Gus. Perhaps. It looks like I am tending that way, though I resent it at the same time.

I have not given much thought to myself, and it looks like I will continue that way. Perhaps I really don't want to. Would it be selfish?

I am not in the best of moods. But Lessia wakes.

Sunday, January 3, 1897.

Two interesting things happened today.

There was a parade up Broadway by suffragists about noon. Women in Sunday dress, wrapped against the cold and holding signs like "Women bring all voters into the world. Let women vote," "How long must women wait for Liberty?," and just "Votes for Women." There was one that especially caught my eye: "The men of Western states and Alaska have given their women the ballot. If they can trust their women, WHY CAN'T YOU TRUST YOURS?"

I didn't know that. I had never thought about voting before; I had just accepted that men ran politics. But why? I was at the curb. Many of the German immigrant men stared sullenly at the parade. Some shouted at them. Some just hooted. A few spat tobacco at the marchers' feet. They did not seem to notice. Occasionally the marchers locked arms and chanted, "Votes for women."

I watched the whole parade. About halfway through, some rowdy stepped out into the street, shouting, "Go back home and tend to the kitchen." In German. A policeman on horseback, perhaps angry at having to spend his Sunday this way, trotted his horse over to him and caught him under the throat with his billy club, forcing him back onto the sidewalk. The man stumbled backward, falling into the crowd.

The policeman then maneuvered his horse so that its flanks moved into the throng, backing them further off. The knot of men murmured. I was only some yards away, and heard them and their curses, the rank smell of beer with the cold, foul air that drifted over to me from them.

I took a pamphlet from one of the marchers. It is in English, but I will try to read it.

I will keep it hidden. Siggi does not approve of women voting. He is turning slowly darker. It would seem to me that a true socialist would welcome women into the party. But somehow, as he sees it, social ownership of the means of production means ownership by men, and since women are producers, it must mean he sees it as men owning women as well. Substituting one form of domination for another. No difference for us.

All this talk from him lately about women being weaker. Where will he be when I, if I, leave with Gus, and Tessie takes my job? Where would he be without us, now, I guess, is the better question.

Such an ignorant, callous little man he has shown himself to be.

Gus and I had a good conversation. I was quite forward, because if I choose not to go with Gus, I must think of something else for Lessia, though I have no idea what that might be. Time will not wait for me.

I asked him if he was thinking of visiting the graves of his brothers and sisters anytime soon, and if he would take a small paper flower there for Leo as well, much as he left a flower for his lost siblings at Leo's grave.

He said he would as soon as the weather warmed a bit and the snow melted.

I nodded and thanked him. Then, I wanted to ask him which of his brothers and sisters he missed the most, but before I could, he began to talk, looking out the front window of Siggi and Tessie's apartment as we sat close to Lessia in her cradle.

"I so miss Fridericka," he said softly. "I was about ten when she was born. She was the first child my mother bore here in New York. We all thought: a new land, new opportunity. New life, especially for children. At the time, we lived down in Little Germany, on Attorney Street, on the Lower East Side. She lies buried in Cypress Hills. My other siblings lie in the Lutheran Cemetery, in Queens.

"A beautiful, warm day in early June. I had been shepherded to my Uncle Charles's apartment several blocks over on Pitt Street. When I was returned, that evening, the midwife, Sofie, was just finishing up, patting my father lightly on his back, and leaving. I remember him looking down at me and smiling so sadly.

"'What do I have,' I asked him, 'a brother or a sister?'

"'A sister, Fridericka,' he said.

"'Can I see her?' I asked.

"My father led me to the bedroom where my mother lay propped up, eyes closed. Without disturbing her, Father pulled down the edge of a squirming sheet. There lay my little sister in my mother's arms.

"'Her head is so big,' I said.

"'Yes, she is our special little girl. She has a frailty. She will need your help and care. Our help and care.'

"Fridericka suffered with water on the brain, as it was told to me. She lived only two years and some months. She died on New Year's Eve. She never left the small drawer we fixed for her in my parents' room, except when I picked her up, held her, and fed her a few small morsels she chewed with crooked teeth.

"I held her a lot. I was her protector and her friend. I would bring her my schoolwork from class, on those rare occasions we had been allowed paper to write on. I would speak the alphabet to her. Sing it. She never said a real word. Only baby talk. But I could tell from the way she looked at me that she knew I was her brother, and that I loved her.

"I still have a ribbon from her bonnet among my things.

"She died, I guess of her malady. Quickly, overnight. We only knew in the morning.

"That was a rough time, because only ten days later my Uncle Charles's son, my cousin Karl, six years old, died of dysentery. Twice, within ten days, our families made the funeral journey to Cypress Hills, in tauntingly warm weather, with the brown earth for Karl soft and loose from Fridericka's grave having been dug out there just a few days before. Two small bodies in small white coffins, one over the other."

Gus looked at me. He was nearly crying. I leaned over and kissed him. On his lips. Slowly.

"I will certainly bring a flower for Leo to Fridericka's grave," he whispered. Then he kissed me. Longer and deeper.

I think, I hope, we will work out!
Just for a few minutes, I started reading the pamphlet from the suffragettes.

Attorney Street, where Pauline and Gottlieb Krieger first settled after arriving from Germany, was on the periphery of Little Germany on the Lower East Side. It was bordered by Rivington Street, Division Street, the East River, and Norfolk Street. That particular neighborhood contained the highest levels of tuberculosis (at the time called phthisis), dysentery, diphtheria, scarlet fever, and typhoid in the entire city. A transitional neighborhood trending downward from an originally outward circle of Old New York, it contained a mixture of mostly private dwellings being compromised by a multitude of erected and under-construction tenement houses and a large complement of liquor stores and brothels, as well as factories, stables, storehouses, and coal or lumber yards. There were a few churches sprinkled through the district. Pauline and Gottlieb were part of the arriving poor that would be attributed to the cause of the neighborhood's decline.

Hydrocephalus was a condition not treatable in Gus's day; the victim would simply be cared for and made as comfortable as possible. The malady could have been congenital or acquired, and since no other subsequent descendant has exhibited that issue, unlike our family's history of diabetes, diverticulosis, and depression, most likely little Fridericka acquired her hydrocephalus. That could have occurred as the consequence of a premature birth, or from tumors, meningitis, or a head injury. Since Kati's narrative includes Gus's narrative of its presentation immediately after birth, it likely was a result of the first factor. However, an elongated head can be the result of labor and subsequently normalizes itself, so the cause cannot be completely determined.

It is curious that Gus does not then tell Kati of many of the signs and symptoms the little girl would have shown, including vomiting, irritability, seizures, and a downward look in the eyes, which doctors call "sun setting." Then again, perhaps he wanted to honor her memory or had blotted those unpleasant moments away.

Hydrocephalus is actually a misnomer. It is not really "water in the head" but a buildup of cerebrospinal fluid, CSF, that causes the swelling. This fluid is necessary to envelop the spinal cord and the brain, but in hydrocephalus there is an accumulation of CSF in the ventricles of the brain, causing swelling and pressure on brain tissue.

Cara Maurer

KT 743-765-8040
Hello, Kaitlyn. This is Doctor Herzmann from Hudson Hospital. I was told you would like to help us care for Margee. Could you please call me at 741-776-0704? I would like to set up an appointment to talk with you.

Dec. 14.

Grggi to KT 743-765-8040
last chance. gonna go 2 Vaile 4 holidaz. C u tmrw?

Dec. 14.

KT to Grggi 875-922-6045
Hit a tree.

Dec. 14

KT 743-765-8040
This is a reminder from Tarry **OBGYN** Associates. You have an appointment with Dr. Samantha Wollenstone on Monday, December 20, 2010, at 2 p.m. Please call our office at 742-837-8370 if you need to reschedule. Thank you.

Dec. 14.

Tuesday, December 14, 2010.

Well, good news and bad news, well, old news. I will be seeing a Doctor Herzmann at the hospital about helping care for Margee. He texted. All real proper words. Didn't even just say help feed, but *care for.* This made my day. I just want to help my BFF, and I know I can. Set up my meeting with him early, like at ten, on the twentieth. Then, I go see Doc Sam to have some blood drawn for an antibody/antigen test at two. I wonder if she could test for pre-disposition to other stuff somehow, like diabetes at least? Nah, maybe not. One challenge at a time.

Could be a day of real ups and downs.

Good school's done now for semester, and I have until the end of January, though I'm not sure what I'm going to do with all that time. Momz asked me yesterday what I was thinking of doing once I graduate in June. I hadn't thought about it much, really. What jobs are out there for psych and lit majors? Maybe I could drop in on the job placement office and find out. Get a feeling for the "salt mines," as Momz tells it.

Momz always reading, sometimes at home. Executive editor for Barman and Mitchell. Makes final say on what gets published, what gets the final rejection slip. She has her staff, she calls them "mother's little helpers," dig through all the stuff that comes in to the office and only send her the finalists. Her specialty is historical fiction, whatever that is. She explained it as stuff that never happened but sounds like it could have. Okay. I've got enough to do now with stuff that shouldn't have happened but sure did.

Speaking of which, I read some more of Kati's diary, and Clueless Cara's remarks. My great-great-grammi's really a tough cookie stuck in some difficult circumstances in turbulent times. (Where does tough cookie come from, anyway? Sounds like another of those oxymorons. Oxymora?)

In any case, here she is, dealing with some misogynistic socialist, oops, another oxymoron, with a child "out of wedlock," which was a hugely horrible thing then. Wedlock, isn't that redundant? Working like ten hours a day, six days a week, as a housekeeper scrubbing floors and cleaning grot out of airshafts. To get out of it all, she's thinking of hooking up permanently with "Gloomy Gus," who she's finally kissed after months and months.

Also, she has her first encounter with the suffrage movement, a sort of forerunner to the old women's lib thing.

She's worried about Gus's preferences. So what does Cara comment on? Gus's kiss? No! The votes for women thing? Of course not!

Cara writes about Gus's old 'hood, some place down south of the East Village, aka Alphabet City now. Though, I cannot imagine having to live in such an awful place. Like parts of Chicago today? Then, she goes off on a riff about what Gus's little sister, Fridericka, died of back in 1870. Hydrocephalus, or water on the brain. Really, Cara?

And especially, nothing about kissing. Was kissing such a big thing in and of itself back then? I mean, could you be satisfied with just a kiss? It would have to be one hell of a kiss for me, and maybe not on the lips beneath my nose! Maybe it's because Kati got used so badly by Willi, she pulled back a lot. Became more cautious. I don't know what I would think if some boy gave me a lace handkerchief and was happy just kissing me.

Or maybe I should be? Well, maybe not that weak.

Anyway, it would have been nice to get her take on that, you know, for her time, and maybe a little more comments on Kati's time and what was expected.

Just what was going on back then? No franchise? Like that would be possible today! Anyway, I'm curious about it. Gonna google it, maybe even ask Momz. Maybe she's run across it in her historical fiction, what she sometimes says poor writers turn into hysterical fiction.

Good ol' Momz.

Going to get a new cell, new number. Grggi. Ugh! Means notifying some of the change, gotta take a look and make my decisions. That'll take an afternoon.

It's warm today, one of those days in winter that get the ground moist without raining. Gray, too. Got Kati on my brain. Thought about Gus and his family heading out to the cemetery to bury Fridericka.

KT

Sunday, January 10, 1897.

New York lies in such an odd climate. In Misingen, once winter arrived, it stayed. Here, one week it is so cold the entire window in Tessie's apartment frosts over with deceptively fanciful fairy patterns, and we all see our breath! A few days later, it is so warm one can begin to smell the horse manure lingering in the streets. It was mild today.

The street sweepers are lazy here. Sometimes they arrive in the morning and work diligently to clear away the garbage and dung. Then, they are absent for a week or more, and if it is warm, or hot, as it was last August, the stench becomes all but unbearable, and the flies are everywhere. The Kleemanns had a hen that pecked the maggots out of the offal and grew quite fat. Then one day it disappeared. Mrs. Kleemann went from apartment to apartment in our tenement and raised such a ruckus, accusing the whole building of stealing her hen. "No eggs! No eggs!" she shouted over and over. If someone did take her chicken, it went into a pot quickly. Somehow, her husband found her another.

So, to come to the events of the day, I went again to Leo's grave with Gus. I decided it will be really the only "courting" I could afford myself without guilt. Tessie readily offered to nurse Lessia if I would go. It would be cruel to ask her to do such if I were to ask Gus to take me to a beer garden, or even on a walk in Central Park.

Siggi went with us. There was a disturbance first.

I was reading the pamphlet from the parade last week. It was not long, more a leaflet than a real pamphlet, but it had some good arguments in it. It started out strangely, titled "Not at Home," with a subtitle, "Woman's Place Is in the Home." This must be a city problem. That would be laughed at in the fields of Misingen. No one could cut hay better than my grandmother. I have heard the western states, the farming and rural states, have already given women the vote. They know. But then came a simple statement, "You were out today!" and a series of questions and statements. I'm just going to list them.

Were you at your children's school? The vote controls the school.

Were you buying your dinner? The vote controls pure food laws and market conditions.

Were you buying ready-made clothing? The vote controls conditions under which clothing is made.

Were you seeking a position by which you can support your fatherless children? The vote controls conditions of woman's labor.

It was put out by the National American Woman Suffrage Association at 271 Madison Avenue.

With the last question, I felt no longer alone in my love for Lessia. How could anyone oppose these reasons?

Well, Gus came upstairs about ten, ready to go to Calvary with me. Tessie already had Lessia in her arms. I was cooing at her, rubbing my index finger lightly on her cheek and making her giggle. Then Siggi emerged, unshaven and rumpled, from the back. He did not say a word, greeted no one, just displayed the usual sullen attitude he had sunk ever farther into since the Tompkins Park riot.

He saw my pamphlet lying near Lessia's cradle.

"What is this? What is this?" he began to shout, his voice getting louder as he repeated over and over, "What is this?"

I was taken aback by his sudden anger, no, more fury, at the simple tract. He scared me, and I backed away toward the door. Gus moved forward a step or two but said nothing.

"It's just a leaflet from last Sunday's parade for women's votes," I said.

"Not in this house! Not in my house!" Siggi was shaking. He grabbed at the little paper, clenched it, and began a broadside harangue. "Petticoat rule!" he shouted. "And next, temperance! Where will a man be able to go if he cannot join his friends in a saloon?" He ripped up the paper. "Not in this house! Not here! Who brought this poison into my home?"

"I did," I said, trying to stay calm. "I got it at the parade."

"Get out! Get out!" Siggi started at me, wagging his finger. I began to back out the door. "This is a man's house!" Then he stopped and moved to Tessie. "Give her back her bastard child!"

I lunged for my baby, but Gus got to Siggi first, turned him around, and pushed him against the wall. I placed myself behind Gus and in front of Tessie. I glanced briefly at her, to see if I would need to take my child from her. I expected her to be crying, I suppose, but she wasn't. Instead, she was staring icily at Siggi, narrow-eyed and angry, gently rocking Lessia, who was whimpering at the noise.

I shifted to Gus's side. He continued to hold Siggi firmly against the wall. Opposite us, in the doorway to the back rooms, Amelia and Elizabeth's faces peered frightened in the shadows.

"Who owns the building? Whose house is this?" Gus hissed.

Siggi defiantly shook his head. "Mine."

"No, you fool, you ass, it belongs to Lausberg. You're just a renter." Gus held him almost off the floor, so that Siggi could only find the raw wooden boards with the toes of his shoes.

"Who pays half the rent on this apartment?" he demanded.

Siggi remained stubborn and silent.

"Kati does. You should thank her."

Siggi shook his head violently.

Then Tessie, unexpectedly and firmly, said, "Bastard child! It was only when I was three months pregnant with Amelia that you married me, you..." Her voice trailed off. The faces of Tessie and Siggi's daughters had vanished from the door-frame. There was some sobbing from the back of the apartment.

Siggi's shoulders slumped. I echoed a line from the pamphlet. "The vote controls the conditions of woman's labor, and I will continue to be a working woman, as well as a mother."

"A better mother than you are a father! What example do you set for your daughters? What support for them is there in your heart?" said Gus.

Gus let Siggi down, and Siggi only hung his head. The scars from the policeman's club that had glanced off the top of his head still wound red through stubbly hair. "Some socialist you are!"

Although I had always thought of Gus and Siggi as equal in stature, at that moment Gus loomed over the crooked, downcast Siggi.

"Get your coat," Gus commanded. "You haven't been to honor Leo's grave since he died. Shave, put on some fresh clothes, and be quick about it."

All Siggi mumbled was, "There's no hot water for my razor."

"Shave in cold," Gus said contemptuously. "Don't expect Tessie to run after you. Fend for yourself."

I smiled at Tessie, hoping in all this she had not come to blame me. But instead, she called Amelia and Elizabeth from the back and had them gather up the little missive Siggi had torn to pieces. She kept close hold of Lessia. "We will be all right," she said. "It is good he goes out today. He sulks too much."

They were standing together, Amelia, Elizabeth, and Tessie, with Lessia in the crook of her right arm and her other around the shoulders of her two daughters bunched by her left side. Amelia held the pamphlet tatters. When Siggi reemerged in the front room, she looked at him with a cold face, lips pursed and eyes set unhappily under reddened lids.

"Let's go, Siggi," Gus commanded.

The hunched little socialist clumped his way noisily down to the street. Gus led, then Siggi, and I followed. A door on a landing below us opened briefly and closed loudly. I turned to see who the nosey neighbor was. All the families had their arguments. At least ours today did not need the police, as many did.

Then Gus changed! As though nothing had happened just several min- utes before, he prattled on with us all the way to the East River ferry about how Delaney's had become so successful that Mr. Delaney was going to open a second eating house nearby, perhaps up in the west forties, and that the owner would need his most reliable employees to work the new location. He complimented Siggi on how he had improved at work, and thought perhaps a promotion would be due him, either at the original business or at the new place. On and on he continued about job prospects improving, business picking up! Small talk about some of their fellow workers.

Then, as we approached Leo's grave, Gus said, "You know, Siggi, it's about time you listened to and loved more those who love you, and not some soapbox revolutionaries frozen in their impotent cant."

Siggi nodded, seeming to agree with Gus, but then stopped walking toward Leo's grave. "This is it?" he asked, causing both of us to look at him quizzically.

"Don't you remember it?" Gus asked.

"My Leo, my little son, Leo. My boy!" Siggi muttered.

Gus put his arm around Siggi's waist. Siggi was still hesitant to move for- ward. I approached from the other side, and we steered Siggi forward, until we all stood silent at the foot of the now slightly concave imprint that indicated Leo's resting place.

"I had a son," Siggi sobbed. "A lovely little boy."

"You still have two fine young daughters," Gus observed. "And a wife more tolerant of a fool than I would ever be."

Siggi kept sobbing and then broke into a steady weeping. I was sure if we had not been there to hold him, he would have stumbled forward onto his knees grave- side. It was cool, sunny, with a soft breeze lolling along the open fields. In the distance, a small funeral procession huddled around a trench. The smell of fresh earth drifted over to us and brought to my mind the day of Leo's burial. Then, Siggi had stood upright and unemotional, Tessie crying softly on his one side, his girls likewise on the other.

"Here," Gus said, handing Siggi a small white paper flower. I guess Gus had expected Siggi just to drop the token over Leo. Instead, Siggi squirmed free from our support and knelt at the edge of the little depression, pressing the flower carefully into the earth with his hands. "For you, Leo. For you, my boy," he murmured softly.

Siggi knelt there a good ten minutes and then startled us by crossing himself. Neither Gus nor I said anything, but we looked strangely at one another. In that moment, Gus let the second flower he had brought for his brothers and sisters loose. He opened his palm and let the breeze take it from his hand and push it playfully across the barren, brown grass.

Then Siggi arose, smiled wanly at Gus, and said, "We can go now. Thank you."

On the way back home, Gus took up his prattle again, but this time Siggi joined in and seemed hopeful that his salary and prospects at Delaney's would improve. Back in the tenement, Siggi entered with his head bowed and apologized to Tessie, Amelia, and Elizabeth. Lessia slept in her cradle. I saw that the pieces of the torn leaflet had been played in carefully ordered strips on top of the blanket near Lessia's feet.

"I will try to do better," he said. There was an awkward silence; the women nodded.

"Excuse us for a moment," Gus said. He led me into the hallway and closed the door.

"What do you think will happen now?" I asked.

"That is up to Siggi," said Gus. "We shall see how he behaves."

He drew in close to me and tapped a finger gently on my nose. "Just promise me," he said. "If he ever acts against you or the Flogts, call me, immediately."

"I promise," I said. "But by the time you arrive, Siggi may have accidently gotten his face ironed."

Gus smiled broadly. "A heavy bucket will do too."

I placed my hand against the back of his neck and pulled him forward. We kissed. A long time.

When I reentered the apartment, it was dark. Noiseless. Deep.

Beginning early in the twentieth century, out-of-wedlock pregnancies came to forefront as a problem of the day. Three groups of women vied with the issue. The first were evangelical reformers regarding unwed mothers as fallen sisters who needed salvation. Conservative and obedient to the cant of orthodox Christianity, they succumbed to the "virgin-whore" dichotomy and the guilt of Eve as temptress and originator of desire. Second, an emergent generation of social workers sought to solve the problem itself, not fit the burgeoning issue within any religious structure. The growing acceptance of romantic love among the middle and lower classes had spurred the increase in premarital sex. Seeking to encourage women to obtain knowledge of their bodies and management and control over them in an era still dominated by men was a challenge. Of course, the third group of women in this issue was the mothers themselves.

Although she may not have been aware of it, Kati was living in what we now term the Progressive Era. The roles of women were expanding. Women's suffrage was becoming a mainstream political movement, thanks to the efforts of pioneer feminists such as Susan B. Anthony, who said, "It was we the people, not we, the white male citizens, nor yet we, the male citizens, but we the whole people who formed the Union." Couching the goals of the movement in traditional American ideals such as this, and explaining the need for enfranchisement for better schools, food, and working conditions as Kati's pamphlet did, garnered some support among the uneasy men of the era, especially the working class, whose insecurity at the threat to the last bastion of their eroding privilege, the home, could be turned into the recognition that the results of suffrage could gain them and their children advantages in their economic struggle. It was not that those claims were specious or a smoke screen for other goals, just that men needed to be made cognizant of their real needs.

Sexual independence was an ideal for Margaret Sanger. She militated for women's rights to their bodies by promoting sex education and birth control, eventually leading to Planned Parenthood. Although her efforts would occur later in Kati's life, after she and Gus had already passed through the most difficult stage of married life (raising young children), her platform nonetheless had been constructed by the forward thinkers at the turn of the century.

Some of the most virulent opposition to the American suffrage movement came from Lutheran and Catholic German immigrants, who were fearful that giving women the right to vote would encourage temperance and thus deprive them of their beloved beer and saloons.

Certainly, the issue of alcohol was a clear, if complex, one. Although reformers of both sexes pointed accurately at the consequences of alcoholism in the destruction of stable family life, especially rampant in urban working-class families during the nineteenth century and into the early twentieth, they did not all adequately recognize or address the cause of the problem: unsafe drinking water.

In New York City, failing to understand that unpolluted land was not an economic free good, ignorant settlers from the Dutch onward placed privies too close to wells, and with the eventual crowding of city life and the construction of the tenements, when wells could no longer be placed far enough from outhouses, and hauling water from distant parts of Manhattan was no longer an option, waterborne illnesses from poor sanitation such as cholera and dysentery would erupt. Children were especially vulnerable.

Avoiding these consequences was often at first limited to avoiding drinking water. It was known that water minimally tinged with alcohol was "safe," although the fact that it killed the microbes associated with disease was not. The early Manhattan Dutch even had a dish called "beer soup" for breakfast. No judicial proceeding could commence without good, meaning strong, beer on hand. When a child passed from nursing to ingesting food and drinking liquids, he was susceptible to cholera and dysentery. Even young children imbibed to some extent. For those predisposed to alcoholism, the results were obvious.

Also, alcohol was, and is, a drug. For many of those immigrants, especially workingmen, crushed under the implacable demands of the industrial capitalism that grew in American cities like cancer, alcohol dulled their pain and their shame at not being able to provide for their families, often large families that sprang from rural habit. Although there were many German families who respectably frequented beer halls and engaged in moderate, social drinking, there were also those of all origins who numbed themselves against the debilitating effects of sixty-plus-hour workweeks through strong drink.

Thus, resistance to suffrage was resistance to temperance for many of these men.

The coming of two essential remedies, clean water and strong labor unions, took until close to World War II to blunt much of this alcoholism. It is not coincidental that the repeal of Prohibition occurred after most American cities had created infrastructure for delivering safe water to all their citizens, and labor unions were finding and exercising the muscle to stand eye to eye with capitalists.

Cara Maurer

Saturday, December 18, 2010.

Howling snowstorm outside. Momz is curled up on the couch in her den, deep into some alternative read about the Nazis having won World War II in alliance with extraterrestrials. It can't be too good. She's giggling a lot. Shaking her head. Smiling. I heard her briefly on the phone with Bob Barman, her boss. She was riffing off a few passages and said something about converting it into a comedy. She mentioned a play called *Springtime for Hitler*. Never heard of it. Getting author to sign off on rights. Options for a movie. Stuff like that. Momz is good with spotting what's really going on in the submissions she gets.

Speaking of riffing. Continued on with Kati's diary and Professor Cara's comments. Not going out today or this evening. Not interested in Grggi. I think I said that before. Well, he is like a bad meal, makes you belch repeatedly. My God, Cara sounded like one of my history professors. On and on. Oh, and thanks for the spoiler alert telling me Kati and Gus get married and have children!

I liked Kati's diary about how she and Tessie and Gus dealt with Siggi better. Reality. There's no mention of Siggi having abused alcohol in Kati's journal, just his wife. Isn't that enough? But otherwise, why would Cara put all of those facts about it in her remarks? Maybe I need to reread Kati, read what my lit professors would call the subtext.

Did pick up a few facts from her, I have to admit. This Margaret Sanger founded Planned Parenthood? News to me. Drawing water from next to an outhouse? Ewwww. Beer soup? I don't even like mimosas on Sunday morning! Well, except when I'm working off a hangover.

Hey, Cara, lighten up! Lots of stuff can be considered addictive. Weed. (?) Booze. Sex. Even exercise and shopping. That reminds me, haven't been to the gym in a long time, and winter is getting on, and Christmas goodies, New Year's parties. Don't want a flab wheel round my middle. What a turn off that is, especially on a guy!

So what's my addiction? Or was? FWBs? I think I'm over that. Alcohol? I only drink at parties. But boy, do I. That's an interesting sentence: *boy*, do I. Haven't been to a party in a few weeks, at least. But it's semester break.

If Cara wanted to connect Kati with her historical context, maybe she should have done a little editing, like ghostwriting added segments into the diary. But, then again, considering her "voice," it would really have been heavy-handed.

Still, wondering if Cara did tamper with Kati's work? Did she leave some passages out? I wonder. Maybe we still have Kati's original. Even if I don't know German, I could scan it into the cloud and retrieve it later. If it still exists, the pages have got to be old. Fragile.

Thought of continuing on with Kati with a little wine, some decent French burgundy, something out of Cote de Nuits, no frat crap. Momz said I could try a new bottle she copped from a recent publisher party. So cool to have a mom who's let me sample some of the swag wine she's "appropriated" from her new author parties over the past several years.

Let me try some pairings at a few of the foodie haunts she's taken me to in the city. Ones that don't ask for IDs.

Will I ever drink anything at a frat party again? GHB is scary. Turns enjoyment, like a "boy, do I," into a "boy, do me." But that wouldn't be me, would it, if I were conscious? Bad joke.

I need to see Margee later. Even if I need to take a cab and let someone from Pakistan drive me a mile to the hospital. Let him sweat it. I have not missed an evening since the twelfth. (See entry.) Not that much has changed with Margee. I'll tell you more after the visit.

Who am I talking to?

Saturday, December 18, 2010. Late.

Got to the hospital. Difficult. Roads were only beginning to be plowed. But the cab came, and Momz gave him a big tip before we even left. She kind of gave me that look: "I'm not so sure this is a good idea, but I've learned not to try to stop you."

Way back was easier. Lots of salt already down. Just some slush.

I know tomorrow's only going to be a week since I first started to help feed Margie. But I had been hoping for more change. I suppose what Della, Sandi, Mike—the aides—and I have accomplished so far is progress, but so slow. Nobody talks to Margee the way I do at dinner, well, gelatin or mush time. But then, why should they? They have so many others to attend. They can't sit and talk. From what I've seen in that ward, mostly old coots lolling in the hallways needing their diapers changed or talking to the space in front of them. Must be some type of mostly Alzheimer's section. But either they're switched around a lot or sent somewhere else pretty fast, many of the faces are different, or seem different, each afternoon when I pass them. It's so sad. Yesterday, I had to stop and smile at a little old lady bent like a comma in an overlarge chair who managed to twist up her head and ask me as I went by, "Beth, could you get me a glass of water?"

She reached up a purple-veined, skinny left hand and waved it, as if she wanted to touch me. She was so thin! The knuckles on her hand and joints in her fingers bulged out white and knobby. There was one ring, a wedding ring, I think, dangling from the fourth digit on her stick-fingered left hand. "Please, Beth, I'm thirsty." I saw she had an IV drip in her right arm.

She could hardly manage to speak.

I stopped. I had to smile at her. When I touched her quivering, out-stretched arm at the wrist, it was so cold and bony. "I'll see what I can do, ma'am," I said.

The old lady stopped looking at me, lowered her head, and let it hover just inches above the tray stretched across the chair. I looked at the band looping around the wrist. Sylvia.

Is this where the really old people wind up? Here and nursing homes, so we aren't bothered, aren't inconvenienced by them?

At the nursing station, I asked Della—thank god she was there. You get better attention if you know someone working—if Sylvia could have a drink of water. "Oh, no, KT," she said without taking her eyes off the screen as she input something or other at a desk. "Oh, you didn't give her any, did you?" She had turned around suddenly, tense.

"No," I said. "I wouldn't do that without asking."

"Good." She pushed herself back from the laptop and walked over to me at the counter. "Sylvia has cancer, KT," she said softly. "Cancer of the esophagus. She can't drink. It would cause her a lot of pain, even though she's morphed up pretty large."

"Oh," I said. I felt disappointed for Sylvia. "Not even a little gulp?"

"No, I'm told it would be like swallowing ground glass, if you can imagine that."

"No, and I don't want to."

"But if you want to help," Della said, "I'll give you a wet cloth, and you can let her suck on it. Careful, she's probably gonna try to bite it, maybe swallow." Della hesitated. "Okay, be careful. Don't tell her why she can't have water. If she calls you Beth, it's because she thinks you're her grand-daughter. Just play along. And thanks."

Della scurried back into a prep room off the rear of the station. They are always busy, and generally behind. When she came back, she handed me a moist cloth.

"Should I have gloves?" I said.

"She's terminal," said Della.

"How long?" I asked.

"For her sake," sighed Della, "as soon as possible would be nice."

I wanted to ask Della why not just stop her IV and give her something to send her over to the "other side." I was proud Della trusted me so much with Sylvia, and sad that, somehow, if even a little bit, I was only prolonging Sylvia's life.

I tried to explain innocently to Sylvia that the doctors wanted her to get a little stronger with her medicine before giving her water. I offered her the wet cloth. She took it eagerly. Her lips were so chapped and cracked that sores had formed on them. Sylvia was actually quite gentle as she sucked on the cloth. Almost, I imagined, like little Lessia might have been with Kati.

I almost sobbed a little when Sylvia said, "Thank you, Beth."

Wow, and I haven't even gotten to Margee. Well, I guess a little progress is better than none, or worse, regression. Della pretty much left me alone with my BFF this evening. I'm getting pretty good at this. Of course, Margee is helping, a little. When I touch the edge of her lower lip, she begins to open her mouth and move it up and down. I gently pass a small, wiggly dab of gelatin onto her tongue, if I can, and wait to see if she's able to swallow it. Sometimes, it comes back out. I keep the spoon hovering just below her mouth, catching any spills, and patiently waiting for the next chance to slip it back in.

It's tough to tell when I can try another morsel, well, that's an overstatement, tiny slice of wiggly gelatin or hint of what I think is finely ground cereal. Margee rejects the cereal more, so I start with the gelatin.

Now and then, she looks in my direction. When she does, I talk to her. About almost anything that comes to mind. This evening it was about the fact she was eating lemon gelatin for the first time I had fed her. Well, it was yellow, so I called it lemon. I went on about how she liked lemon ice and gelato, especially for dessert at Lucia's up in Yorktown. I couldn't wait until we could go back up there, and wasn't the crème brûlée also scrumptious? Then I stopped. Was I entertaining her or depressing her? Did she even know what I was saying?

I could tell she'd lost weight. "Just a little more, Margee," I urged her. "It's Christmastime, girl, it's expected you fatten up a little!" As I said it, I almost choked on it. I was being, what's the word, insensitive. No, callous.

So I cut back to the day and the weather and all the snow outside. But by that time, Margee had stopped looking at me and was just gazing around the room as she loosely gummed her food.

I wondered what was going on inside her. Was she thinking? Was she dreaming? Or was it like she was sleep-waking? Like some people do on Ambien? Had she already entered that theater I had dreamed of? Was she already sitting in nirvana? Sitting in a row of casualties? In a row of like victims? Silent, screaming souls contorted within the frustrations of their unexpected, sudden demise. And if it had happened to me? Would Margee have accompanied me to my assigned seat to witness the torturous boredom of eternal silence?

I'm trying to forget it, even now. I still keep wondering if Margee can hear me or see me or even understand me. Or if she's lost somewhere in herself, drifting around her past life like Joe Bonham did. And I hope, if she is, she's down on the Jersey shore with me late after our high-school prom, giggling quietly as Billy and Jed call out our names frantically, thinking us lost. Our bare feet splashed by the lapping waves, damp as we lie in our wrinkled dresses on the beach. The moon lying just at the edge of the sky over the ocean. Light from coming dawn slowly over-washing it. Holding hands.

And not, oh god no, not that night at Lammi.

So, it's late, actually early Sunday, but who cares. All I have to do is see Margee this evening. So I tried to find any more info on Tompkins Square Park that would tell me there had been a labor demo, well, riot, in December of 1896. Couldn't find a thing. Then again, I'm tired. Try again some other day. Why is this bothering me?

Still, I was so depressed by Cara's descriptions. I decided to try something easier. I drifted around the net looking for information on food immigrants ate at that time, German immigrants. Not a lot specific to the time. I wandered downstairs and was surprised to find Momz on her couch in the den, slowly scrolling through something or other on her laptop. I asked her if we had any books on the topic.

"Books, KT?" Momz asked. "Books?" She was smiling.

I explained I was checking up on Cara's commentary.

"Oh," she said and looked at me quizzically. "Checking sources?" But she said nothing more. She has soooo many books around that room. On shelves. On her desk. In tall, crooked piles. Sometimes they fall off. Some on the floor.

Some wind up in the kitchen, not that we really cook much, or in the living room or in cars.

Momz switched on the big ceiling light and poked around a low shelf on the far wall. "Here, try this," she said. "It's all I've got close to what you want."

"Thanks," I said.

"Oh, wanna go out for Christmas dinner, or maybe on the eve?" That was unusual. We usually celebrated separately. Maybe she had noticed I was staying pretty much to myself over the past several weeks. Margee and all.

"Sure," I said. I knew I wasn't going to be up for much fun. "Who else'll be there?" I expected Momz'd say Winnie, or maybe Winnie and Steve, or Hattie, or Max.

"Just us," she said. "We can talk some more."

"On the day, then," I said.

"Great," said Momz. "Get some sleep soon, hon."

"Sure," I said.

Well, Cara, either Kati and crew were among the most destitute wretches in all NYC, or you really like to pick the sorry parts to translate.

Or maybe Kati was the "sorry Sally." Not sure. Or maybe they were the poor of the poor.

Anyway, this one volume said, above all, lunch was the big meal of the day, and the evening meal, dinner, was mostly boiled eggs, bread, and maybe some cheese. Lunch included stews with some beef, veal, or pork, along with dumplings or noodles! The book even had recipes in it, stuff that was heavy, but much more than the simple starvation regime Cara, or Kati, records. Veal, beef bones—real paleo stuff, butter, onions, parsley, beef stock, celery, carrots, or another root vegetable.

They also had snacks of beer and herrings, pickled. Sometimes the herring had mayo. Ewwwww! Fart city!

Yeah, I'm tired now. Damn, I wrote a ton. I wonder if Margee is really asleep now. If Sylvia is, well, at ease.

Haven't seen Mr. or Mrs. O. in four or five days.

Good night!

KT

Saturday, February 20, 1897.

So much has happened! I keep wanting to write it all down, but then something else happens, and I forget or postpone it. Well, a diary should reflect life, right, not substitute for it!

Gus Krieger and I are marrying tomorrow. I might as well start at the end, and then bring matters up-to-date from the beginning. I even had to go back to my last entry to catch the date, January 10, to bring things into good order.

I am uncertain if I have made the right decision. So much unknown yet with Gottlieb and Pauline, though we will live with them, at least for the time being, in their home in Paterson, in their very apartment, in fact. So much I do not know about Gus. And yet, so much I do know, and know about Lessia, and how she definitely knows me, and recognizes Gus, and needs the respect of this ugly world that demands a father as well as a mother.

Have I abandoned Tessie? How will Siggi be? How will Amelia and Elizabeth respond?

So many misgivings. Yet, if I had hesitated or decided to let Gus go, what would my and my daughter's future be? Housekeeper scrubbing my hands red and bleeding into my old age? Lessia only getting the education I had, and then out into the work world, earning less than a man at her job, but expected to do as much or more. I am not sure if I could provide her with the guidance she would need as a young woman regarding men, and having found out about her own birth, would she even consider anything I would say valid?

Has this been an opportunity, or will it become a disappointment, or worse?

What path have I begun to strike out upon?

Well, to relate. The next Sunday, January 17, Gus did not show up until late in the evening. When he did enter our apartment, he was slope-shouldered and sighed as he shrugged off his bulky overcoat.

"I've had a sad day," he said to me softly before even sitting down. "Parents are expected to care for their children, and then, eventually, if both survive, children must take in their parents."

I felt nervous and felt my stomach knot. I was afraid perhaps Gottlieb or Pauline had fallen ill.

"Is it Pauline?" I asked. "Is it Gottlieb? Are they sick?"

Gus sat on a bench to the other side of Lessia's crib and smiled down at her, sleeping calmly under her ruffled woolen blankets. He stayed silent. "She is such a beautiful child," he said quietly. He playfully touched a small lock of her thick auburn hair, a curl that stuck down below her sleeping cap. "Is anyone else up?" he asked.

I shook my head. "Can I get you a cup of coffee?" I asked him.

We talked in whispers, leaning in close to each other.

"No," he said. "It will only keep me awake, and I need to return to Paterson fairly early tomorrow."

"What is it, Gus?" I asked. "What's happened?"

I sat down in the chair near the head of Lessia's cradle.

"My parents just can't maintain their home anymore without help," Gus said. "Freddie, well, Freddie means well, but he's not dependable. He's involved with some woman now and spends a great deal of time with her. He has promised

much, but with little results." Gus stroked his chin, scratched the stubbly goatee he had grown recently, and sighed. *"I need to move to Paterson."*

I nodded, and my heart sank.

"I know I can get a good job at Pelgram and Meyer. I was a ribbon weaver, and I know the Jacquard system. My father became foreman there. I will explain it all to Mr. Delaney tomorrow and then leave for Paterson. I will be back in a few days." Gus leaned back, turned, and looked down into the blackness beyond the door leading to the back of the apartment.

"How has Siggi been this week?" he asked in a whisper.

"The same," I said. *"Gloomy, unhappy, silent. He comes home and just retreats to the back. Tessie, Amelia, and Elizabeth stay here, crowded as this room becomes, until sleep."*

"Has he gotten angry, lifted a hand against anyone?" Gus asked.

"No," I assured him. That was true. Siggi was not eating much at home. I didn't think he was eating much at work either. It had begun to show before his outburst over the pamphlet.

"Do you notice any smell about him, alcohol?" Gus asked.

"No," I said. *"But I do not try to approach him."*

"Keep this from him," Gus said.

"What is wrong, Gus?" I asked. *"Can I help?"*

"Well," Gus began, *"I was thinking, well..."* He stopped. He looked down at his shoes. Just now the last bits of snow from the sidewalks were melting off the tips and the sides and staining the wooden floor dark and wet.

"My father," he said, leaning back toward me, *"he's become weak. Feeble of mind. He's sixty-four and worked hard his entire life. Hours and hours. First at a loom in Misingen, then as a street sweeper, and then as a ribbon weaver, here and in Paterson. About six months ago, he was let go from work. He had become forgetful and just could not keep up the pace. Now, often, in the night, he's begun to leave bed and wander about the house. My mother says he calls out for Lina, Mary, or my other passed brothers and sisters. This past week, when Pauline tried to bring him back to bed, he resisted her. He didn't know who she was."*

"You fear for him," I said. *"You are a good son."*

"I fear for my mother," said Gus. "She is frailer than he is. But she has her wits yet. There is a gun in the house, a revolver. I had her lock it away in the bedroom safe. Paterson is not Manhattan. No gangs to fear. It is not needed."

I was going to lose Gus; I knew it. It was a moment when I had to make a decision. I began to talk to Gus, thinking softly but clearly out loud. I did not want to lose him.

Sometimes I think it is good that we are put in circumstances that make us come to a decision. The only danger is that in retrospect we review it too severely. Form regrets and "what ifs" that we knew at the time we could not tolerate.

I am trying not to do that.

"I will go with you," I said.

"But—" began Gus.

"Hear me out, Gus Krieger," I said firmly to him, picking up my chair and moving it close to him. I set it down carefully to avoid waking Lessia. "Even if you do move to Paterson, even if you do live with your parents, you will be working. Your mother will still be alone with your father. Not much will change, because you will need to sleep at night.

"I will go with you. I can help Pauline with the house and with your father. You know I am proud of my work, my job, but if you will be proud of me, if you will respect my contribution, at least through this crisis, that will be reward enough."

I took Gus's hand and held it firmly. "I want to marry you. Will you have me as your wife, because I want you for my husband? And, to be frank, Lessia needs a father. You impress me as a good man."

I held my breath. Gus was looking at me blankly. Then he smiled a bit, nodded his head, and said, "Yes."

We embraced.

"Not a word to anyone here, not yet," said Gus. "I will be back midweek."

Then, he gazed back into the blackness that blocked out the back rooms of the apartment. "Tessie?" he said softly.

"I can recommend she replace me to Mr. Lausberg. I am sure he will agree, and Amelia and Elizabeth are old enough to support the household. Working will give Tessie influence against Siggi."

"But no word until Wednesday," Gus said. He wagged a finger at me, and that worried me.

"You know I will not tolerate being anything less than your, than an equal voice to yours," I said. "I do believe in votes for women, and I will participate in suffrage. I will not neglect you, but I will neither neglect myself."

Gus nodded. "I am not threatened," he said.

We hugged.

Much more has happened. I will relate that in future entries. The minister tomorrow is Lutheran. He is coming to Garrison Street in the afternoon. He thinks, as do Gus's parents, that I am a widow. That my husband died in Misingen, which in my opinion, he did. There is no paperwork to be had. And Minister Langhaar, a jovial old man with a taste for brandy, has said Gus's word is good enough for him. I guess mine would not have sufficed.

Mary doesn't mind. Lessia will have a father and be a citizen. All we will need is the marriage certificate.

I hope I have made the right decision.

What we today call depression was called melancholia in Kati's day. It was a broadly accepted affliction often called Hamlet's disease. The word "depression" only began to make itself known in the early twentieth century. And understanding it as a chemical imbalance somewhere in the brain only surfaced midcentury.

Freud described melancholia as a type of mourning and wrote a paper about it in 1917. He balanced objective loss against subjective loss. To him, if a person lost someone through death or—for example—divorce, then that event caused the depression. He went on to create an explanation relating it to narcissism, an unconscious process he referred to as *libidinal cathexis of the ego.* The sufferer would not only turn negatively to the outside world, but begin to denigrate himself as well, feeling unworthy or inferior or impotent against outside forces, or even blaming himself for the original trauma.

This was possibly Gottlieb's issue, and to some extent Siggi's. But Gottlieb could also have been suffering from what we now call

Alzheimer's disease. Although the malady is becoming increasingly prevalent, due perhaps to extended life-spans, it has been known since the research of German doctor Alois Alzheimer back in 1906. The condition was named for him in 1910. It was he who, upon examination of a brain at autopsy, first described brain tissue shrinkage and the accumulation of foreign material in and around nerve cells.

This doctor was also the one who first described the symptoms: failing motor skills, loss of a functional sleep/wake cycle, disorientation, profound memory loss, and unfounded suspicions about those around the sufferer.

In Kati's time, there would have been little for a family to do except to extend Gottlieb comfort and love. Considering all the heartache and burden Gottlieb had borne in life, he very likely had both illnesses.

Could some of his later disability have had physical causes? Likely. Pollution in the Paterson area, later becoming known as part of northern New Jersey's Cancer Alley, was rampant in those days.

Cara Maurer

Sunday, December 19, 2010. Late.

Yesterday I was feeling okay. I mean, I'm going out for Christmas dinner with Momz, and that's the first in a long time. That was something I was, am, looking forward to. Thinking about where Margee may be, prisoner in herself because of some dickhead fratboy, was pulling me down. But I got through the day thinking maybe this evening, maybe this time, Margee would smile at me. Recognize me. Even maybe start eating without slobbering too much. Maybe. Maybe. Maybe.

But now. This must be depression, or at least the start. I didn't eat dinner, the Chinese takeout Momz had left for me on the kitchen counter, smiley face "yum yum" with dishes and silverware. I can't think of anything except Margee. Not so much that I've lost her, but that she's gonna be taken away from me.

The roads had cleared up Sunday, so I drove over to the hospital. Thick black ribbons chopped into high layers of blanketing snow glistening in the moonlight. Clear, black sky. Streetlights playing off the puffy snowbanks and seeming to twinkle as they were briefly blocked by the stiff branches of the tall, skeletal oaks lining the highway as I drove forward passing them. Writing about it now, it seems so grim, but is that my change? As I drove along then, it seemed enchanting. Charming me in a way. Now, I think of it as the road to death. Or maybe, worse, a suspension of life, and for how long, Margee?

As I walked down the corridor toward Margee's room, Della called to me.

"There are a bunch of people, lawyers I think, in there with Margee's parents."

"Does that mean I can't go in?" I asked.

Della just shrugged and said, "I don't know. But you may want to wait."

What wasn't she telling me, I wondered as I slowed my walk down to a hesitant shuffle. I passed the doorway to Margee's room and saw the backs of Mr. and Mrs. O. Facing them were two tall men, middle-aged with long white hair pushed back, in long, light-tan overcoats, straight and severe, and with long faces. I kept walking and stopped in the waiting room only a few doors down at the end of the corridor. I sat inside the door, where I could not be seen, and listened intently to the voices drifting down the dim, softly lighted corridor.

Mr. O.'s gravelly voice was indistinct at first, except for an occasional "yes," "no," or "I agree," when he raised it firmly. He seemed to be leading whatever matters were being discussed. I never heard the word "Margee," just an occasional "your daughter." Mrs. O., if she was saying anything, I could not hear her.

The other two were definitely lawyers. That became clear when one voice rose up above a stew of hushed, indistinct conversation to say, "Oh, no, the fraternity bears at least half."

More low mumble.

"I disagree," I heard Mr. O. say. "The university should."

Then, I heard, "Well, they both have deep pockets."

Yeah, they were discussing a lawsuit, Margee's lawsuit. Right there. And what could Margee say? I tried to hear more, wanted to hear more, but unless I sneaked up to the door, it would not be possible. So I stayed in the waiting room, near the door, quiet and hunched over, straining to hear any word I could.

They weren't there long. Maybe another ten minutes or so. The volume of the voices rose. I looked at the reflection of the corridor in the window of the waiting room. First the lawyers backed out from the room, then Mr. and Mrs. O., and they stood there talking more.

But now, I could hear it all. I wish I hadn't.

"At least fifty to sixty million," said one of the lawyers.

"Together?" asked Mr. O.

"Each," came in the voice of the other lawyer.

"Do you think they'll go to trial?" Mrs. O. asked.

"No, especially if we can keep your daughter alive through depositions." (Lawyer.)

"This is getting expensive." (Mr. O.)

"If you take her off her tubes now, expect to halve the settlement." (Lawyer.)

"A picture of your daughter out to the media would nail them. They won't want that. They'll settle big time." (Other lawyer.)

"Well, okay. And how long?" (Mr. O.)

"We'll try to push this along. We have all the ammo here." (Lawyer.)

"What about my daughter's friend, Kaitlyn Cantori? Will she need to be deposed?" (Mr. O.)

"Maybe. We'll try to keep her out of it." (Lawyer.)

"Good. I don't know about her much. I think she's sort of a party girl. Might get taken up by media if this thing gets out." (Mr. O.)

"What if she starts talking on her own?" (Mrs. O.!)

"I can have her in and have her sign an agreement to remain quiet. Tell her it's in your daughter's best interests." (Other lawyer.)

"She'll go for that. I think she feels guilty, the little skank, for not having been there herself." (Mr. O.)

"They were quite a pair, huh?" (Lawyer, laughing briefly.)

A "humph" from Mrs. O.

I watched the huddle move down the hallway and past the nurse's station. I bent over in the chair in the waiting room and stared down at my feet. I closed my eyes and fell into myself, oblivious to everything. All I saw was the flushed orange of the inside of my eyelids, and coldness, a coldness that wrapped me completely yet did not sting. I imagined myself in Margee's room, and then I was Margee, hearing over and over: "Fifty or sixty million. Your daughter. Your daughter. Your daughter."

I sat up in the chair. I opened my eyes. "Oh, please just say my name," I said.

But there was no one there. No one.

"I'm coming," I said. "Skank's on the way."

I went to the nurse's station and asked Della if maybe this evening I could feed Margee some ice cream, if that was allowed, and that evening that's exactly what I did. I talked to her, on and on, about school, about the coming semester, about bringing something from home to fill up her blank, cold room. And yes, about what skanks we had been partying last year! Those vodka coolers at homecoming. Barfing out the window at Sigma. Losing our shoes at Halloween somewhere behind the bushes of the chem building. Kinky Ron and wobbly Will.

All of it!

Margee didn't eat more or less than any other night. Her lips twitched into a smile several times as I gently scooped a small blob of melty vanilla pudding between them. Did she see me? Was she even alive?

It was almost nine o'clock when I left Margee, saying her name over and over as I patted her cheek and then stroked her hair. It needed brushing, so I took out my own brush and lightly teased her unwashed locks back into a gentle wave. This time at good-bye, I kissed her over each eye. "We skanks gotta stick together," I whispered in her ear.

Mine was the last car in the visitors' lot.

Am I being selfish? Am I mourning you, Margee? Damn, Cara, you and your commentary. And Freud, go fuck yourself, you misogynist troll!

But if Kati could bear up under all the shit slung at her, so can I. Even if I test positive, there are drugs now. But, from where I am, what's the way forward?

KT

Sunday, February 21, 1897.

Not much time to write. I took a lovely, hot, and soapy sponge bath; Gus is taking one now. We have an entire bedroom to ourselves! No need to worry about intrusions as I wash! Gottlieb and Pauline are already asleep. Lessia sleeps deeply in her cradle in the corner of our bedroom! Our own bedroom!

I was so worried today that someone would ask about my circumstances. Having a five-month-old child and remarrying already as a widow. About my first husband's death. How I could have wanted to emigrate so soon, pregnant. Maybe someone would be from Misingen? That somehow, it would all come apart, just as we were to marry.

But it didn't. Gus assured me it wouldn't. His father was so forgetful and confused, he kept on asking when Gus and I had Lessia. Pauline was happy just to hold a grandchild at the ceremony. She kept on saying, "Liebes Enkelkind. Liebes Enkelkind." Minister Langhaar spent most of his time slapping Gus on the back and saying, "Congratulations, sir! A real man now." He also drank most of the brandy Gus had set out, and devoured the tiny sugar cookies he had purchased at Kooiman's bakery down at the corner on Belmont Avenue.

The ceremony was short. I remember nothing of it. We both nodded yes often, and then we got the treasured certificate with Gottlieb and Pauline as witnesses. That was it.

We survived a surprise party thrown by Freddie in the downstairs apartment early in the evening. My old fears about being found out resurfaced. I told them to Gus. "Don't worry," he said. "We are all members of the working class. We all carry scars. No one asks how we got them."

Most of Gus's friends turned out to be from Silesia. Far away from my Misingen. Even Langhaar, who speaks like he is gargling.

I am writing so fast! How will Gus be as a lover? Part of me hopes for a strong, experienced partner mindful of a woman's needs for touch, embrace, and a gradual, steady consummation. Part of me worries that means too much gained familiarity and a danger for fidelity.

How I worry! Would I want a fumbling, naïve boy? Of course not!

Oh, I think Gus is finishing up. He did shave that prickly goatee, I hope.

From the *Paterson Morning Call*, Tuesday, February 23, 1897:

"Newlyweds Gustav Adolph Krieger and Kati Scheu Krieger were tendered a surprise party on Sunday evening, February 21, at the home of the groom's parents, 67 Garrison Street. The soiree was organized by the groom's brother, Frederick Krieger. An informal program of song, fancy dancing, and accordion music was enjoyed. Numerous toasts were spoken by the assembled guests, with fervent wishes for a happy marriage the theme.

"Among those present were Mr. and Mrs. Gottlieb Krieger, parents of the groom, Mr. and Mrs. James Thetge, Mrs. William Loewenherz, Mrs. Mary Swartbach, Mr. and Mrs. Josef Roth, Alvin Thetge, Albert Roth, Leo Haefell, Joseph Groeger, Rudolph Groeger, and the minister Ludwig Langhaar, who had the pleasure of marrying the happy couple.

"Toward the end of the evening, a fine collation was served."

A collation would be a light, informal meal, likely consisting of cold meats, cheeses, bread, and lager beer, followed by some pastries and coffee.

Cara Maurer

Fuzzi to KT 743-765-8040
Hey, KT? How r u? Long time sinz i saw u. Txt me.

Dec. 20.

Monday, December 20, 2010. Late.

I was really up this morning. I thought at first the appointment with Dr. Herzmann had gone really well. She had already talked to the floor staff in Margee's unit. She said she was impressed with my dedication and optimism for my friend, and also how I respected the directions the staff had given me.

Wow, I thought. I had no idea they had written this all up, or at least remembered me so much.

I think Dr. Herzmann was then more interested in just getting an idea of who I was and what I was thinking. We talked about Margee's prognosis. She emphasized Margee may never come out of her unresponsive wakefulness syndrome. I nodded, somehow happy that this doctor had used the term "wakefulness" and never used the word "vegetative."

I probably impressed her as naïve. Or practical and resigned to Margee's fate, because I just went on with her about what other foods I might be able to feed her.

Then, Dr. Herzmann asked me if I might consider becoming a volunteer for the hospital in general on a more regular basis. I was surprised by her question and told her I really had not thought about it, and for now I just wanted to help Margee.

She smiled and said something to the effect that Hudson could always use good people like me, and would I please think about it.

"Sure," I think I said.

And that was that. For the moment.

But then, back at home, I googled "unresponsive wakefulness syndrome." I found out it was simply a new term, a euphemism as far as I'm concerned, for "vegetative state." And that soon, Margee may be considered in a persistent vegetative state, and that in a few months she may be reclassified as permanent. My Margee. No more aware than a...I can't say it. That sent me down, way down. For an hour, I just sat and stared out the living-room window down far across the lawn to Camelia Lane. Our street, so prissy and cute.

Why did I think Dr. Herzmann was going to be a man? Name alone? Authority figure implication? Me, KT, the small and meek?

I had to pull myself out of self-analysis. It was like all the concepts from my sosh and psych courses were coming out to torment me! I picked up Kati's diary. At least she had a happy wedding, I guess.

No limos, destination wedding, or even a caterer.

Then I had to go get my blood drawn, and Doc Sam was at the hospital, some crisis in the ER. I was in and out quick. I had wanted to talk with her.

Well, my blood *has* been drawn, and I should know tomorrow, Wednesday at the latest, what my immediate future holds, at least in pills and drugs, and for—well, let's just leave that alone for the moment. If I am positive, the first thing I want to do is find Ken and neuter him. Minimally. I thought about that, I really did, while aimlessly trolling the malls for something to bring to Margee. Her room is so sterile. I will do what I can for her.

I don't know if I turned the Ken thing into a full-blown, delicious nightmare because I just was coming up empty store after store, stall after stall for Margee, or because I started to think of how, just how, I could cut off Ken's dick and get away with it after passing through a good kitchen knife display at Bed Bath & Beyond early on shopping.

Lure him on a pretext? Where? A dark alley in Chinatown? Nowhere that dark down there. Even at three in the morning. Say what first? I'm sorry, sorry, sorry, I was worried about myself, and then what? I want to be FWB again? Until your next cheap condom breaks? I would have to leave a text message trail.

I could not think of a practical way to do it. So I just enjoyed the moment, stayed in the moment, as Buddha would advise, and imagined his shriek when he saw his dick in my hand.

But that would be so bloody. Ewww. Hire Princess Leia and her light saber? A soldering iron would do. Hot coals. I got really dark.

I caught myself giggling through an image of Ken howling down my street with his pants smoking. By then, I had enlisted Momz in my quest. Held him for me while I stuffed the coals down the naughty child's crotch and then pushed his pants shut. Coals for Christmas, naughty boy. I think in my little revenge play I was shouting, "Burn, balls, burn!" Just how I got there I forget.

But when I looked down, I saw I had wandered into a Toys"R"Us and had one of those soft, cuddly Beanie Babies in my hand, a giraffe by the neck to be exact. Whoa! Then, I saw a bulldog. Our college mascot! The plushies had been rummaged through, some looked soiled. But many looked really cute. I pulled out a holiday bear, another small bear looking like an "M," a dog that looked faintly like the Sigma mascot that had barfed on Margee's feet in September at a mixer, and a fuzzy little bat. On Halloween, Margee had dressed up as a bat.

I finally had my gifts for Margee! A memory tree! A little Christmas tree, no lights, and the stuffed animals attached to it. There were so many small trees to choose from. Pink ones, white ones, blue ones, and finally, a green one. Only about eighteen inches tall. Perfect.

Maybe it will help her remember. It will also give me a few things to talk with her about when I see her this evening.

I got so into it, I forgot to do what I really have been meaning to do, get a new phone. Especially since I got a text from some jerk I don't even know, or minimally remember, while I was in B B & B. Oh, well.

KT

Wednesday, March 3, 1897.

Pauline has made Lessia a doll! A small doll, about eight inches long, expertly sewn in firm white cloth stuffed with cotton, I think, with little black button eyes, a wide red "w" nose, and a cross-stitched mouth smiling broadly. It has long woolen hair in soft, light auburn, much as Lessia's is now.

There are no eyebrows though, so "Fridericka," as Pauline calls her, does look slightly unfinished. A small matter.

Fridericka wears a simple knee-length dress of sturdy dark blue. I suppose. She has no obvious knees, but the dress comes down to about an inch above her feet. Pauline overlaid black thread at the bottoms of the doll's legs to imitate shoes.

It has been lovingly created. I find it precious, so much more than the German bisque dolls in fashion at the finer department stores. Those are so preformed and cold. Mass-produced for money, not out of love, and overly fragile. Attached to cloth bodies, their heads loll unless solidly cradled. They shatter easily and will not survive active play. They impress weakness and daintiness on the girls who are given them. Such dolls require quiet sitting, no running about and frolic allowed! I prefer Pauline's sturdy present that allows Lessia's imagination to transform the cloth, thread, and buttons as she will. A doll she can take by the hand and run with. Once she is old enough!

I know Pauline must have been working on this gift for a while, undoubtedly thanks to Gus's encouragement. He had to have been talking about me with her, and evidently with praise and love. She has so much else to do.

I was so happy that Pauline showed such kindness to Lessia I wished to hug her when she showed me Fridericka. I wanted to hug her firmly, squeeze her, but as I put my arms around her, I felt how slight she was. How bony! I felt her shoulders, her collarbones, sharp through her heavy gray wool dress, and I relaxed my enthusiasm in a soft embrace and a light kiss on her cheek.

Pauline manages such strength despite her age and the wear that twelve pregnancies and unremitting household work have put upon her. She works hard at every task, occasionally humming or singing mostly Swabian songs, so she is likely not from Gottlieb's immediate land. I have only been living here some few weeks, but already I catch myself mumbling off-key, as Pauline does mostly, "Muss i denn, muss i denn, zum Städtele hinaus, Städtele hinaus, Und du, mein Schatz, bleibst hier?" Sometimes, she sings "Das Lieben bringt gross Freud," and I wonder about Gus's and my future.

Would my own mother have borne up so well over time? Will I? I look at Pauline, a strong face, thin but not gaunt, resolute blue eyes set deeply to either side of a sharp, thin nose. Below fine, gray brows lighter than her thick, steel-colored hair pulled back into a long, graceful ponytail. She still maintains a mouth of strong, if yellowed, teeth. Her chin juts out slightly, but not haggishly so. Taut skin that reddens when she stirs the steaming wash bucket.

Her hands show age and insult. Her fingers are knobby-knuckled, one might say gnarled, and thick purple veins course along the backs, hidden in part under irregularly patterned brown splotches and crazed, mottled skin. Her left pinky finger was broken some time ago. It sticks out wide from its base and then curves back in again. Callouses mark her palms.

However, hers are still capable hands. Very capable hands.

I'm sure Pauline is also happy because I have started immediately taking over household work. But it is our house. Gus says I should consider this my home, *my house too. I assured him I do. "We are a married couple now, two together," I answered.*

Only one family, if extended! Not the twenty-five in Manhattan. There will be two, one downstairs once Gus chooses a tenant. He says nothing about what happened to the prior tenants. He is particular. But even then, just two families! No air-shaft to clean out. No hallways to scrub free of old, chewed plugs of tobacco, vomit from the occasional drunk unable to reach the outhouse, or trash dropped from a bucket.

An indoor toilet. No chamber pots. A cold-water tap in the kitchen.

In the backyard a chicken coop, which Gus and I will restock with hens in the spring! A backyard with grass. A fence. Lessia's own little park! I will plant a garden.

No gangs!

I am so happy at this moment.

Poor Gottlieb. He sleeps often during the day and calls out at night. Gus sits him in a chair in his parents' bedroom and puts a string across the doorway with a bell attached. When Gottlieb wanders, he trips the "alarm," and either Pauline or I attend to him. We take turns, and if Gottlieb has had a bad night, we can sleep in the morning, since there are two of us now to tend the home.

The poor, poor man. So bent over and frail. Sometimes, we can hardly get him to eat. Hollow-eyed. Brow sometimes knotted and suspicious, even of his lifetime partner, whom he fails to recognize often. He bounces from chair to dresser to wall to door, and we are usually at him even before the bell rings. To whom he is talking when he rests in his chair we can only surmise as friends and family from his youth. Ghosts and memories. He sees them before him. He points at them. Sometimes he laughs, and at those moments he seems to revive. But briefly, and then he is gone again.

He soils himself. He wears a white cotton cloth underneath his pants. Like a child, he is in diapers again.

There is a park, a beautiful park with a labyrinth garden I want to walk in the spring. Just down the block on Oxford Street.

Gus is leaning toward renting to a married couple: Alvin and Lois Thetge. Gus asked me what I thought of Alvin. He was here for my wedding surprise party. He is a policeman. He seems quiet, polite, and well-dressed. I am pleased Gus asked me. It is a good sign.

He is proving to be a good man. I am withholding nothing, so I wonder if, and hope that, Lessia may have a little brother or sister soon.

Gus is working as a ribbon weaver at Pelgram and Meyer. They produce such beautiful silk fancies much beyond what we can afford.

Das Lieben bringt gross Freud	Love brings great joy
das wissen alle Leut.	All people know that.
Weiß mir ein schönes Schätzelein	I know a pretty treasure
mit zwei schwarzbraunen Äugelein,	With two black brown little eyes
das mir, das mir, das mir mein Herz erfreut.	That brings joy to my heart.
das mir, das mir, das mir mein Herz erfreut.	That brings joy to my heart.

Sie hat schwarzbraune Haar	She has black brown hair
dazu zwei Äuglein klar.	And also two clear eyes.
Ihr sanfter Blick, ihr Zuckermund	Her soft glance, her sugar mouth
hat mir mein Herz im Leib verwundt,	Has hit me in my heart.
hat mir mein Herz im Leib verwundt,	Has hit me in my heart.

Ein Brieflein schrieb sie mir,	She wrote me a little letter
ich sollt treu bleibe ihr.	I should stay true to her.
Drauf schick ich ihr ein Sträußelein,	So I sent her a small bouquet
schön Rosmarin und Nägele,	Sweet rosemary and button blooms.
sie soll, sie soll, sie soll mein eigen sein!	She should so be my own.
sie soll, sie soll, sie soll mein eigen sein!	She should so be my own.

Mein eigen soll sie sein	She should my own be,
kein'm andre mehr als mein.	No one else's, just mine.
So leben wir in Freud und Leid,	So we will live in joy and sorrow
bis uns Gott, der Herr,	Til God Almighty separates us.
auseinanderscheidt.	
Ade, ade, ade, mein Schatz, ade!	Good-bye, my dear, good-bye.
Ade, ade, ade, mein Schatz, ade!	Good-bye, my dear, good-bye.

This particular Swabian folk song surfaced about 1825. It would have been popular especially when Pauline was a young girl.

Cara Maurer

Fuzzi to KT 743-765-8040
Hey KT. How r u?

Dec. 21.

KT to Fuzzi 756-818-2102
bz. Fuzzi who?

Dec. 21.

Fuzzi to KT 743-765-8040
Hahaha? Knok knok?

Dec. 21.

Wednesday, December 22, 2010.

I'm negative! Found out this morning! Such energy. Optimism!

Just spent early afternoon wrapping up Margee's stuffed animals and the little tree-in-box. Ribbons and all. Used up all of last year's paper and then had to go out and buy new for Momz's cape. It's sturdy and bold. Woolen knit in a Navajo-inspired style of interwoven blocks. Instead of earth tones, subtle shades of mauve and deeper violets barely discernable. Something Momz can wear with a more striking top or leggings. Damn! That's it! I should have gotten matching or complementary leggings. She loves them, out of fashion and all. Probably could not find any, anyway. Maybe online? I love to shop, but got to get to Margee.

Maybe I can find it online from a mall store nearby and pick it up? Hhhhmmm!

Wow! What made Kati happy way back in the day! I cannot imagine pooping in a pot around two in the morning, or peeing into one. How did that go? Did you squat? Like, with this poo-and piss-pot on the floor between your legs? What if you lost your balance? What if you were drunk, and you tipped it over? Did they have TP back then? If not, then…Stop! Stop! No wonder ol' Kati got happy over a bathroom. She doesn't mention bathroom, though, just toilet. Earlier, she mentioned taking sponge baths, so I guess there was a tub, no?

Happy over a chicken coop? Again, wow! There was this store down in the older part of town that sold freshly killed chickens. It's closed now. I mean, when you drove past it, even from the roadway, the smell in summer was so foul, haha, your head nearly snapped off.

And the doll! So easily satisfied. I guess this was way pre–child safety, buttons on the face.

Women back then, well, I guess working-class women, had no choice but to look old. Like, wicked witch of the west old. Too bad we have no photographs. And these TV shows worry us about the wrinkle wars!

They really weren't that old, though. Scrubbing floors in an unheated hallway loaded with tobacco plugs, vomit, and just plain garbage. I think I'd either go postal or jump in the Hudson.

I wish I knew German. Cara's translation of that Swabic folk song is pretty bad, I think. And no translation of "muss i denn." I got room on my schedule. Does the school have a course in German? Or maybe I try Rosetta Stone? Or *German for Dummies*? Are there any real Germans around I could be tutored by? There is a German School in White Plains.

See what fits. Margee's top priority with my time scheduling.

'Til God Almighty separates us! And this is a happy song about the joy of love? Those Germans were really dark, like their "fairy tales." Sticking kids in ovens and having women eat poison apples.

KT

Wednesday, December 22, 2010. Late.

I was so up, and now I'm so down! Am I depressed? Going bipolar? Do I need to see someone? If I can hold out a few more days, maybe I'll even out.

As I was walking down the corridor to visit Margee, I realized I hadn't seen Sylvia yesterday. So I stopped at the nurses' station and just asked, "Where's Sylvia?"

Della wasn't there. Nobody was that I was familiar with, and some strange little lady pecking on a laptop at the back of the station squeaked at me, after hesitating, "Oh, she's no longer on this floor."

"Where did she go?" I asked. "I let her suck on an ice cloth a few days back. She thinks I'm her granddaughter, Beth."

The squeaky little lady looked at me annoyed over harlequin bifocals teetering on the end of her pointy nose. Then, she sighed and walked over to me. "Sylvia passed," she said in a low tone.

"Oh," I said. "Sorry."

I wasn't sorry, but it was a quick way to end the conversation. "She's passed." What an absurd term! Like, "She's no longer with us." "She's gone to a better place." "She's departed this life." What's wrong with "She died"? I mean, that's all we know for sure.

But then, what would I say if Margee died? Thinking that made me cold as I passed down the corridor. What if I entered the room and didn't find her? If I had to return to "Squeaks" to hear, "Oh, she's passed."

But there she was, propped up in her chair, her reflection in the window showing that her eyes were open. Just like many times before. "Hello, Margee," I said. There was a small, gratifying twitch at the corner of her mouth, but her eyes did not acknowledge me. The hissing oxygen flowing from the regulator in the wall through a slim green tube and out of the little prongs just beneath her nostrils was the only sound in the room. Margee still had that tracheotomy tube wobbling on her throat as she breathed, capped. It seemed so vulnerable, she seemed so vulnerable, and briefly I wondered again how it would feel to have some tube like that stuck in my windpipe and protruding from my neck.

I pulled up a chair next to her, as I had each day before. "I have some presents for you, Margee," I said. "Some Christmas presents. It's three days before Christmas, and I couldn't wait to give you my presents."

Margee's eyes turned to me. She blinked. For a second, I was hoping to hear her speak, but could she with that tube?

"Margee," I said, holding her left hand gently, the one without IVs penetrating it. "Squeeze my hand if you can hear me." Impulsively, I stroked her hair with my other hand.

Margee didn't respond. I looked down at her left hand. It had grown thinner. I could see a few veins purple and crooked beneath her skin. Her knuckles had raised, and her fingers were so white. And cold.

"Well, Margee," I said, "here they are!"

I set down the wrapped Christmas tree on the metal window sill just beyond Margee and me.

"Can you guess what it is? Do you like the wrapping? I chose your favorite colors, silver and green!"

Margee stared out the window. I wondered what was going on inside her as I slowly removed the crinkling paper and opened the box, setting the tree on the sill. "Look, it's a tiny Christmas tree. Sorry, no lights, the hospital doesn't want lighted trees, real or artificial, in patient rooms. You understand?"

Margee stared out the window. Was she thinking?

"Ohh, what's next?" I said to her, picking out a small, lumpy package from my Macy's bag and holding it up for her to see. "What could it be?" I unwrapped it slowly, picking the paper off its head first so it appeared to hatch out of the wrapping. "Oh, look, it's a Margee bear! 'M' for Margee." I placed it next to the tree.

Margee took a deep breath, and the tracheotomy tube quivered and swayed. Was she dreaming?

"What's next?" I picked up the bat gift and removed it from its holiday packaging a little faster. "Oh, Margee, remember on Halloween when we went trick-or-treating frat to frat? You were a bat, and I was the Count." I clumsily imitated a Transylvanian accent and said, "I want to suck your blood."

Margee blinked, but her head didn't move at all. I paused briefly. The annoying hiss of the oxygen made me start to talk again. What drugs was she on? Did they make her sleep-wake? Like some people do on Ambien? The bat leaned against Margee bear.

I pulled out the holiday bear and fumbled off its wrapping. "Oh," I said. "A holiday bear! Ho, ho, ho, Merrrry Christmas, Margee!"

I turned away from Margee and took out the ribbon I had brought along, tying each little plushie to the tree, my hands shaking as I rearranged them to balance on the branches. I brushed my cheek with my shoulder, hoping Margee, if she could see, and if she was with me, did not see the several tears escape down my face.

When I turned back to her I couldn't help but wonder. Could Margee hear me, or see me, or even understand me? I flashed back to the Jersey shore again late after our high school prom. The giggling. Splashing in the lapping waves at the water's edge. Holding hands.

So I kept the dog, the stuffed dog that looked like the Sigma mascot that had barfed on Margee's feet in September at a mixer in my bag. She should not go there.

And not, oh god no, not that night at Lammi.

"Those are very thoughtful gifts; can I thank you for my daughter?"

Startled, I turned quickly and held on to my chair with both hands.

"I didn't mean to upset you."

It was Mr. O. How long had he been there? He was leaning against the doorframe, slumped and stoop-shouldered, his long overcoat uncharacteristically rumpled.

"Oh, that's all right," I said. It wasn't all right, but what could I say? I'm trying to keep your daughter alive, I wanted to say. You know, for the fifty or sixty million? Or is it getting too expensive? Maybe we should let her pass on, for, say, twenty million? You can kink her oxygen tube, and look here, there's a valve for the IV. You can turn it off!

I just stared at him.

"Have you helped her with dinner?" he asked.

"I was about to," I said. Helped her with dinner, I thought. Helped her with dinner! Small, sloppy bits of loose ice cream and gelatin that dribble out of her mouth.

"Then I won't interrupt you," said Mr. O., and then apologetically, staring at his shoes, he added, "I had a late day at the office."

Yeah, I thought, threatening to release a picture of my Margee to milk the college and the frat. I looked beyond him down the hallway. No Mrs. O.

"Do you think I'll need to be deposed?" I asked, trying to front an innocent, weak smile. I added vaguely, "I was there."

"You," Mr. O. began, straightening up and taking one step into the room. He stopped, looked at me quizzically, and then retreated. He turned away. "I don't know," he called back to me as he disappeared into the darkness. I heard him repeat it as his footsteps faded away. "I don't know."

When I looked back at Margee, she seemed to be gazing at me intently. As though she knew. "I will not leave you, Margee," I said. And I fed her. But she was able to take no more than she had yesterday, or the day before, or the day before that.

I'm so down, all I keep thinking about is hoping that Mr. O. dies a slow, paralyzing death trapped in his own body. And I wish somehow I could then give him that gift, for Christmas, he wants for Margee's life, and sit him in front of sixty million dollars in crisp, new twenty-dollar bills he can never touch, let alone spend.

And the thought just popped into my head, why are you so happy about the latest test? There's another one on January 20, then February 20, and a "semifinal" one in March now. Another in June!

Mrs. O. too, same fate. Maybe sitting right next to Mr. O. And I'd wave little dollops of gelatin and ice cream in front of their eyes. Let it melt off the spoon, or coat their lips with it, and make them lap it off. Go "Tch, tch, tch," when it dripped onto their chins.

I need to get back to the gym. It's been nearly what, two months? Kickbox. Elliptical. Hot yoga.

Even if I do, I don't think I'll ever be strong as Kati was, physically or mentally. I wonder what happens next.

KT

Sunday, March 14, 1897.

So much to write about. Such a confluence of happiness and apprehension. Sweet and sour. Optimism and trepidation.

I have spent much of the day preparing our vegetable garden bed and sowing the first seeds. Gus was beside me. We have recovered from our first difference. That is good.

I stepped out into our backyard the Saturday before yesterday, March 6, late afternoon, as a falling yellow sun illuminated it in a sugary golden texture. It had been a warm day, an early one just at the edge of spring, enticing me from the house where I had been fixing dinner for us. I stepped slowly over brittle brown grass about the back steps. To one side of the empty chicken coop lay what must have been Gottlieb and Pauline's garden. Roughly bordered by broken bricks forced to zigzag by freezing and thawing earth, it was weed strewn, with the sad, stiff remnant of a wild seeded tomato plant bent backward in one corner against a raw, wooden-slatted fence marking the rear corner of their property.

I will garden this year, I decided. The nearby park on Oxford Street will allow Lessia recreation. There is room here for at least three four-by-six-foot patches. I reached down to test the soil. It was fairly rich and dark. The aroma of it crumbling in my hands was wet, heavy, and promising. It sent me back to Misingin, to the fields, and their deep, pungent announcement of spring in the tilled and manured furrows ready for wheat.

A hoe, some cow manure, seeds, hay, and strenuous tilling, the type of work that leaves one tired and yet calm and satisfied, and I, no, we, will have a garden, I thought. I stood there musing about my first vegetables to go into newly worked earth: spinach and lettuce.

A few weeks later, I'd begin to add kale cabbage, turnips, carrots, peas, broccoli, and onions. Several plantings, in case a hard, late frost should penetrate the hay blanket and retard our hopes. Then, as the soil warmed and winter receded to memory, I would add parsley, cauliflower, and spinach, followed on the edge of summer by cabbages, beans, lovages, celery, and rutabaga. Beautifully contorted thick purple-black tomatoes, also some pink, some dusty yellow, heavy and pulling on the vine in late July. A perfect salad with thinly sliced onion in a light comple-ment of drizzled vinegar! A small bouquet of parsley chopped and strewn over all.

Gus will build a root cellar. I will preserve our harvest. We will save money.

At the farmers' market along Main and Market Streets, we will buy four or five Rhode Island reds. Gus says those were the chickens his parents had good suc-cess with, and they produce five to seven eggs per week apiece. Yes, we will need to buy feed, but such nourishment for so little cost.

We have agreed to spend next Sunday renovating the coop. Work has reunited us where friends made a rift.

Although I have not written about it, we did not leave Tessie, Siggi, Amelia, and Elizabeth adrift in Manhattan. We exchanged some letters with them after the marriage, and we invited them to visit us for a Sunday dinner. It took some time, and I was at first surprised that Tessie was demurring, usually about the exhaustion from her housekeeping duties at the tenement and need to catch up on home chores on her "day of rest." (I had put in a very good word for her with Mr. Lausberg, and she did take my old job!) Or it was that Siggi was not feeling well. I wondered.

Finally, she agreed to visit. We set a date. Sunday, March 7. Gus even picked them up at the nearby North train station and accompanied them the several blocks uphill to our home. Pauline and I had bustled up quite a feast, perhaps weary of a long winter, and knowing Easter would not bring its celebration until mid-April. I do not think Pauline had had the opportunity for much socializing or merriment over the past several years, tending to Gottlieb.

Pauline had directed me in preparing the courses for the table, and I happily obeyed the suddenly animated work-worn woman happy to welcome guests again. It was quite an undertaking. It had been a long time since I had put together, or dined on, rabbit stew, so I was relieved to be guided in marinating the rab-bits in vinegar, with onions, cloves, allspice, and peppers adding their tang on Thursday for a three-day steeping. While they were then boiled to tenderness that

Sunday, I made a gravy. That accompanying roux of butter, flour, and marinade broth stirred and cooked to a smooth creamy sauce sent a thick, lingering smell exuding well-being and security throughout the house.

Pauline baked fresh bread. Instead of potatoes, she insisted on her Swabian dumplings, a delicious spring dish I was unfamiliar with. She took some parsley and some dried spinach, some chervil and chives, chopped them all up enthusiastically, and steeped them in butter for several minutes. Then, she added them to old, grated rolls and some egg and placed them gently and expertly into the simmering rabbit stew, guiding them gently among the bobbling meat and vegetables until they lay on its surface, plump and swollen.

Gus had provided good beer.

On the kitchen larder board sat a wreath cake I had baked Saturday evening, double-ringed and observantly baked, with a thin frosting of egg white and sugar. Ready for coffee and conversation.

Gottlieb slept in the back bedroom the entire time, and no amount of noise or laughter woke him.

I was so eager to see Tessie and her girls, Siggi the unfortunate appendage, I kept moving to the living room and looking down the street. That, I think, was the high point of my day. When I did spot them, I saw quickly Siggi was absent.

Although Tessie, Amelia, and Elizabeth hugged and smiled at both Pauline and me inside our warm, welcoming home, I knew Tessie was lying when she said, "Siggi is not feeling well."

So there was an empty chair throughout the meal. An empty chair Tessie pointed to whenever a question was asked about Siggi. What was ailing him? How was his work going at Delaney's? Was he finding it too strenuous? We would visit soon and bring some delicacies to help his spirit.

It was then, after the meal, which our friends ate voraciously, while I noticed a pallor and shakiness of hand that Tessie had never exhibited before, that the truth of their situation came forward. Gus and I were pressing for a date to visit and had suggested this coming Sunday. To keep up acquaintance. To share our growing happiness and springtime celebration. If not then, perhaps Easter itself? A walk in Central Park?

Tessie sighed deeply and said, "Siggi has disappeared. He has not been home for close to three weeks."

I reached across the table and held her hand. "How can you possibly be managing?" I asked.

Tessie just shook her head, keeping it low to and facing her now empty plate streaked lightly with the few smudges of gravy she had not sopped up with large wads of bread. Both her daughters looked sadly at their mother. "We're not," she said.

"Have you notified the police?" asked Gus.

"Poor dears," said Pauline. She rose and stood behind Tessie, putting her sharp, bony hands on Tessie's shoulders with remarkable tenderness and kneading them softly.

"The police care little about a lost immigrant," Tessie said.

A snore erupted from the back bedroom where Gottlieb lay.

I knew what I must offer my friend. For all she had done for me while I was left abandoned and big-bellied, I must do the same for her. I looked briefly at Gus. He seemed perplexed, perhaps more in thought about how to retrieve Siggi, likely either lying in self-pity for his bereft manhood in some lodging house, or floated out somewhere in the harbor from a gang robbery or offending someone with his socialist cant.

"You must come live here. We have an empty apartment downstairs. I am sure we can accommodate you."

"Oh, no," said Tessie. "That's too much."

Gus was staring at me, startled, shaking his head, as Tessie continued to look down at her empty plate. It was not a look of anger, just confusion. Disorientation.

"Yes, you can," I insisted. "You are a hard worker. There are jobs available at Pelgram and Meyer, aren't there, Gus? Since Mr. Pelgram let go a number of activists?"

"Yes," stuttered Gus, "but—"

"You will not be a charity case on us, Tessie," I asserted. "We will indulge you several months. You will need to buy some furniture. Other items. Amelia and Elizabeth can help us with our new garden and chickens. Yet stay in school."

Amelia and Elizabeth broke out in unforced smiles for the first time since they had arrived. "A garden!" laughed Amelia.

"It's settled then," I said. "We will obtain two beds, and you can repay us once all is settled. Now, let's have some cake, coffee, and smiles."

Pauline kept patting Tessie on the back, rather robustly. When she broke out into a grin, I laughed too. I had resigned myself to being prepared for whatever storm ensued, and that I would return to Tessie and her daughters, permanently, if Gus's behavior forced it. I would not step down!

By the end of the evening, we had agreed that the trio would move in on March 21. Gus did not display anger or look displaced and offended, the way Siggi had over the pamphlet stir, just confused. He said little and nodded his head now and then as we talked about old times on Forty-Seventh Street. Clearly, Tessie did not mourn or miss Siggi. His disruption of her life had banished love or even pity for him.

Tessie, Amelia, and Elizabeth insisted on leaving us at home and returning to the train by themselves about six that evening. After we had waved them down the street, Gus closed the door and looked at me, his forehead wrinkled, with his palms outstretched in bafflement. Pauline leaned on the railing at the second-floor landing to our apartment, watching us. I doubted briefly it would still be "ours" for long.

"What have you done?" he asked, his voice uneven and bewildered.

"I have given my friend my shelter and support, just as she gave me hers when I was—"

"Okay, I know," said Gus, cutting me off and glancing back up the stairs at his mother, his eyes wide, with a "don't tell her about your history" look about him. "I know, but I was just going to offer the apartment to Alvin and Lois. They'll pay good rent!"

"So will Tessie. Do you doubt my trust in my friend?" I answered sharply.

"No, but—Alvin and Lois. You should have talked with me first. Us, together."

"There was no time," I said.

"Do you remember when your father and I were evicted down on Attorney Street, Gustav Adolph?" came Pauline's voice slow and firm from above us.

"Well, yes, Mother, but—" said Gus, looking now upstairs at Pauline.

"And your Uncle Charles took us in?"

"Yes."

"You know, son, we didn't make our share of the rent for three months, until your father found work."

"Well, that was family."

"And who is she?" said Pauline, pointing a finger at me. "Is she some maid in your kitchen?"

"Well, no—"

"I like her, Gustav Adolph; she is a hard worker and treats your father like she would her own, and she is planning a garden, and our chicken coop, and knows how to take my directions in the kitchen. I like her."

Gus nodded.

"Besides," said Pauline, "do you know who inherits this house should your father die before me, which, God forgive me for saying this, he probably will?"

"You will, Mother," said Gus.

"So come up here and help us," said Pauline. "There's some hard scrubbing to be done, my back aches, and your wife can't get it all done alone."

As Gus and I climbed the stairs, she added, "Don't forget your roots, son. Don't put money in front of family."

I sighed, glad I had made a favorable impression on Pauline. I would need to watch myself. Need to please Mother Krieger. It was a new wrinkle I had not seriously considered before.

Gus was reserved for about a week. Today, after we finished in the garden, he asked me, "What would you have done if matters had turned out otherwise?"

"I would have returned to Tessie," I said. "To be her support."

Gus stood there silently, taking in what I had said. "I hope someday you will be able to consider me as worth that level of loyalty."

It was my turn to be silent. Some feathers remain ruffled.

PS in all this, I realize I have not said much about church since arriving in Paterson, or Minister Langhaar. It's because there's not much to say. Gus has gone to services once or twice. I have remained home with Lessia. He is not much of a churchgoer. That is fine with me; it's just a tool of fearful old men, anyway. I do not miss it.

Sunday, April 4, 1897.

Quite a bit of bustle about 67 Garrison Street. Tessie, Amelia, and Elizabeth are working well into the household after joining us two weeks ago. The children, upon returning from school each day, have been excellent help hoeing over the soil and mixing in manure. A bit late I have planted spinach and lettuce and quickly followed up with the first of several plantings of kale, cabbage, turnips, carrots, peas, broccoli, and onions. Last Sunday, Gus cleared out the coolest corner of the cellar and built racks for our root vegetables. We have tilled four beds out of the earth! Four!

As for beds, I am becoming more confident in and proud of Gus. Saturday afternoon before the arrival of our new renters, we went downtown to Meyer Brothers Department Store. I had intended to purchase two of the most economical beds for the Flogts. Gus, however, was hesitant, remarking that the least expensive of those offered for purchase seemed spindly and likely to collapse easily. He made his point by sitting down on one put on display, and we both laughed as it groaned. The headboard and footboard started to sag inward to him.

"No," he said. "We purchase for durability. I want something that will last. Strong and reliable." He winked at me as the flustered little salesman flitted to another model close by. It was not until we found a model capable of supporting him that we bought it. The same drama unfolded with the mattresses.

"A mattress, not a throw cushion," Gus insisted.

We paid directly and arranged delivery on Monday. Then, Gus took me by the hand, and we stepped down the grand staircase of that lovely department store and seated ourselves in the restaurant for coffee and French crullers. I was a bit apprehensive.

"This will be much more a cost than Tessie anticipates, I'm sure," I said.

"Give her a price that you think she can afford," said Gus. "Tell her we were able to find a bargain, and impress on her how durable the furniture is."

The crullers arrived, sweet fluted and ring-shaped airy pastries dusted in sugar and cinnamon. I dipped mine in the hot, thick coffee, bit by bit, savoring every taste.

"Are you courting me, Gustav Adolph Krieger?" I giggled.

"I love you," he said. We held hands across the table.

Seated next to us, a stiff, old couple looked down their noses in our direction and sniffed. Gus just calmly showed them his plain, round wedding ring and turned my hand to show them mine. He looked at the man and said, "I love my wife; don't you love yours?"

They looked away as we laughed.

Back home, Lessia had napped contently the while. I nursed her soon after we returned, and mused on the fact she would soon be sampling food: a small dollop of mushy oatmeal, a teaspoon of pureed carrot or squash. So quickly she was growing. So playful she was becoming.

Sunday evening, since the beds would not arrive until the next day, I slept with Pauline, the Flogts snuggled into our bed, and Gus slept on the living-room sofa. Pauline snores.

Gottlieb had taken to sleeping in a chair we had moved into the parental bedroom. On the Tuesday after the Flogts visited, he became particularly agitated early in the morning, about four o'clock, and pushed Pauline away violently, causing her to fall back, luckily into bed. The poor old lady hardly got sleep that night, what with his moving about and calling names, some of whom I recognized as Gus's dead brothers and sisters. Gus called for the doctor, helpless in the face of his father's severe episode.

Now, in the evening, before bedtime, we give him ten drops of tincture of laudanum, as Doctor Kanntlos advised. It has settled him, giving us much relief overnight. It has also made his stool firmer and easier to clean. Beyond that, he seems somewhat peaceful, and as of late he has entered one of his better periods, as he does at unpredictable intervals, recognizing Pauline and his own home. Sometimes, he mixes past and present and talks to us as well as others from Misingen whom he apparently sees in our home.

Yesterday, he even ventured out of the house in the evening, and Gus got him as far as Oxford Street Park on his spindly, wobbly legs! Then, back home, he retreated into a dark spell, calling out names and crying pitifully until the laudanum, which he took disguised in a small amount of warm milk, quieted him.

Amelia and Elizabeth are kind with him and encourage him to eat those evenings he is mentally somewhat among us, bringing him his dinner, mashed so he can digest it easily, and even offering him it spoonful by spoonful.

Although I do not have a perambulator, I carry Lessia now for walks in Oxford Street Park, winding our way down a labyrinth-like path loaded with the promise of spring blossom—azalea and forsythia are swollen and ready—as well as summer resplendence to come: rose bushes in abundance but still scrawny in winter retreat. For now, daffodils grace the path.

Today is soft, warm, and full of promise. I have missed my time of the month. I am hopeful but will not tell Gus until another missed cycle assures me.

From the *Paterson Evening News*, Saturday, April 10, 1897:

"Man 62 Years Old Commits Suicide

"Gottlieb Krieger, of Garrison Street, Was Despondent over His Failing Health and Lost Children

"Shot Himself in the Head

"Tragedy took place this morning in Oxford Street Park, where the aging man had gone to brood. Sat on a rock as he fired revolver.

"Grief over his failing health and the loss over his lifetime of many of his sons and daughters is thought to be the cause of the suicide of Gottlieb Krieger, sixty-two years old, of 67 Garrison Street, who shot himself in the head with a revolver as he sat on a rock deep in a garden in the Oxford Street Park, about nine o'clock this morning.

"The old man's grief at the loss of so many of his offspring, ten of the twelve borne to him by his wife, Pauline, had been so poignant that often in the night he would leave his bed and go about the house calling their names. He lived with his son, Gustav Adolph, and wife, Pauline, but had never hinted to either that he was thinking of taking his own life.

"However, he apparently had left the house early in the day, unbeknownst to any of the household. His wife had gone to the backyard garden to sit and watch downstairs neighbors Tessie, Amelia, and Elizabeth Flogt till the soil. His son, Gustav, was at work at the Pelgram and Myer ribbon factory on Lane Street, while his daughter-in-law and grandchild were returning from Coleridge's Drug Store on Belmont Avenue, where they had obtained medicine for the old man. He was soon dead beside the rock he had visited just a week before in one of his occasional spells of lucidity, according to his son.

"Workmen in the street did not notice Krieger going to the park. Suddenly, a revolver shot broke the stillness of the neighborhood, and the workmen dropped their tools and followed the sound to Krieger and saw the old man had fallen.

"A night watchman at Crescent Mills, who happened to be in the vicinity, ran to Patrolman Timothy Brophy, on post on nearby North Seventh Street, reporting that a man had shot himself. Hasting to the scene, the officer found the man lying face downward on the ground with blood flowing from a wound just above his right ear. He breathed his last as the officer turned him over on his back. A .38 caliber revolver lay on the ground beside its victim. It contained four exploded cartridges, but the workmen said they had heard only one shot.

"Patrolman Brophy notified police headquarters by telephone, and Lieutenant Pforzheim, on desk duty there, informed Coroner Illes of the shooting. After viewing the body, the coroner ordered it removed by P. H. Carver and Sons to the son's residence.

"The son and his wife, carrying their young child, came to the scene of death from work and home before the body was removed, some persons having carried the news to them. The son said his father had seemed in better spirits often lately. He related to Officer Brophy that he had kept the revolver locked in a safe at his home. Although his father had known the combination to it, he had not thought the old man in his present condition would have remembered it or possessed the presence of mind to open it. Visibly upset, he was comforted greatly by his wife.

"Krieger had lived in Paterson for some ten-plus years, coming here when he had removed from New York City. He was born in Germany but came to this country in his early thirties and had been employed as a silk weaver before his mental and emotional upsets disabled him. Another son, Frederick, also lives in this city. The funeral is to be on Monday."

A similar story ran on Monday in the *Paterson Morning Call*. Both were headlined, front-page articles.

At his death, Gottlieb's will, written on September 1, 1894, bequeathed his home to his wife, Pauline, and five hundred dollars each to his sons, Gustav and Frederick. His handwriting was shaky, tilted from the horizontal, and uncertain, unlike the strong hand that had vouched for Gus's citizenship in 1884. On Monday, April 12, Gottlieb's remains were cremated at Little Pond Crematory and Columbarium, Hawthorne, New Jersey. His ashes were returned to Gustav. Their current location is unknown. I suspect they were strewn in a corner of the backyard at Garrison Street. Gottlieb's death certificate lists his father as Gottlieb Krieger and his mother as Mary, maiden name unknown.

As religion of the day viewed suicide as a grave sin of self-murder, there would have been no religious service.

Cara Maurer

Sunday, December 26, 2010.

Yesterday, Momz and I had a fantastic dinner at Lucinda's in Larchmont. We sat down for appetizers at five and didn't leave until after nine! I think we closed the place. Nobody minded. It's where Momz brings new authors often and holds occasional book parties, so she's a customer everybody at the restaurant wants to please. And even though the food was superb, better than some of the one or two stars Momz treated me to in Paris last summer, what we talked about over dinner is really what I want to write about here. And then later at home about Dad.

Of course I was carded, being just twenty-one and all, and the sommelier apologized over and over about it until we laughed and Momz just said, "I don't mind, just please flatter me and card me next time too!"

We ordered some seasoned fried squid in a tart, lemony sauce with a hint of heat and, of course, Momz favorite PEI mussels in garlic and white wine. We opened a bottle of Veneto sauvignon blanc, refreshingly grassy. Those Californian whites are just too fat and sweet.

"So, Momz," I asked just as we started into the first course, "how did you first meet Dad?"

"Well, that's out of the blue," Momz said.

"I've been reading about Great-Great-Gramma Kati's experiences," I said. "It's especially interesting about how she and Great-Great-Grampa Gus met."

"How's that?" asked Momz.

"You never read Grandma Cara's translation of Kati's diary?" I asked.

"No," said Momz. "Tell me."

So I did. Everything I had read so far. Right up to Gottlieb's tragic suicide and how I had actually cried when I had read it.

"Hmm," said Momz. "Maybe I should. Do you think you'll be getting to the rest of it soon?"

"I'm trying," I said, and explained I was so focused on Margee, and somewhat distracted and unable to concentrate too much at any one time with these HIV tests, that a few pages at a time was my max at the moment.

"So you didn't see Margee today?" asked Momz.

"At lunchtime, while you were on the phone with London."

"And how are your tests going?" Momz asked. Leaping from topic A to topic B directly.

"Negative so far," I said and went on a riff about the schedule of tests and antibodies and antigens, and how nice my new obi-wan was.

Momz just nodded and then asked, "Are you still active, I mean having sex?"

"No," I answered. "I'm not."

The conversation lagged. We each made a stab for the last mussel, which Momz ceded to me; then she chuckled. "Obi-wan, that's cute." A pause. "I think you're being smart, until you get your final test, on, what, March twentieth? Or?" A pause. "Do you miss it?"

"What?" I asked, forgetting briefly what we had been discussing as the plates were cleared.

"Sex," said Momz. "Well, I guess not, you've forgotten it already!"

"No, I really don't," I said, and then added, "They're not very good at it, mostly.'

"Is that because of the alcohol?" Momz asked. "Or the—"

"Maybe," I said quickly, "because of the alcohol, but, no, no drugs."

Momz smiled. "Then you haven't done anything I didn't do, party girl."

That took me aback a little. I mean, that was Momz, my high-powered, rapid-reading, brutally honest book-reviewing mother, slicing through bullshit with her wicked pen-wand each day on her laptop. Well, in a manner of speaking.

"Time for salads?" she asked.

"Sure," I said. "Can we share one?"

We chose a simple mista to go best with the sauvignon blanc. We were nursing the bottle. Using water laced with lemon for thirst. At the same time, we ordered our dinners: branzino—Mediterranean sea bass in an herbed white wine sauce with capers for Momz, and scarpariello—chicken with sweet peppers, balsamic onions, sausage, and rosemary for me. I knew I was pushing the limits of a white wine with the sausage, but so what!

"No rose?" asked Momz. "That sausage might be a little off-balancing."

"Nah," I said. "Nothing looks right on the list, and the reds all look too heavy. Besides, I think I'm gonna limit myself to a 'genteel sufficiency.'" I laughed. That was always Momz's term when she was a little buzzed and starting to turn off her tap late in the evening. "I may have to drive you home."

"Are you giving me license to swill?" Momz laughed.

"Go for it," I said.

"Not tonight, KT," said Momz, looking at me with that soft gaze I always get before she hugs me or kisses my cheek. "Not tonight."

As we dug in enthusiastically to our main courses, guiltily interrupting our enjoyment with a forkful of greens from the mista at intervals, I talked about Cara's translation. "It's just that, occasionally, I find the diary too well crafted."

"How so?" asked Momz.

I described the scene as Tessie leaves with Amelia and Elizabeth, with Pauline at the top of the stairs, imparting her wisdom as the venerable elder to her son, as her probable chosen replacement, Kati, gained her approval. "It's just too perfect," I said. Then I told her about what to that point remained the wrongly placed description of the Tompkins Square labor riot. "It reads well," I said, "but some of it doesn't seem to add up. Also, I'm not saying Kati is stupid or anything, but either the translation is embellishing Kati's words, or Kati is one hell of a self-taught, incisive writer."

"Which do you think it is?"

"I'd like to believe Kati's pulling herself up."

"Why?"

"It's such a good story! I'm beginning to really want her to do well, not really identify with her, I don't think, but want to see her succeed. She's going through so much shit."

I think I retold almost all of what I had read so far, concerning Kati's trials, in between the branzino and scarpariello, sharing and praising both dishes done excellently. "Moist and fresh with just enough seasoning to complement the substance of the entrée," I said as we were finishing up, and I was chasing an errant caper across Momz's plate.

"The diary or the bass?" Momz asked.

"Oh, please!" I giggled. "The bass!"

"So you're gonna finish the diary?"

"Yes, definitely! But I wish I knew German, and whether Cara was really giving us Kati, or herself."

"Hmmmm," said Momz. "Dessert?"

"Oh, crèma bruciata, for sure," I said. "And espresso, please. How about you?"

Momz chose the Italian cheesecake, with an espresso as well and a dry grappa Alexander.

"You better get on that bicycle and spin, Momz!" I said. "Join me at the gym tomorrow!"

"I just might," said Momz. "You know, I could have Walther down-town translate Kati's original diary, if we find it."

"Where would we do that?"

"Well, maybe in those boxes in the corner of the attic we didn't get to."

"I want to look at them tomorrow," I said. "I forgot about them. But if we find anything, I want to see for myself."

"But the German?"

"I'll take an extra course this spring."

"Extra course, spring semester, last semester of your senior year?"

"Yes!" I said.

"And speaking of which, any ideas about graduate school? Or what you want to do after you graduate?"

"No," I said. "Not yet."

Momz gave me that "you'd better get on it, girl!" look, and then dessert came. I wondered if Momz was thinking about that diary as a "commercial potential." Well, not before I finished it, but that meant I would have to focus on it. Momz was not one to be stalled when she wanted something.

"So tell me," I asked Momz later at home as we settled in to watch some silly ancient Scrooge movie in black and white in the media room, "did you actually date Dad? I mean, that's what I asked you at Lucinda's, and then we got lost in Kati and all."

"So you did," said Momz. "Yeah, I actually dated. Once I got over my party girl phase and decided I wanted something more than just sex."

"Momz!" I said.

"Well," said Momz. "That's the truth."

"So what was your first date like?"

"Well, it wasn't much of a date, more like a disaster," said Momz, snorting her "private snort of sarcasm" she reserved for her privileged inner circle, me. "I was a lowly assistant editor at Green and Robles downtown living in a postage-stamp studio apartment with only a wall for a kitchen. Hot plate. Two burners. No money. Your father was a wholesale marketing assistant for Ballacio of Italy. We were set up on pretty much a blind date the first time at this place called Mama Leone's in midtown, old friends you never met. Terrible, kitschy restaurant with oversauced food and plastic statues…and grapes on the wall. For the second date, or first real date just the two of us, to save money, since I could tell by his pilled collar your dad was on a budget, I invited him to my little grotto for dinner."

Momz stopped, snorted again, and said, "Here, this is great overacting. Here comes the ghost of Scrooge's business partner."

It was, too, with Marley in histrionics over his misdeeds to Scrooge, some British actor named Alistair Sim.

Then, as Marley vanished, I asked in a low tone, "So-ooooo, what happened in your little grotto?" I giggled.

Momz tossed a throw pillow at me. "I had cooked up pasta, to go with some meatballs I had fried up earlier."

"Fried?"

"Yup, two burners, nothing very haute cuisine then. Well, I had this little, stubby-legged folding table I kept in the closet. I pulled it out and set it. We were going to eat cross-legged on the floor with it between us. Well, your father was already squatting at its edge when I tripped and spilled the pasta—thank God I had rinsed it incorrectly in cold water—over him and his pants in particular. He got up and did this funny dance, whooping and saying, 'Hot, hot, hot!'"

I began chuckling, then cackling, and finally roaring in fits as Momz continued. "He took off his pants and ran off to my tiny bathroom to douse himself with cold water."

Momz was trying not to laugh but couldn't stop herself as I fell off the sofa laughing.

"I didn't like those pants anyway," she said. "Blue-and-white plaid. Just awful. But at least it answered the question of boxers or briefs."

"And what was that?" I asked.

"Briefs, low-cut black ones."

"What did you do for dinner?" I finally asked, after wiping away tears and calming down slowly.

"Meatballs and a Gallo burgundy," said Momz. "Your father wore my bathrobe until his pants dried."

"And he asked you out again, despite that?"

"Well, it was more I asked him. He kept his calm, if not his dignity. And he wasn't overly concerned about his balls."

"And so it began."

"So it began," said Momz with one final titter. "So it began."

The Spirit of Christmas Past rose up on the TV to torment Scrooge.

"This week, sometime, let's check out those remaining boxes," said Momz. "I have Knicks tickets too. Sometime mid-January. I'll have to check exactly when."

KT

Sunday, May 2, 1897.

I have tried to open and write in my diary several times, but I have been unable to find the capacity, the strength, to say what must be said first, and what has kept me from writing, that Gottlieb took his own life in Oxford Street Park, on Saturday morning, April 10. For the details, I have kept a copy of the Paterson Evening News, *hidden in my dresser drawer, so Gus should not know. Keeping it under my diary, I will perhaps someday be able to transcribe it respectfully in a separate entry. Just not yet.*

The consequences of that horrible moment were harsh. For each of us, it struck differently. For Pauline, it became the grief of losing her life partner of near forty years. For Gus, it was the reassertion of occasional gloom and melancholy that had gripped him so often before in the loss of his brothers and sisters, and from which I had thought I had perhaps freed him. For Tessie and her children, it was the shock of waking the patched corpse of the spent old man in his parlor, if only for several days.

For me, it was bearing all of their pain, and my own pity, as well, for a man who had endured so much disappointment and hardship in his life and then let it all consume him.

We each blamed ourselves for not having noticed Gottlieb leave the house. Thankfully, no one was so distraught as to thoughtlessly try to place guilt on another. There were others to exact our anger upon.

First was the careless and sensational News, *whose reporter had managed to arrive quickly at the scene from police headquarters, where we presume he waited for any morbid story of interest to his readers. Neither Gus nor I had wits at that moment to realize that the insistent little man in the bowler hat and bow tie was more than a morbid onlooker as he peppered us with questions while we stood at the rock.*

Second was the coroner, so quick to have Gottlieb's bloodied body practically thrown upon an open cart, the only conveyance Undertaker Carver had been able to muster up at so short notice. His careless remarks, including, "How inconsiderate to risk injury to others," and, "Doesn't look like he'd have the strength to lift such a gun," and "How did he get loose, anyhow?" had even Police Officer Brophy, a white-haired, hard-bitten veteran of the force, staring at him disapprovingly.

Third was Minister Langhaar, who later at the house offered prayers for all of us except Gottlieb, whose body had since gone to Carver's for some cleaning prior to the wake on that Sunday. "He has committed a grave sin, an affront to God who gave him life," said Langhaar. "One we can only beg the Almighty to forgive, but which I cannot."

"Just one small prayer," Gus pleaded. "One intercession of his hard work and faith on his behalf."

"Very well," said Langhaar. But he remained adamant that he could not attend any burial, recommend any consecrated cemetery, or perform any service. "My congregation would have me dismissed," he said.

So, after a short, mumbled entreaty in our parlor, Langhaar turned to leave. "This has been very thirsty work," he hinted.

"You have left us all thirsty," said Gus. "I will see you to the door."

Gus has not been to church since. I am fine with this. Religion has continued to disappoint me in its lack of comfort to those who need it most. "Insofar as ye do it unto these the least of my brethren, ye do it unto me." That exhortation is lost in rules and respectability.

Of great comfort and help were Gus's friends, many of whom I had met at our wedding surprise party. Mrs. Roth, especially, came and helped us with receiving mourners, few for Gottlieb, but many to condole us. She saw to all the kitchen work and cleaning, aided by Mrs. Loewenherz and Mrs. Swartbach, who made a lovely raisin pie. Leo Haefell and the neighboring Groegers smoothed all the arrangements with the cremation, especially with the Sterbekasse, and Albert Roth assured Gus that if he needed any extra money, he could provide it. Alvin and Lois Thetge, along with Alvin's mother, Mrs. James Thetge, were noticeably absent. I have not brought that up with Gus.

I know it hurt Gus to have Gottlieb cremated, a means for disposing of vagrants, criminals, and atheists. We keep the ashes in a corner of the parlor safely back on a shelf in a weighted vase. I have caught Gus a few times close to the urn, staring at it.

So, until yesterday afternoon, we went about our work and about the house as sleepwalkers, toiling dull and dead at any menial task to avoid more than a weak smile or nod to each other. Tessie did not venture upstairs, nor did the girls come to play with Lessia. Pauline sat in her kitchen chair and stared out the window toward Oxford Street Park. Easter passed unacknowledged.

I imagine each, save Gus, was thinking of how indulgence in the moment had let Gottlieb slip away from us. I know I did.

At night, Gus lay stiffly on his side of our bed. When I rolled to him and put my arm around him, he patted it, nothing more. When I kissed him gently on the neck, which would have initiated love play for us, he sighed and shifted his shoulders. There was no "good night." No "I love you." No talk of how the day had gone. Nothing.

I determined this had to change.

"Gus," I said about four this afternoon after he had come upstairs, "I have something to tell you, but you must come with me." I carried Lessia with me.

Gus looked puzzled but nodded. He followed me downstairs and out the front door but stopped when I headed to the street.

"Come," I said. "Come with me."

"What is it?" he asked.

"Something good, something you will want to hear. Come."

Gus hesitated for several seconds, his hand tapping the gate post, and then moved to me. I took him by the arm, and we walked locked together down Garrison Street to the corner with Oxford. When we crossed to face the park, he stopped abruptly.

"No further," he said. His voice rose.

"We are going into the park," I said.

"No, I will not go there, ever again, even with you. Nothing you can say will make me," said Gus. He looked angrily at me.

"Do not become angry with me. Do not oppose me. I mean it. You need to hear me; you need this," I said firmly. I pulled at his arm, which he had released from mine, and said to him, "You either come with me, or I will scream what I have to say to the whole neighborhood, Gustav Adolph Krieger." Lessia whimpered.

I had never addressed him so; only his mother had. But he relented. I think he expected me to scold him in some way. Perhaps it was Lessia he did not wish to upset. We walked into the park, down the labyrinth-like path to the rock where Gottlieb had taken his life. I led the entire way. Along the way, spindly yellow forsythia pointed up their hardy, tiny flowers into a light afternoon breeze. Squat, crimson azalea hid the brown leaves remaindered from winter still scattered upon the soil. Most of the daffodils had withered away, but an occasional spike of hyacinth lifted its heavy, purple mass of flowers and let their heady fragrance drift up into the evening.

Gus kept his head down as we stood in front of the rock.

"I am pregnant, Gus. We are going to have a child."

Gus kept his head down for a minute or two. He did not move, but he did turn his arm and take my hand to his, clasping it softly. A perplexed look calmed to one of acceptance, and then a smile, broadening and deepening slowly.

Finally, he looked at me and said, "Why here?"

"Because now I will need you more than Gottlieb did in his decline. Of course I expect you to honor him and think of him, the many memories I hope you will share with me over time. But I need your presence. I need...you. Do not disappoint me!"

When he said, "Our Lessia will have a brother or sister!" and kissed me lightly on my cheek, I knew I had made the correct decision in marrying Gus.

"Come," I said. "Let's sit. Let's talk about names."

So we sat where Gottlieb had sat, where only a few weeks ago, his blood had run onto the rough surface of the rock. Where the revolver had lain smelling of gunpowder. Hand in hand, with Lessia clucking and fussing until I relented and started to nurse her, we discussed names. It will be Charles Gottlieb if a boy, and Helen Maria if a girl. We discovered we both want American first names. We laughed at Krieger and Scheu. Such burdens: "warrior" and "shy"!

Back at home, we announced our happiness. The mood in the house changed immediately.

Monday, May 3, 1897.

This evening there was much to discuss. Nothing that important, just the usual stories of the day. Tessie's complaints of low wages and fumbling coworkers halting the spinning of the silk. Gus worried about another work action at Pelgram and Meyer by, as he tells it, the less skilled and most recent immigrants, from whom he always now distances himself. Amelia and Elizabeth proud of a history test on the American Revolution. Their school is very progressive. Pauline annoyed at the price of onions.

"Soon we will have our own, fresh from the ground," I said to Pauline. "Tomorrow, Mother Krieger, let's you and me go and buy some chickens for our coop. It is ready now, thanks to Amelia and Elizabeth."

Pauline, whom I had never addressed as Mother before, smiled and nodded. "Of course, daughter, and what are you thinking of buying?"

"Rhode Island reds," I said.

She nodded again, deeply. She approved. "Fresh eggs with onions!"

For the first time since Gottlieb's death, there were no leftovers at the table.

"I should bake a pie," I said. "Mother Krieger, there is rhubarb growing along the Osford Street fence of our yard. Do you know a recipe?"

"Yes, I do," said Pauline. "You may have it. Would you bake one with me?"

Amelia and Elizabeth's progressive school was Public School 14 on the corner of Union Avenue and Coral Street at the southeastern edge of Paterson's Second Ward. Built in 1894, it was named after the feminist author and reformer Lillie Devereaux Blake. Her daughter, Katherine Blake, served the school as principal from its founding until 1928, thirty-four years. She was an avowed pacifist and insisted that the song "I Did Not Raise My Son to Be a Soldier" be sung at every school assembly. Lillie Blake argued fervently that gender roles were learned behaviors and that both genders shared a common nature. Responding to the diatribes of male clergy of the day, who argued for biblical support of women's inferiority because Eve was created after Adam, she noted that in such a case, Adam would be inferior to all the beasts of the earth, as they had been created first.

Later in my childhood in Haledon, New Jersey, there were several houses I passed walking up Barbour Street on my way to Absalom Grundy Grammar School that grew rhubarb. Those two-family, wood-frame houses, built on a plan similar to Gottlieb and Pauline's, had side yards, and they had their rhubarb growing along the walkways that passed from the front porches to the back steps of the residences.

Rhubarb was one of the first plants to break through the soil in late March and early April, right after crocus and concurrent with daffodil and hyacinth. It was a welcome sight in the drear, chilly gray mornings while tramping up to school: bright-red stalks emerging with heavy leaves. They defied the crisp crust of frost or late dusting of snow some springs laced upon them and other early garden growth. Rhubarb was also grown by my paternal grandmother, Nellie Maurer, in Wayne. She baked many a rhubarb pie.

Rhubarb was essentially an immigrant crop. Easy to grow, easy to "fruit" into a pie. It was no wonder it occupied Nellie's garden as a throwback to her paternal grandparents' days, emigres from Minden, Germany, or those gardens adjacent to homes on Barbour Street, built by wealthy industrialists to sell to first- and second-generation weavers from Paterson and to guide them toward a financially accountable lifestyle with mortgages, which would make their employees less likely to radicalize against them. Or so they thought.

Rhubarb also had a long history as a cure-all medicine. The root of the plant was ground up and dosed to sufferers of all nature of ailments, including dysentery and constipation. Since medical potions of the day were mostly palliatives against inevitable death from fearsome diseases, the practice continued through Kati's time. In fact, rhubarb was one of those trade goods that arrived in Europe via the Silk Road from China. The tsars of Russia monopolized its trade. It was praised as early as 1403, when Ruy Gonzalez de Clavijo, an emissary, reported that the best of all merchandise came to Samarkand from China, including silk, satin, perfumes such as musk, precious stones such as rubies and diamonds, and rhubarb.

As a child, I learned that rhubarb could also have disquieting laxative effects, especially as a leftover slice of pie from the refrigerator. I was warned early on that its leaves were poisonous. Nonetheless, it was allowed to grow close to where children played. It made its way to our table either as stewed rhubarb or as a meringued pie.

Although Krieger domestic life may have seemed quite boring, it was still demanding. The wages for workers were oppressively low; home economy was seriously practiced. Domestic workers played a cornerstone role in the success and preservation of a family. Additionally, sharing news and events at the dinner table gave breadth and depth to each participant's understanding of the world at hand and at large. A newspaper was a vital link to the world, as well. Activities in the evening required involvement and skills: reading, knitting and sewing, home repair, preserving vegetables and fruits, piano. This went far beyond mere entertainment. To build a picture of the immediate and metropolitan world of the Kriegers, consider:

1. Paterson at the time had six English-language newspapers: the *Daily Guardian*, the *Daily Press*, the *Evening News*, the *Morning Call*, the *Weekly Press*, and the *Sunday Chronicle*. Furthermore, two German-language weeklies, the *Staatszeitung* and the *Volksfreund*, were available.

2. Social and fraternal organizations abounded, including the Turnverein, a German gymnastics society, and Masonic lodges for various ethnicities, such as the Beethoven Lodge for German Americans. Each had a building devoted to its activities. The Turnverein had a hall located on nearby Totowa Avenue.

3. People took the opportunity to celebrate birthdays and holidays with parties. For example, one party for Halloween at the Turnhalle included two male choruses, a yodelers' ensemble, and a music club presentation.

4. Some other facts of note for the times:
   * There was no radio or television.
   * The life-span of a white American was about forty-eight; that of an African American was thirty-three.
   * The automobile was a mere curiosity. There were no traffic lights. Travel was by boat or train. No airplanes.
   * Football was a college sport, with few spectators. Basketball was a means of keeping athletes fit in winter; it was a sport in its infancy. There was no American League in baseball, no World Series.
   * Even silent films were in the future: *The Great Train Robbery* debuted in 1903. Music was recorded on wax cylinders. Hand-cranked phonographs, or gramophones, were referred to as talking machines. They played cylinders or discs. They were priced well beyond the means of Kati and family.
   * Telephones, likewise, were seldom found outside of commercial establishments or affluent households.

Lastly, popular music of the year included "Asleep in the Deep," "Beautiful Isle of Somewhere," "On the Banks of the Wabash Far Away," "Our Lodger's Such a Nice Young Man," and "The Stars and Stripes Forever."

Certainly, the first verse of "On the Banks of the Wabash Far Away" would have struck a deep chord in Kati's heart. The memories of

Misingen would have come back bittersweet to her, transcending the gender of the child being greeted:

Round my Indiana homestead wave the cornfields,
In the distance loom the woodlands clear and cool.
Oftentimes my thoughts revert to scenes of childhood,
Where I first received my lessons, nature's school.
But one thing there is missing from the picture,
Without her face it seems so incomplete.
I long to see my mother in the doorway,
As she stood there years ago, her boy to greet.
(Chorus)
Oh, the moonlight's fair tonight along the Wabash,
From the fields there comes the breath of new mown hay.
Through the sycamores the candle lights are gleaming,
On the banks of the Wabash, far away.

As regards Tessie's complaint of low wages, wage disparities between men and women were large, especially in silk. The following comparison dates from 1913, sixteen years after Tessie's complaint at the dining table. It was taken from a July 1916 publication of the Bureau of US Labor Statistics, volume 3, number 1. Male broad silk weavers earned $13.31 per week, women $10.58! Male ribbon weavers earned $16.05 per week, women $13.14. Additionally, loom fixers, considered a male occupation, earned $17.92 per week, while soft silk winders, considered a female role, earned but $8.14!

Cara Maurer

Fuzzi to KT 743-765-8040
Hey! KT itz Fuzzi. Txt me!

Dec. 27.

Sunday, May 9, 1897.

Our chickens have begun laying eggs! The first batch we gave to the Groegers, who lent us their cage to bring back our fine sturdy reds from market. The next batch we used in part for our first rhubarb pie for yesterday's dessert! Dessert on Saturday! We made two. One for today as well.

Pauline sat and dictated the recipe and watched as I made it. Pauline cannot read. She carries all these recipes in her head. Precious Swabian delights I am writing down each time I can. It is quite funny. I keep a pen and paper on a small table safely away from the flour and butter, and all the other dangers baking or cooking present at the main table and the stove, and move between the two as Pauline dictates and laughs good-naturedly at my efforts.

Well, rhubarb pie is quite simple really. It is, to Pauline, more important to harvest the proper stalks to cut for the filling. So down the stairs she insisted on coming to supervise me. I was hesitant. Stairs! More wobbling and support from me. What if she falls? I had so worried about that earlier in the week.

Last Tuesday it rained; no chickens! On Wednesday, when I was getting ready to walk down to Market Street to buy our chickens, Pauline was adamant in accompanying me. Progress was slow. Her legs are bandy; she wears large, bulky shoes and walks awkwardly with a cane. I had forgotten Tessie telling me it took her and both girls to lead the old lady downstairs to the garden. It took several hours to reach the farmers lined up in stalls along the side of the thoroughfare hawking their boisterous, clucking fowl. Of course, I let her choose the animals, but then, very worried about her, I insisted we take a cab back. It was very expensive, and at first Pauline scowled. "A waste of money!" she said. Then, she said, "You insult me. I can still walk the distance!"

My heart sank. If I let her walk, would she make it up Hamburg Hill to Garrison Street? If anything happened to her, what would Gus do? I am pregnant, and although still vigorous and healthy, I try to conserve energy for the whole day. But by forcing a cab ride on her, had I disturbed her sense of thrift and turned her against me?

She did not talk to me the entire ride back. I left her sitting in the cab and hurried upstairs for extra money to pay the cabman. It took forever to escort silent

Mother Krieger upstairs. Then she sat down in her favorite kitchen chair. I rushed back downstairs to the caged chickens I had left at the curb and fairly threw them into the coop with some feed after them.

Coming rapidly back upstairs, I found her already asleep. I removed her shoes and elevated her swollen feet to a cushioned stool. She slept for near three hours. I watched her closely. On waking, all she said was, "Are the chickens in the coop?"

"Yes," I said apprehensively.

"Good," she said, and smiled. That was it. No further mention of the little dispute.

When I told Gus that evening, he shrugged his shoulders. "She will go out fighting," he said. "I'm surprised you got her into the cab." Then, he said, "Thanks for looking out for her," and kissed me solidly in front of Amelia and Elizabeth, who had come upstairs to play with Lessia.

Lessia likes tiny, tiny bits of mashed carrots, and peas!

Well, quite a digression! Back to harvesting rhubarb! To Pauline, the stalk must be the right shade of brilliant red. She managed to stand quite well, despite my misgivings, leaning heavily on her cane and pointing out each stalk to cut from the plants lining the small border garden between the house and the path to the back. Each one I harvested she insisted I snap in half before placing it in a basket on her arm.

I suppose I was fortunate. She rejected only two. "Too weak," she said. "Overripe."

Cutting the stalks into one-inch pieces, enough for four cups of fruit per pie, takes most of the time, as well as tossing the pieces in sufficient sugar and flour, one and one-quarter cups of sugar and one-third of a cup of bleached flour per pie filling, and letting the mixture steep for nearly half an hour. I quickly assembled enough dough for two double-crust pies.

Pauline said to dot the pie with butter after filling each crusted pan, before placing down the top crust and fluting it. I said nothing, thinking however that might make the pie taste too oily and slick. But it doesn't. Baking was slightly challenging. The pies needed to bake for nearly an hour in a moderate oven. The Krieger oven is temperamental and tends to burn hot. I kept constant eyes on it.

Success.

This afternoon, I asked Pauline if she would teach me to tat. She assented. Tatting is such an art. Besides, we can do it without the challenge of the stairs.

Next Sunday, there is an afternoon suffrage meeting at the Turnhalle. I am going. I think I will bring Lessia.

Monday, December 27, 2010.

So sore! Back to kickboxing and the elliptical. Got up late and settled down in the sofa to read more Kati. I get confused. Sometimes she's very forward and authoritative; then, she turns so domestic, especially with Pauline and rhubarb pie! I haven't become a total "fact checker" on Cara, but I have become a little suspicious with how neatly her story line flows, sometimes, so I looked up Lillie Deveraux Blake. I got lost in her story. At least an hour. Quite a feminist. But her daughter was a principal at School 6 in Manhattan. Everything else checked out, just the location. Huh?

Wow, that took balls—hey, what am I saying—what could I use as a female equivalent, brass knockers? Sounds lame. Anyway, Katherine really politicized the school! Try doing that today! Her head'd be on a pole in front of, what is it, School 14?

Oh, and I trolled on about Paterson and the silk industry. There were earlier periods of labor unrest, including 1897. Big blowout in 1913. No mention of that there, the 1897 issues, so far. You would think Kati, or Cara, her Grand Explicator, would mention that. It would fit into the drama nicely. Unless I'm wrong on the labor stress. I don't think they would be oblivious to it. Chickens and a veggie garden. They were trying hard, but still on the edge, economically.

And, of course, this misplaced Tompkins Square riot that I know I'm right about.

The stats about wage disparities were correct, and the source. Depressing.

So I went up to the attic, dragged out what amounted to six boxes of "stuff'" Momz and I had not gotten to, dusted them off, and lugged them downstairs to the den. I so want to open them up by myself, but I think it was understood at Christmas dinner Momz and I would do that together. I think.

Another annoying text from an idiot named Fuzzi. So, made a list. One: get phone. Two: look at postings on placement office wall, just to get an idea and think about, hmmm, life after graduation. Three: get Momz leggings.

Pretty quickly, it was time to see Margee. Nothing has changed. Someone had shifted the stuffed animal tree out of Margee's sight, so I repositioned it so she could see it. If she can see anything.

I am losing hope for her. She's soon to be classified "persistently vegetative."

Never lose hope. Never lose hope. Never. Never. Never lose hope!

I have to stop now; I'm crying.

KT

PS: Momz called. I had been staring at those old boxes. Me sitting on the floor in one corner of the den, the dark one, the boxes in the other, catching the last light of a weak afternoon's sun. Got me out of my hole.

I told her about Blake. The Paterson strike unrest in 1897. My doubts about Cara's reportage. Also started in about how "plot-like" the whole thing with Gottlieb's death and Kati's pregnancy seemed. Momz a good listener. She put me onto a website called Familysearch where I could check up on family history items like births, deaths, census records. Not that they have everything, but that it's a good place to start.

Momz had called to tell me she was gonna be late, very late. Some blowup about a promising author, advance for a second novel, no novel, no advance left. Lawyers. I listened. Got to admit, I lost most of it, thinking about fact-checking Kati's pregnancy on this site, apparently run by the Mormons. Like the Angel Moroni in upstate New York. More golden tablets and all.

Sure!

Anyway, guess what? A Kati Scheu Krieger, in Paterson, did give birth to a girl. Named Helen Maria! Father Gustav Adolph Krieger. On December 12, 1897. It fits!

What the hell is going on?

Like I said, I did not want to start looking in the boxes without Momz, although I was tempted! And lurking about the house all evening would only bring me back to Margee, so I went out to Nieman and bought Momz some really nice leggings. Lululemon. And one quirky pair for her exercise classes that had all the muscles of the legs and butt printed on it. Weird and funny.

Well, item three accomplished. Just like me, start with the easiest thing to do. Well, most fun!

Poor Margee! I wonder what I would really do if I found the asshole who did this to her. Better anger than sorrow? Better for me, I guess.

Sunday, May 16, 1897.

I walked to the Turnhalle on Market Street for the early afternoon suffrage meeting. It was a pleasant, warm day, as it has been this past week, causing the rosebuds to swell to a promising red-edged fullness harbingering bursts into early blossoms this year. As I started out, I felt a light-headed sense of belonging to this country, really belonging to it, for the first time. Democracy. The voice of the people, not just men!

In the end, being practical, I left Lessia with Elizabeth. Left her to play and nibble at a few mushed carrot flakes and sip a little boiled milk. We have bought an ice box!

The Turnhalle is no grand temple like the Congress. It is large, stuccoed, gray, and square. It occupies about half of the front of the block between Main and Grand Streets, with a modest, wooden double-doored entrance several steps above the sidewalk. There is a cornice, and a pillar to either side, ground to roof, simple and plastered gray as well.

I noticed all this as I approached it, because so much had been written in the newspapers about this place as a den of "dangerous ideas" and "threats to Christian order" on the editorial page of the Morning Call. *My English has become good. Emily and Amelia have helped me. Often evenings, Gus returns from work with a newspaper, and we spend some minutes reading and speaking the news by gaslight in the kitchen. Pauline listens—she cannot read or write German or English—until she falls asleep, and then we whisper but read on.*

The Turnhalle was built for the German Turners, gymnasts. They are socialists. Many of the union meetings for the silk workers occur here, and their marches start here, according to Gus. So it makes sense that the hall should be given over to suffrage meetings as well.

I expected a more robust building. And as I approached it, I worried. I remembered the march in New York, how the women marching then had much finer clothes than I carried now. My light-blue shawl darned in several places and tired from many washes. My shoes worn at the toe and flaked under the best polishing I could provide. Not the current year's style, or last year's, for that matter. My dark-blue dress plain and practical, patched at the sleeves.

Did I really belong? How different things seem in our heads, in our dreams, than when we start on to their hoped-for achievement. Is this what I should be doing? Or am I really just a ragtag immigrant, a poor reject? Unworthy?

I walked so slowly down the block to those unpretentious doors, studying the Turnhalle, noting few women about the entrance. Nervous. Unsure. Thinking maybe the meeting had been canceled, and I could walk back home comfortably relieved in the evaporation of this once-wished moment from my routine. I could always agree with my sisters from afar.

I hesitated at the entrance, clenching the edges of my shawl with my rough, work-worn hands. I drew a deep breath, trembling under my working-class attire. I walked in.

The hall was a patchwork of dark wood illuminated at intervals by light streaming in from long, narrow rectangular windows to either side. The shafts of sunlight fell in bars across a large crowd of bonneted women, some seated, many standing. All seemed better dressed than I. A speech was being given. It was very quiet. All were attentive.

I felt some relief in the extent of the crowd. Reassurance I was among comrades in ideas. But awkward in my person. An outsider.

I wondered if anyone was looking at me, telling me by glance I should leave. That I diminished them. That I did not belong. No one appeared to have noticed me, several minutes late as I was.

First, I noticed the American flags hanging from the supports of the indoor wooden track that circled the perimeter of the hall. Large flags. Also, red, white, and blue bunting. At the front of the hall, on a stage and behind a stand, a woman spoke, forcefully and audibly. Her fist in the air. Behind her looped a large banner saying: In order to form a more perfect Union!

I began to listen to her words. I had just missed her introduction, I suppose, as she was thanking the organizers for inviting her from New York and saying that she was happy to see so many progressive citizens.

I looked around me. No men. Obvious, I suppose, by the lack of the rank odor of alcohol and tobacco. And no side talk.

I did not catch her name, but I did listen well to her words. A speech delivered by a woman called Susan B. Anthony, about twenty-five years ago, after she had been arrested for voting! I found it reasonable, logical, and deserving of my approval. Of everyone's approval.

Afterward, there was talk of a march in several weeks, to City Hall. There were calls to sign up to distribute leaflets, as well as to participate in the march. I left at that point. I was elated but fretful. Proud to have attended, but concerned some stumbling, angry man might challenge me as I walked back up toward home. What would I say? How would I respond?

What of Gus? What did he really think? He has actually said little to strongly support the vote for women. For a moment, I felt disappointed in that, but then I thought, isn't it I who should lead? Where to? And I was uncomfortable again.

Lessia was sleeping at home, in Elizabeth's arms. Her lips puckered in a smile. Fleck of carrot in the corner of her mouth.

Here is the text of the speech Kati heard that day:

"Friends and Fellow Citizens: I stand before you tonight under indictment for the alleged crime of having voted at the last presidential election, without having a lawful right to vote. It shall be my work this evening to prove to you that in thus voting, I not only committed no crime, but, instead, simply exercised my citizen's rights, guaranteed to me and all United States citizens by the National Constitution, beyond the power of any State to deny.

"The preamble of the Federal Constitution says:

"'We, the people of the United States, in order to form a more perfect union, establish justice, insure domestic tranquility, provide for the common defense, promote the general welfare, and secure the blessings of liberty to ourselves and our posterity, do ordain and establish this Constitution for the United States of America.'

"It was we, the people; not we, the white male citizens; nor yet we, the male citizens; but we, the whole people, who formed the Union. And we formed it, not to give the blessings of liberty, but to secure them; not to the half of ourselves and the half of our posterity, but to the whole people—women as well as men. And it is a downright mockery to talk to women of their enjoyment of the blessings of liberty while they are denied the use of the only means of securing them provided by this democratic-republican government—the ballot.

"For any State to make sex a qualification that must ever result in the disfranchisement of one entire half of the people is to pass a bill of attainder, or an ex post facto law, and is therefore a violation of the supreme law of the land. By it the blessings of liberty are forever withheld from women and their female posterity. To them this government has no just powers derived from the consent of the governed. To them this government is not a democracy. It is not a republic. It is an odious aristocracy; a hateful oligarchy of sex; the most hateful aristocracy ever established on the face of the globe; an oligarchy of wealth, where the rich govern the poor. An oligarchy of learning, where the educated govern the ignorant, or even an oligarchy of race, where the Saxon rules the African, might be endured; but this oligarchy of sex, which makes father, brothers, husband, sons, the oligarchs over the mother and sisters, the wife and daughters of every household—which ordains all men sovereigns, all women subjects, carries dissension, discord and rebellion into every home of the nation.

"Webster, Worcester and Bouvier all define a citizen to be a person in the United States, entitled to vote and hold office.

"The only question left to be settled now is: Are women persons? And I hardly believe any of our opponents will have the hardihood to say they are not. Being persons, then, women are citizens; and no State has a right to make any law, or to enforce any old law, that shall abridge their privileges or immunities. Hence, every discrimination against women in the constitutions and laws of the several States is today null and void, precisely as in every one against Negroes."

The speech was actually given in 1873. Anthony had been arrested and fined one hundred dollars, a large sum in the day, for her voting in the 1872 presidential election.

Cara Maurer

Monday, May 17, 1897.

I am angry and disappointed in myself. Why did I leave the meeting yesterday without participating? It is not enough to just be there. Have I become too comfortable in my newly found fortune? Am I worried about losing it? Am I worried about Gus's approval? Is that not what yesterday's meeting was about? Freedom of choice? Independence?

Shame on me. So what if I am not as rich as many of the other ladies who attend. I have been through much. I have attained much. But I need more. For myself. For pride. I will go to the next meeting. In a week. And I will be heard.

If Gus loves me, he will not oppose me. If he does disapprove and opposes me, I have made a mistake. I have made others; I will go forward alone.

But I cannot. There is Lessia, and her brother or sister growing inside me. And if Gus should not really love me, should I abort? How, and where? There are laws. And if he disapproves but does not oppose, is it only because he awaits his child? What does that make me, a fruit tree for his cultivation? We need to talk. But not yet.

Am I unduly harsh in my lack of expectations of Gus? Or practical?

If I am willing to abort this baby, I may die. What would happen to Lessia? Does my willingness to take such a risk mean I am selfish, that my motivation in pregnancy was to secure Gus and become captive as well?

I need to attend for more than just the vote. I need to find support. A second family? My community. I must attend and participate.

Perhaps. It is still early; the sun is large and yellow on the horizon, about to set over Oxford Street Park. I must go there, to the labyrinth. To Gottlieb's rock. But to think.

Wednesday, December 29, 2010.

I am so nervous. So alone. I don't think I will sleep much tonight. But I need to. I really do. I want so much to cuddle into Momz and just hold her and cry. But then, I'll probably wind up telling her everything, and I can't do that. No more. She'd just lawyer me up and prevent me from doing what I need to do. For Margee, and for me. And it'd be a step, huge step, backward from Monday.

Maybe if I just write all this down, what happened Monday evening and then yesterday, then, I can rest. Maybe.

So, when Momz got home on Monday, she saw I was upset. She sat next to me in the den, on the sofa. I did cuddle into her, like when I was a kid. I guess that was what I was Monday.

"Margee still?" Momz asked.

"Does that bother you?" I asked. "That I care so much about her?"

"You need to care for yourself, KT," she said. "Don't let her misfortune be your heartbreak."

"But it is," I said.

"Then you need to mend it," Momz said. "Continue to see her as you do, but, well, tritely put, get on with your own life." She paused. "At least then you'll have more to talk about with her."

I just sighed.

"You can be her way into life, if she does hear you. Be an example. Be strong for her."

"I feel so alone," I said suddenly.

Instead of pulling me closer, Momz just sighed very deeply, kissed me on the top of my head, and then said, "Life's a bitch, KT, isn't it?"

Momz humor. What's the word? Sardonic?

"Glass of red?"

"Sure," I said.

"So, what about a career, and your new phone? Tomorrow?"

"Oh," I said, remembering my Neiman's purchase, "I have something for you."

Momz liked the leggings and laughed and giggled over the muscles. Impulsively, she got up off the sofa, pulled off her pants, and slid them on. "How do I look?" she asked.

"Like, disturbing," I said, laughing. I was actually bothered. Momz is still slim, and she looked, well, MILFy in an undead sort of way. If that makes any sense.

"Just a hunk of meat, KT," she laughed. "We should go to the gym and work out together. Maybe you can introduce me to some of the younger guys."

"Momz," I shouted and tossed a throw pillow at her. "Take those off, now!"

"You are back at the gym, right?" asked Momz as she plunked herself back down onto the sofa.

"Yeah," I said. "Kickboxing mostly, and elliptical for cardio."

"Good," she said. "Time for a postworkout pick-me-up. Malbec or chardonnay?"

So that was how Monday evening went. So yesterday, with Momz working from home and agreeing to go through the remaining attic boxes with me this coming weekend, I drove over to the student union, where the placement office is, just to get an idea from the bulletin board in the hallway outside the office. What would be available for a psych-English major, anyway?

Like, nothing. Why even bother? I should have gone straight to the hiring desk at Walmart. All the good stuff, higher-paying jobs, was like environmental engineering. Math needed. Biomedical engineering. Science and math. International marketing. Languages and, yes, math! Over and over, anything with a salary that would allow me to live on my own, like at least $50K, math, math, math, science, and math. Sorry, Monty Python.

There was just one flyer up for interviews for someone with my degree. With Westchester County Social Services for a social worker trainee. Psych major. At last. Last, for sure. Starting salary: $32K. $32K! And I'd have to pass a civil service exam and get a master's in social work inside of three years.

There was also a position for an English teacher at the Cambridge School, snotty little enclave over in White Plains for white flight from the publics. Starting in September. No salary listed. Don't you at least need a master's to teach? And state certification? Besides, teach? I remembered how I was in high school. No way!

That was depressing. I meandered downstairs to an almost completely empty food court and entered it via the back door. Only the Mickey D's was open. Mostly the campus cops, janitors, and office staff types grabbing late breakfasts and coffee on the run. I so wanted some double frappe thing doused in cream that would impel me guiltily over to My Fitness crosstown. But Mickey's coffee was good. Just honest coffee without pedigree was probably what I'd have to resign myself to anyway, I thought, if I was going to wind up living on $32K a year, in my postage-stamp-sized studio with a hot plate in some ungentrified hovel stocked with pork and beans and cheap red wine.

I grabbed a large and shuffled off to a booth. One on the far side of a double row just to the other side of the concession row. Well, what do I do now? Graduate school? In what? Continue down the path of the unrewarded? Social worker? Case load of eleventy billion societal outcasts all venting on you? Broken families. PINS. Needles! Children whose major accessories were their parole officers? Abusive alcoholic fathers?

God, no! No. No. No. But what? MBA? Mammon worshipers. Then again, like I ever had to do without? The thought of jumping onto one of those Metro North commuter express trains, cattle cars to Manhattan, with all those anxious types in suits pecking away at their laptops and tablets, bleary-eyed and twitching from caffeine poisoning at seven in the morning. No, again.

Why was social work so underpaid, I wondered, staring at my half-empty cuppa joe. Hell, they were heroes, in their own way, even if not for me. Just for the hell of it, I googled "gender breakdown of social workers" on my soon-to-be discarded phone. The answer came up: 80 percent female. Hmmm. I couldn't find an easy breakdown for international marketers, but I hit on a *Forbes* article, some business magazine online, about the twenty jobs with the biggest gender pay gaps.

Motherfucking unreal! I mean, I knew it was a thing, but in surgeons!? Financial managers? You name it, it was there. Like, I always thought it was more a blue-collar thing. Nope. I felt like an ass. Like where my head had been.

And now what? I had no answer. I stared down at the table. Head down. Droopy. Looking at the scratches, names and phone numbers, and streaks of congealed ketchup from leaky quarter pounders that had dried unwashed from who knows how long ago.

What now? Susan Anthony's oligarchy still flourished. In economics. The oligarchy of wealth is the oligarchy of sex now. Sure, what was that stupid economics term my high-school teacher insisted was real and that most of us snickered at? Psychic income. Yeah, eat that!

No oligarchies, Susan B., not in race either, you old bigot. Was I being mean in thinking at least that's one wall I didn't have to face?

Then I wondered what had led me to google "gender breakdown," anyway? Was it Kati, or more precisely, Kati and Cara? Maybe Cara felt more for Kati than I had realized. And what did I know of either outside of that diary?

"Hey, Fuzzi, c'mere."

The voice startled me, and I picked my head up. There was somebody sitting on the other side of the booth wall on my right. Calling to Fuzzi, the name of the jerk who had been texting me. I was about to stand up and glare at the ass when whoeveritwas in the hidden booth said, "Sit down, my friend; I'm out."

Out? Of what?

Fuzzi, I presume, sat down fast and violently, hitting the booth barrier between us and rattling it. "Shut the fuck up, you asshole," said this Fuzzi. I wondered. Was he hairy like a bear? Maybe about as smart. Did he wear a weird porkpie hat? Apologies to Kermit and friends. There couldn't be more than one idiot with that nickname on campus. No? Yes?

"Stickin' it out at Lammi? Got some bitchin' townie tucked away?" An arrogant, snickering voice rasping out its lechy dig.

"Shut up, jackass; somebody could hear you!"

"Place is empty."

"Oh, yeah?" One of the two was getting up.

I ducked down fast under the table in my booth, bent over and stuck uncomfortably in the dirty, dark space. I held my breath. My dimly lit retreat grew darker. A shadow from overhead. Fuzzi? Or his sidekick, blusterin' Bill? The floor was gritty. Unwashed. My hands pressed down on ossified French fries. It stank there, sour and sharp.

"Yeah, you're right." The shadow disappeared. I heard a thunk. It had to have been Fuzzi.

Should I stay here, I thought. My butt had to be visible from the aisle. If somebody passed by, or, Jesus, sat down at my booth! I worked my way up slowly back to my seat, afraid I might make the table move and squeak against the stone floor. I was nimble, or lucky, or both, because I was able to get back into my seat quietly, listening to them hiss a conversation as I did.

"I'm outta roofies," said blusterin' Bill.

"No can do, gotta make more."

"When?"

"Probably tomorrow."

"Why not tonight?"

"Parents still home. What am I gonna say? Hi, Mom. Hi, Dad. Just gotta pull stuff outta my room and go make some date-rape drugs in the basement. See ya in a few!"

"Goin' into the city for New Year's Eve. You'll have some for me?"

"Can't guarantee it. Score with Rags."

"Rags is gone until after the break. Skiing somewhere in Europe. Besides, your stuff kicks ass! Like, you wiped out that Margee skank."

"Fuckin' shut the fuck up, you fuckin' dick!" hissed Fuzzi.

I crammed myself back down under the table. I was shaking. I am now, just thinking about it. I felt this sudden surge of—rage, I guess. I mean, I had never felt it before. It was like I was getting, well, not numb, but lighter, all tensed. I felt almost outside myself. Not feeling my body, but ready to pounce, attack. I felt like I could break right through the table, the wall, between me and these two Neanderthals and rip into them. Literally.

The shadow came back. Hung over the table until Blusterer said, "Sit down. Whatta you lookin' for, the skank patrol? Feelin' guilty, mighty Joe Dick?" Blusterer snickered. The shadow disappeared. Clunk again as Fuzzi sat down.

I crept back up. Looked around. Nobody.

"So, whatta ya gonna do with her phone?"

Damn. Fuzzi had Margee's phone? So that's how he got my number. But wouldn't Mr. O. have had it turned off?

"Dunno. It went dead. But I copied out all her text numbers. 'Specially this KT bitch."

"Huh?"

"Probably her BFF. Definitely the bitch who 911'd on the frat."

"Yeah, and?"

"Well? Have ya heard anything about all the shit that went down? Huh? Nuthin'! Like, did Margee talk to this KT before she went veggie? Are the cops gonna nail my ass soon?"

"Yur paranoid, buddy. If they had sumthin' on ya, ya wouldda been taken in by now."

"Not so sure. Not so sure."

I had heard enough. So little Fuzzi wanted to meet me? Okay. I wasn't sure exactly what I was going to do at that moment, but I did know he was going to get his wish. Soon. I was still in rage mode. I moved quietly out of my booth and kept low, drifting silently to the end of the row of booths. I was now at least fifty feet away. A group of maintenance workers came into the food court. On break probably. I popped up, using them as a shield, and exited the union, brushing my hands clear of grot.

Now what?

I still had no idea what they looked like, only voices. That would be laughed out of any police station, trial, etc. Fucking lawyers. No justice, just sophistry. Okay, so I needed to act. I thought briefly about the fact that nothing had gone public from the Lammi disaster. Just lots of money changing hands, or about to. Hands wringing. Hands shaking. The O.s' hands full of money.

There was only one other way out of the food court: up the main stairs and past the main entrance. Fifty-fifty chance on how Fuzzi would leave, except the parking lot was in front of student union. I sat down in a chair close to the stairwell, pulled up my hoodie, and made like I was texting. It didn't take long. Fuzzi and blusterin' Bill exited the stairwell and pushed out the main door, laughing. They spoke. Clearly them. Voices now burned into my consciousness. Arrogant, snickering voices.

I waited a few seconds, got up, and followed. Into the parking lot in front of the building. Passed them as Fuzzi unlocked the door on the big-ass, old turdy car he was driving. Banged up right front fender. Maybe the dick had run over somebody's grandma. Ugly shade of orange. New York license plate: FUZ 2U. Didn't look up to catch the car itself. On the bumper, a pretty new parking-permit sticker for that dumpy little boat club on the Hudson, in our town!

"Goin' back home!" I heard Fuzzi shout out.

So Fuzzi probably lived in town, or close to it. Should I follow? No, too soon. Give it a few hours. So I did. Around three o'clock I started driving through our neighborhood. Three blocks over and six blocks down, there was FUZ 2U parked in a driveway: 75 Ridge Way. Back home, I pored over the local telephone book that gets thrown on the steps every year. Yeah. There it was. T. Fuznekza. 785-6723. So the spawn had parents?

Should I text him or wait for him to text me? He was going to cook up more roofies? Text him. Now. Give him incentive. Hang out bait and wait. I decided to read a little of Kati's diary. As I did, I went deep and dark into how I was going to end Fuzzi's life, googled "medieval torture," and then wikied into modern methods.

KT

KT to Fuzzi 756-818-2102
Hey, txt me. bord.

Dec. 29.

Thursday, May 20, 1897.

This evening, I sat with Mother Krieger, with Lessia in my lap, and took my first tatting lesson. She is so often napping now, her gaunt form fallen into the corner of the worn chair in her bedroom, where Gottlieb had previously languished, or her kitchen chair, where she sits closed-eyed toward Oxford Street Park, the failing sunlight shadowing her cheekbones as growing dusk fills her deeply recessed eyes with dark pools of coming night. She seeks to help about the house, but she cannot stand long and is too weak to scrub dishes and work laundry.

Waterboarding. Hmmm. What's dry drowning? Well, lots of pain, damage to major organs. Brain damage from oxygen deprivation. Oh, like HAI. Excellent. To me this Fuzzi is an extrajudicial prisoner.

I fear she is letting go. When she is sitting in the kitchen, she stares often now for long periods toward the park. I know she is thinking of Gottlieb, her life partner, by how she lightly touches and turns her simple gold band wedding ring with the skinny index finger of her right hand and smiles. I think she is feeling she will join him soon.

She holds her abdomen and quivers briefly now and then. She refuses to admit any pain. "Just a bit of gas," she insists. "Your excellent cooking." And then she will offer a compliment to the meal. Gus and I look into each other's eyes, worried. Gus asked her if she wanted the doctor yesterday. "Doctors mean death," she answered and dismissed his question with a wave of a hand and a scowl.

How quickly she is fading...

Sleep deprivation. Fatigue, clumsiness, bad effects on thinking. Not enough.

There is so much work, now with a flourishing garden, cackling hens, and a prosperous household, many chores, despite the help of Amelia, Elizabeth, and Gus, though Gus has been working extra hours, training as an assistant factory manager, and often arrives home when only I am still awake.

So this evening, with dinner dishes still to be washed and Tessie's children sent off to mind the henhouse and draw water to moisten the garden, I decided it was time to pick up a skill from Mother Krieger, and of all the wonderful old woman can offer me, none is dearer to my heart than learning, if only rudimentarily, the art of tatting. When I asked her, she smiled broadly, her eyes flashed with happiness, and she asked me to fetch her shuttle and some thread from the top drawer of her simple, splintered dresser opposite her bed.

Tatting, huh? Tats. Maybe I could "tat" Fuzzi, like all over his body. Real crappy stuff. In, like, day-glo colors. Especially his dick and balls. Solid, bright pink. This is not on the net. Maybe I should contact the CIA, for a fee.

Sound. Like what they did to Noreiga outside the Vatican embassy in Panama. History professor ranted about that my freshman year. Course, Fuzzi probably likes death metal.

"Watch me," she said, grasping the tiny oblong tool firmly in her animated hand. "We will start with an exercise I first learned from my mother, Margarethe, when I was ten." I know she tried to slow her work for me; still, it seemed so rapid I could barely catch her rhythm. Although it was still light in the kitchen, I lit a lamp and placed it on the nearby window sill to help me see her work. "Ring five

double stitches," she said in a light, sing-song lilt, "three picots." The metal shuttle flashed in her hand as she manipulated it so fluidly. "Then separate this with five double stitches, five more double stitches, close, turn, space. We call this the first ring in Hens and Chicks."

"I see," I answered Mother Krieger. "I see."

Mother Krieger laughed. "Would you like to see this again?"

"Yes, please."

I heard Amelia and Elizabeth clomping energetically up the stairs and into our apartment. They brought in several onions and announced that tomato seedlings had broken through the ground in the garden.

Solitary confinement. Had no idea there were so many terms for it. Hole, hotbox, punk city. Administrative segregation. Cute. Already used a lot in US prisons. Diminished impulse control as a consequence. Too late. Fuzzi's already there.

"Come here, ladies," I said. "Would you like to learn to make lace?"

"Yes, please," they said and gathered behind Pauline and me at the kitchen window facing the park. We patiently watched Pauline repeat her instructions several times more. Then I tried the exercise, exasperated at how clumsily my red, thick fingers fumbled the thread and botched the knots. Lessia followed my fingers and grasped toward the thread, making my efforts more challenging. Elizabeth followed, then Amelia. They were better than I, quick to absorb the instruction from Pauline. Intuitive in their imitation. Their first efforts came out whole, irregular, but whole. Mine looked to be the work of a drunken spider. I said so; we all laughed. Lessia cooed with us. Amelia tickled her lightly on her tummy. Lessia liked that.

We practiced Hens and Chicks together, alternating turns and producing an awkward run of several repetitions that nonetheless began to yield the promise of capturing whimsy and delicacy in lace. Pauline grew more animated and encouraged as our work proceeded, happy with our effort and devotion. Lessia lay quite patiently against me, watching our lace grow, her eyes following our work intently. It was then, after nearly an hour at her side, that I heard dishes move on the sideboard and turned to see Gus near the sink.

"Oh, how long have you been here?" I asked.

Pharmacological torture. LSD. Panic attacks and anxiety. How about paranoia? Fuzzi's probably already used it.

"Just arrived back," he said softly. "Go on. I'll eat and then work the dishes." He took the plate I had prepared for him earlier after Pauline and I had eaten, and sat at the far end of the kitchen table, watching us. He ate more quietly than normal; the lack of a clattering fork or sound of a knife grating off sections of beans or potato against the plate made his presence so unobtrusive that I turned several times as Amelia and Elizabeth took turns, to check on his progress. Gus was watching us as he ate, and he said once between chews as I looked at him, "Five double stitches, five more double stitches, close, turn, space!" We both giggled softly. Gus had never giggled before.

"Let me show some of my work," said Pauline. She handed me her shuttle. "I'm getting tired."

"Would you like a cup of tea?" I asked her. It had become her habit before retiring.

"No, not yet," she said. "Go to the top drawer of my dresser, to the right. Lift away the pillowcases, and bring me the small wooden box inside."

I went into her bedroom and did as instructed, bringing back a fine, rectangular box, fairly deep and wide, carved on top, if primitively, with a wreath of slender, indeterminate leaves surrounding a large, fat-petaled rose. When I placed it in her lap, she looked up at me and said, "My Gottlieb carved me this when I was fifteen." She gazed down at it, ran her fingers across the uneven depictions of the foliage, and said, "It was so, so long ago. And he was such a beautiful boy." I put my hand on her shoulder, so vulnerable and bony.

"It is very beautiful," I said.

I have to stop this. I have to be practical. I feel like Kati's somewhere around me. She's not happy with what I'm googling.

"Oh, nonsense!" she said. "Thank God he was a better weaver than carver, or we would have starved to death!" She sighed faintly, a nimble sigh balanced

between mirth and regret. Then she flipped open the box and began to show us some treasured work.

Such masterful work. She let me hold each piece.

A lovely star, small and fragile in gossamer thread of pure white. I held it up reverently across my palm. It was so light I barely felt it resting against my skin. Lessia reached out for it, and I lifted it well above her head to protect it. "That was to be on a pillow for Lina," said Mother Krieger.

A supple butterfly in redolent blue-gold interweaving, exceptionally balanced in color, its broad wings ready to bear it happily into flight. Tiny stars and delicate, cavorting fillips filled its span. "This would have been Mary's," said Pauline.

Pansies in yellow and lavender, small expressive faces centered among the petals in deep black. Four in number, bold and substantial, angling quickly to a firm, dark-brown stem. "For Fridericka."

Soft, flattened baby booties tatted of marvelously crafted loops and frilled edges. A miniscule rose crafted of almost imperceptible scarlet strands at each toe. "For Paulina." I remembered Gus's words at Leo's grave. "One for Leo," he had said. "And one for my dead brothers and sisters: Lina, Gottlieb, Mary, Fridericka, Rudolph, Adolph, Charles, Karl, Paulina, and Sofia."

What lay in that box, that tiny mortuary, for Sofia? I glanced back at Gus as Pauline returned the booties to their resting place. He sat motionless, his hands cupped before his mouth, looking sadly at his mother's hunched back. Our eyes met, and his were moist. He shook his head very slowly, and I knew he had no knowledge of those relics.

I turned back to Mother Krieger. "You will take care of these once I die?" she said.

"Of course," I said. I leaned over and kissed the tightly pulled-back steel-gray hair on the top of her head. "Of course."

"I am tired now," said the old lady, "I need to sleep."

I took the box from Pauline's hands and moved to the bedroom. Amelia and Elizabeth steadied Pauline at her sides and escorted her to rest. As we readied her for bed, I could see Gus's back as he pumped some water into the kitchen sink, steam rising from it showing he had already added hot water from the stove. Then, very quietly, he began to clean the pots, pans, and dishes.

Kati, why do you have to be so decent? Damn it! So moral and so noble. I'll stop! I'll do something. Something to catch this Fuzzi. No lawyering. No bargaining! And I think I have an idea. Meanwhile, get to your suffrage meeting, girl! Tatting! Really?

KT

Shuttle tatting was the original form of this handicraft. It first appeared in the early 1800s. In German, tatting is called *Schiffchenarbeit,* which translates roughly as the work of the little ship, since the word *Schiffchen* refers to the English word *shuttle.* The work itself is *l'art pour l'art,* with its sole purpose being a decorative effect on such items as handkerchiefs, pillows, and the like. Tatted articles such as doilies or booties were often produced purely as mementos and show pieces, as they would be damaged or destroyed by practical or constant use.

The work itself is a combination of chains and rings over a guiding thread. The double stitch is what we call a half-hitch knot. Spaces between these knots are called picots. The picots serve to space the stitches and provide locations for connection.

Kati became an expert tatter, inspired by her mother-in-law's work. Although she was able to benefit from only a few sessions under the tutelage of the doyen, she resolutely practiced at stolen hours and eventually had almost an entire cedar chest of fine, delicate lace work. I treasure her heirlooms, which I preserve to this day.

Cara Maurer

PS: Yes, I've got an idea. And where could Kati's lace work have gone? Maybe in those boxes left in the den? I so want to open them now. But no! Margee first. Come on, Fuzzi, answer my text! Is Pauline going to die soon? The cops will have to accept my plan.

KT

Fuzzi to KT 743-765-8040
Hi, KT how r u?

Dec. 30.

KT to Fuzzi 756-818-2102
Bord. U?

Fuzzi to KT 743-765-8040
Same. wanna get 2gthr?

KT to Fuzzi 756-818-2102
Yeah. How do i no u?

Fuzzi to KT 743-765-8040
frat bash. Howz bout 2mrw?

KT to Fuzzi 756-818-2102
Nu yrz eve? OK. earli. Got planz. Like coffee n bs?

Fuzzi to KT 743-765-8040
Sure. 1 or 2 or so?

KT to Fuzzi 756-818-2102
G8t. Koffee Korner near Main n Stella n town? 2 pm.

Fuzzi to KT 743-765-8040
G8t.

KT to Fuzzi 756-818-2102
Sending u a pic. So u no me.

Fuzzi to KT 743-765-8040
Wow. Thnx.

KT to Fuzzi 756-818-2102
How bout ur selfie?

Fuzzi to KT 743-765-8040
Sur. Here cumz.

Dec. 30.

Thursday, December 30, 2010.

Thank you, you dickhead Fuzzi, for texting me this morning and sending me your magnificently ugly little leering face, zits and all. Fuck ugly worm! I was able to get over to the police station by noon.

First, I stopped by Hudson to see Margee. It was early morning, about eight, and most of the other patients on the ward were eating, or taking meds, or already seated in the hallway, most of those talking to no one in particular as they lined up outside their rooms in new white linen gowns. There was noise: hollow clattering of plastic trays onto tables, chattering aides and nurses making rounds, doctors being paged over the intercom. The morning sun shone brilliantly through the east-facing windows on the left side of the hallway as I walked my way through the bustle to Margee's room.

"Oh, KT," said a familiar voice as I passed the nurses' station. I turned to see Della leaning over the counter edging into the hallway. "You're early. Visiting hours don't really start until ten."

"I've got a meeting with the police today," I said. "I don't know how long it will go. Please, can I see Margee?"

"Come here," said Della. "You need to know some things. I don't want you to go into her room and get startled."

I took a deep breath. I knew that what Della was going to say would upset me. "What's that?" I asked tersely, knowing Della was surely right and that I had to listen to her, but unsettled simultaneously, and resenting her disruption of my hopes, as her words must be.

"Let's take a little walk," Della said. She came up to me and took me by the arm and began to walk me away from Margee's room. "Everything's okay with you, I mean, the police and all?"

"Yeah, no problem there. Just a follow-up on Margee's case. Are Mr. and Mrs. O. there? Lawyers?" I hoped desperately it was something that simple.

"No," Della sighed. "Look, KT, last night, late, Margee had, well, an episode. She seized. Her parents were called in. It looked bad. Margee's stabilized, but she's slipping from us. Slowly. Her parents just left. For some sleep. They'll be back. You need to know she's DNR; that's do not resuscitate. Her breathing rhythm's irregular. We call it Biot's rhythm. Margee will take a number of shallow breaths, then stop breathing for a period of time, apnea. We think she had a stroke, major one, from lack of movement, maybe DVT, deep vein thrombosis. You following me?"

"Yes," I said. "She's going to die soon."

"Yes, I'm afraid so. Maybe it's good you came early today. Later, I'm sure there'll be her parents, maybe other family members, who knows who else."

"Death watch. How long do you think Margee has?"

"Could be hours, could be a few days. Are you okay?" Della put her hand on my shoulder and rubbed it lightly.

"No, but I'll be a soldier. For her. I promise."

"Good girl," said Della. "Just stay about fifteen minutes or so, no longer, okay?"

"Okay."

So we turned and walked silently back down to the nurses' station and Margee's room beyond. Della left me, calling out to a nurse at a meds tray across the hall. "This one's spending a brief time with Margee. Oh, and three twenty-seven, bed two, refused her Tylenol."

I walked down alone and crossed the threshold into Margee's room, dark and silent, blinds down and a small night light leaking weak illumination from a socket in the far corner. I looked at my Margee; her now gaunt form had fallen into the corner of the bed. She sat closed-eyed, her face toward the shuttered window. She was so ashen, and her cheekbones protruded prominently above the shadows blanketing the rest of her face, especially her deeply recessed eyes, pools of night.

"Oh, Margee," I whispered to her. "My dear Margee."

An ugly, obscene DNR sign hung crookedly over the top of her headboard. Her chest fluttered lightly. She continued to take quick, light breaths, imperceptible save for the slight motion of the smooth sheets covering her otherwise motionless body.

Then she stopped breathing. She lay there, mouth open, still and frozen, the texture of her face pale and glossy, doll-like. I waited, holding my own breath, waiting. I counted seconds as a child does playing hide-and-seek. One one thousand, two one thousand. I reached fifteen, and then Margee took a long, if thin breath. A faint, brief gurgle broke midway into it.

My Margee, bent like a comma in her overlarge bed. IV still dripping some palliative elixir into her purple-veined, skinny left hand limp above her covers. The knuckles on that hand and joints in her fingers bulging out waxen and knobby.

I lifted a chair up that stood in a corner and placed it as noiselessly as possible next to her. I sat down slowly and reverently. I brushed her hair gently from her forehead to the side. I whispered close to her ear. "Margee, it's me, KT." Margee took a deeper breath. Her lips parted faintly wider. Had she heard me? Or not, just her body slowly failing her. "It's after prom, Margee. Remember, we're down on the Jersey shore? Remember, Margee?"

Margee stopped breathing again.

"You're at the edge of a new ocean, Margee," I said to her lying so still there. "We don't know what it really is or where it brings us. We call it eternity, nirvana, death. It wants to wash over you, Margee, and when it does, it's okay to let go and join it. It's okay to let go and join it."

I leaned over and kissed her on that taut, slippery skin. On her forehead. Briefly. Tenderly. "It's okay to let go," I said again.

Before I left the room, I noticed that my little Christmas tree with the plushies leaned against the far corner of the window. I untied the Margee bear and placed it next to my girl's limp hand tied to the IV. I left head down.

I knew then I was a soldier for her. On a mission. I drove directly to police headquarters.

It was a beautiful morning today. Sky bright and azure. A gentle, cool breeze wafting up off the Hudson. Almost no cars on the road. As

I parked and locked the Beemer, I took in a deep, delicious breath of moist air promising spring, as days in New York irregularly can through the bitter stretch of bleak winter. This was one of them, undoubtedly originating from a front pushing up from the south and drawing its moisture in off the Atlantic only a few score miles to the south.

It refreshed me; it strengthened me with its soft yet supple promise.

I walked inside the police building to reception. There was that same unhappy cop at the front desk, behind this thick plexiglass. He asked me what I wanted. "I need to see Officer Bozel," I said. All he did was call back into the station. He didn't even look up after that, just kept typing something into his laptop.

"She's just getting off shift," he said. "Give her a minute."

Five minutes passed. Ten. The phone rang at the desk. "Yeah, okay, sure," said the cop. Then half an hour had passed. Some hunched-over little man in droopy pants and a flat, wide hat came in to complain about a traffic ticket. On Social Security, he complained. No money. The unhappy cop just told the little man he would have to go to traffic court to contest it. Bring a lawyer.

"Lawyer?" The little old man trembled. "I can't afford a lawyer." He went on about a sick wife, medical bills, the price of food and car insurance, hanging on to the narrow counter before him as he did.

Finally, the unhappy cop said, "Let me see the ticket."

The little old man pulled out a pink, crumpled slip from a wrinkled, faded overcoat and pushed it with difficulty, his hand trembling, into the tray under the thick plexiglass. The unhappy cop unfolded the document slowly, watching the little old man grasping the counter. The cop unfolded it sullenly, almost as though he was waiting for his complainant to lose his grip and fall to the floor. He then took a long, long time to read it.

He sighed. "Sir, you were driving the wrong way down a one-way street. That's very serious. Three points on your license. I suggest you pay the fine and be happy your license wasn't taken."

"Three points!" the old man fumed.

"Three points," echoed the officer flatly.

The old man shuffled out of the station, muttering to himself, slowly negotiating the several stairs to the street. I watched him go, anxious he would fall. After he passed out of view, I turned back to the unhappy cop. He was munching on a sandwich, tuna fish. Its heavy, overcooked, and oily smell made my stomach queasy. Or was it him, I wondered. I looked up at the clock behind him. Nearly an hour gone by.

The phone rang again. Mr. Charm said without looking at me, "You can go in now." I sprang up and walked quickly to the access door to the offices. I don't know if this cop, whom I was beginning to dislike deeply, toyed with me or not, but while I was still somewhat far from the entry-way, he hit the toggle to buzz me in. I hurried and lunged for it, but it switched off before I could grasp the doorknob. He was ignoring me! I had to ask, please, for him to hit the button again.

He sighed and did.

I really wanted to complain about him to Officer Bozel but let it slide. Enough to do. I worried only that if the others on the force were as cold and ignorant as he seemed, I might have made a bad plan, unlikely to get any reception there. After all, how much did I really know about this police force, their competency? If the unhappy cop at the desk was an example of it, maybe that was at least part of the reason nothing had happened, at least publicly, on Margee's case.

Officer Bozel sat at her desk. I sighed heavily as I sat down in that little, no-big-deal room, painted light green, no windows, just a messy bunch of desks with laptops in bins, and the smell of burned or stale coffee. After the tuna-fish smell, that acrid odor was not helping.

"How are you, KT?" said Bozel, smiling at her desk. "Please, sit down."

I had waited long enough. I was feeling nervous, uncomfortable, unsure, so I simply answered her directly. "I have information on the boy who roofied my best friend, Margee."

Bozel looked startled. "Oh?" she responded.

I sat down quickly and immediately related all that had gone on yesterday at the student union with Fuzzi and his sidekick, "blusterin' Bill," and this morning with Fuzzi's texts and my answers. It must have come out all right. Bozel immediately found a pen and began writing it all up on a yellow legal pad.

I told it all as it had happened but added a new detail. When I got to the part about sneaking out of the food court, I said that I got a good look at Fuzzi first by passing him and his friend with the maintenance workers, and then I waited for him out front.

Voice recognition in court, if it came to that? I knew who Fuzzi was. I was clear. No ferret lawyer was going to stop me!

"And," I said, "I have his picture. I'm meeting him tomorrow at two at Koffee Korner."

Officer Bozel sat back in her chair and stared at me. She dropped her pen onto the pad. A slight smile formed at the edges of her mouth. "KT," she said. "That's great work; I think we might have enough for a warrant for his home. But no way you're going to meet him tomorrow!"

"I'm setting him up for you," I said.

"I know," said Bozel, matronizingly. "But we'll set him up with one of our younger women on the force." She patted my hand. "Nice work, hon."

"KT," I said. "And you can't. He already has my picture. I'm the only one he's going to see there."

Bozel exhaled through rounded, pursed lips. "You—" she began and then stopped. She put her head between her hands and massaged her temples. Strands of her long, blond hair pulled out from her ponytail as her sharp blue eyes glowered at me. I met her stare. This time it was I who leaned in from the edge of her desk.

"My best friend is gasping for her final breaths at Hudson with an obscene DNR sign perched over her on her headboard," I said. "I do this."

Bozel collapsed back into her chair. "What do you know about police work?" she asked icily. "Some *Law and Order* episodes? Bang-bang. Shoot-shoot. Lawyers testifying in court and witnesses breaking down on the stand, KT? Really? Do you know how dangerous this asshole might be? Probably is?" She hissed, "The whole fuckin' world's an expert in police science today, including..." She stopped again. "Are you even twenty-one?"

I pulled out my driver's license and showed it to Bozel.

"Just," she grunted. "End of September last year!" She looked at me now more with exasperation than anger. "Stay here." She went down the hallway and brought back the police chief.

Talking with the police chief, Cody Greene, took over an hour. He was even more belligerent than Bozel, but I held my ground. He disappeared. Bozel stayed with me in that little ready room. I asked if I could go eat. I was hungry. I must have been making progress, I thought at that point, because instead of letting me go, they asked me if Burger King would be okay, and I got a Whopper with cheese, onion rings, and a chocolate shake courtesy of the town. Bozel ordered almost the same thing.

Bozel watched me eat as she did too. "Nervous, KT?" she asked.

"No, sir," I said. "Angry, and out for justice."

Bozel raised her eyebrows and began to rub her temples again. "Well, I'm nervous, sprout," she said. "You have no idea..." She stopped again. "I'm getting a headache." She huffed, irritated. "The headache you should be getting." But she finished her burger, some of her fries, and her soda before I did.

We tried small talk. It worked for a while, then awkward silence.

"What are we waiting for?" I asked.

"An ADA from White Plains," Bozel said. "That's an—"

"Assistant district attorney," I interjected.

"Yeah," said Bozel tersely.

"Can I finish your fries?" I asked.

Bozel pushed them over her desk to me, shaking her head.

About half an hour later, a young, lanky woman in a very Burberry gabardine trench coat, warm for the day, but I suppose the uniform of the county district attorney's office, broke brusquely down the hall and let her Bally briefcase fall near my feet. "Is this the one?" she asked Bozel, pointing backward to me without looking at me.

"Yes, I'm the one. Would you mind addressing 'her' directly?" I asked.

Young Miss Huff 'n' Puff turned. "Oh," she said. "Hmm."

I stood up. "Kaitlyn Cantori," I said. I reached over and took her hand, shaking it firmly. Huff 'n' Puff at first wanted to pull it back, but I held firm. "And just who are you?"

"Uh, ADA Rowell, Ms. Cantori."

"Nice coat," I said. "Burberry, no? Bally briefcase. I deduce you don't have any student loans."

"What the?" said Rowell.

"Look," I said, keeping on the offensive. "I don't like the way you walked in here. I'm giving you the opportunity to make a poster boy out of this Fuzzi character. Strike a blow for justice, you know? Get you a charge of at least depraved indifference, if not manslaughter, and, perhaps, just maybe, get you in on a date-rape drug ring that will sit nicely in the press."

Behind Rowell, Bozel broke into a wide grin, ear to ear. She nodded at me but pulled back the few remaining french fries and nibbled on them. "I told you she was unusual," Bozel said. "Sit down, Rowell."

Rowell sat.

"KT," said Bozel. "What do you know about 'wearing a wire'?" Bozel put the phrase "wearing a wire" in imaginary quotation marks with her fingers.

"It's no longer a wire," I said. "Powerful little transceiver. Practically invisible."

"What do you know about entrapment?" asked Rowell.

"Causing someone or inducing someone to commit a crime they would not otherwise have done," I said. "Factual deception could lead there."

"Oh, my dear little girl," sighed Rowell. "You have no idea."

She turned to Bozel. "I think it's too big a gamble."

Bozel gave Rowell an "are you sure" skeptical look and shrug.

Rowell said, "We can pick him up based on what Ms., uh—"

"Cantori," I said.

"Yes, what Ms. Cantori said." She looked at Bozel again. "See if we can shake something else out. Maybe get a warrant for the house..."

"Talk to me," I said, putting my fist down hard on the table. "It's my best friend near death at Hudson. It's my college laced with this roofie crap. It's my life I'm willing to hang out there publicly, to testify."

Rowell turned back to me, unhappy at being challenged.

"If you do what you want, Ms. Rowell, his lawyers will just attack my character. That I'm some raging party bitch out for vengeance for my girl. That I could not have heard what I heard. No other witnesses. All that line of crap."

Kati, if I had not gotten into your diary, your life, I don't think I could have done this. I know I couldn't. I am your legacy, and I must make you proud.

Rowell said, "And it's my office I'd be putting on the line, and if you fail, we'd look like idiots."

"You'll look like bigger idiots if I take this to the *New York Investigator* and it winds up on the newsstands and the net that you let this boy go."

"Are you—" started Rowell.

"I'm telling you what I'm going to do if you don't give us all a shot at this hump," I said.

Kati, how you stood up to Rau. To Siggi.

Bozel sat there, entranced. Behind Rowell's back, she raised a fist and pumped it briefly. "We'll get her set up tomorrow morning," said Bozel. Rowell turned around, fighting from two sides now. "It's your job to get a judge's approval for a wire. How about it?"

"I'll try," said Rowell.

"Try hard," said Bozel. "There could be unnamed sources corroborating KT's story."

So, eventually, I was allowed to leave, with a judge's permission given for my meeting with Fuzzi to be recorded, and got home just before Momz, at seven. I so wanted to tell her but knew I better not. She might squash everything. Bubble me in a cadre of lawyers. This is my war.

Well, with the help of Officer Bozel, our war, and, I suppose, even ADA Rowell's war. After all, she did get the judicial order: Bozel's write-up, the picture from my cell, the text exchange, our pressure, and whatever Rowell added got it.

There's a strange car parked on the street across from our house. Probably a cop. It's late. I'm tired, but I'm curious. Kati, don't let me down now with your suffrage thing. Go to the meeting, girl! Go!

A little Briscoe and Logan, then diary. Kati found more to think about than just the vote, and Cara gave me more to consider, along with Momz's comment, "When I wanted something more than just sex."

KT

Sunday, May 23, 1897.

I am glad that I went to the suffrage meeting this afternoon, but I am disquieted too. Such a gap between men and women that I had not sensed before. Would I ever have seen it, felt it, if I had not watched that parade just after New Year's? If I had not taken the pamphlet? And been repulsed by Siggi's ranting?

This time, I left Lessia sleeping and Gus picking beans. I simply said I was going to the Votes for Women meeting at the Turnhalle and blew him a modest kiss. He rose briefly from harvesting and waved his hand weakly. Should I wonder what he thinks? Should I really care? Did he step in at Tessie's out of respect for me, or out of paternalism? Me and my child, the vulnerable sex? I thought I had made the correct decision in marrying Gus. Had I?

I arrived in time for the full meeting. There were a few chairs, but most of us stood. I looked around but saw no familiar faces from the neighborhood. I had not expected any, and no one walked with me down to the hall from Garrison Street. They were all back home at Sunday activities, I suppose. Wendolin, the dyer, and Maria Walter. Wendolin sitting content in the backyard with his pipe and large belly, waving over the dividing fence to us on such a day as today was. Watching wife Maria hang up laundry on her poles. Calling over, "How are you all doing? How is Mrs. Pauline? Looks like you have some prize onions there!" Maria silent and smiling, laundry always out on a Sunday by two if the weather permits.

The Groegers to our other side. Joseph, the painter, and Elsa and their young children: Mary, Ester, and John. Joseph admiring and inspecting the swelling fruit on his cherry tree. Fed by chicken manure. The pollinated flowers having been set fast by the lead arsenate with which he dusted the fading blossoms in late April. Early bloom and harvest this year. Elsa brushing back her long blond hair with the heel of her hand as she exits their chicken coop with eggs for a light dinner. Mary and Ester content in a corner with two moppet dolls and a crude, make-believe stone table with tiny rocks for teacups. John clattering with a stick-sword around the lilacs fragrant and full, the rich, honeyed perfume from their outsized spikes drifting to our yard.

The Schwartzenbergs. Emil, the weaver, and Josephine. The Stignes. Joseph, the mason, and Teresa. Old like Pauline. But Joseph still working as he can. The Garrets. Charles, the carpenter, and Bertha. Four children in school: Mary, Charles Jr., Gertrude, and Gladys.

All the men with occupations. The children blithe and happily in the moment. The women keeping them all. Serving them all.

Inside the Turnhalle, the meeting commenced with the reading of the Preamble to the Declaration of Independence, leaving out the word "men." There was the usual beginning to any meeting: a call for any unfinished business from the last, the reading and approval of the minutes, and a reading of the financial report. Next, the chair, one Harriet Garret, rose in soft Sunday finery complete with a spray of red rose and pink gypsophila fresh against the white satin of her flowing dress. She exhorted all to attend next week for a march on City Hall.

Many clapped. I joined the applause.

Then, an older woman, named Clarissa, rose to speak. She had been a disciple, apparently, of a woman named Charlotte Gilman. Clarissa spent a good half hour reflecting on Gilman's ideas, especially on economics.

I strained at the back of the hall to hear her. She did not project well, but I did catch a number of phrases and ideas that have me thinking now. Clarissa called herself a humanist. I am not sure what that means, but she did say that she was a reform Darwinist, alleging the original scientist had only included male in the process of evolution, overlooking the development of the female brain. "There is no good reason for the continued assumption of male and female roles in society," she argued. "We are long past the time when belligerence in men and maternalism in women are constructive to society."

That drew large applause and cheers, and I, thinking of Willi, heartily took part.

"There is no such thing as a strictly male or female brain," she added. "Is there a male or female lung?"

Laughter and more cheers.

Then, Clarissa spoke about economics, economics of the household, and sex. From what I heard, I understood her to mean that a woman's survival in today's family meant she had to please her husband with sexual gifts to ensure his continued support of her. So, I thought, this meant marriage was religion's way of making prostitution a virtue? That troubled me, but I could not argue against her reasoning as I heard it.

More on the marketing of toys to inculcate children into accepting roles in society, as the games they played and the clothes they wore did also.

It was quite a lot for me to digest, and I noticed the applause growing more tentative as she progressed further into her speech.

At its end, however, she was cheered long and loudly. She offered for sale Charlotte's book: Women and Economics. *I had no money to buy it. But I did take a copy of a short story Charlotte had written, "The Yellow Wall-Paper," copies of which were offered free to all attending.*

As we left, the chairwoman, Harriet Garret, stepped into a chugging motorcar waiting for her at the curb in front of the Turnhalle. A motorcar!

Independence. Economic independence. How that could change my life! How that is necessary, I am beginning to think, to be what one wishes to be in full. Or is it? Harriet is obviously wealthy and immune to so much of what society demands of the average woman. I love my children, my Lessia and the one to come. I love my husband, I think. But is that because of who I am now and how I am now? And what if I change? What then, so thickly intertwined in the ties that bind? What then?

I am glad that I went to the suffrage meeting this afternoon, but I am disquieted too. So much to think about. I was glad, at home, to find a pile of green beans on the kitchen table and Lessia smiling at me as I picked her up. I mixed some of the beans up with onions and eggs for dinner and then prepared and put the rest up. It was late when I got to bed. Gustav was already asleep. He needed to be up for work early.

But so did I. I will march, I decided, as I lay beside him. Something impels me. Forward.

Charlotte Gilman was certainly not the first to consider the issue of sex and equality in an androcentric society in America. One of the early proponents of a divergent life structure, if an extreme one, was Mother Ann Lee of the nascent Shaking Quakers, or Shakers. Before her rise to eminence within the Shaker sect, she had a difficult, poverty-stricken youth and tragic marriage. Apparently uncomfortable with sex, she forestalled marriage until 1761, when her father forced her into marriage with an Abraham Stanley. All four of her children died in infancy. After arduous times and persecution in England, she immigrated to America with her husband, who then deserted her. Already, by then she and a small band of followers, who had come with her from England, were advocating the abandonment of marriage, while practicing celibacy and pacifism. Mother Ann considered sex a "lustful gratification." Tangentially, she thought it essential to pursue perfection in all the chores of life.

Mother Ann was given to revelations and visions, establishing herself as the core of the Shaker sect, who envisioned the imminent second coming of Christ as a female. Her doctrine led to the core habits of the various Shaker communities that sprouted in New England: equality between men and women and keeping them separated in labor and living arrangements.

This charismatic leader also suffered persecution here, including physical violence, which led to her early death at age forty-eight in 1784.

By contrast, Charlotte Gilman's propositions seemed mild. She was firmly convinced that lack of self-sufficiency contributed to mental, emotional, and physical illnesses for women. As a remedy, she proposed communal-style living open to both genders. Both would be afforded independence but enjoy the benefits of companionship and a social world. Marriage could occur within her structure, without compromise of individuality. Housekeeping, cooking, and childcare would be handled by others for pay, exempting women from those traditional roles except by free choice.

At the opposite pole of Mother Ann Lee stood free-love advocate Victoria Woodhull, who was the first woman to run for president of the United States in 1872. Free love was, and is, not the counterculture promiscuity practiced in hippie communes that encouraged multiple sex partners and fleeting relationships. Rather, it stood for freely entered-into sexual relations, meaning as an example no spousal rape, with a woman free to use her body as she saw fit. There was no place in this movement for government or ecclesiastical regulation imposing restrictions such as marriage, or punishment for adultery, birth control, or abortion. Woodhull would eventually back away from this social view.

There was a welter of proposals and demands to adjust the behavior of a male-dominated society in Kati's time, as there still are today.

Cara Maurer

Friday, December 31, 2010.

I was up early. Got to police headquarters by nine and got lectured by Rowell about entrapment and all that. Signed a bunch of documents exempting the county from liability should anything go wrong. Stuff like that. Read it quickly. Usual legalese bullshit designed to protect cowards' asses.

As we finished up, Rowell emphasized, again, "Better to be cautious. If nothing happens this time, maybe next."

"So this may turn into a 'mole' type of thing?" I asked, startled.

"If you're willing," said Rowell. Was she testing my resolve?

"Fine," I said. "Here comes Donna Brasco. But I'm not gonna get laid by that hole, or blow him."

That took Rowell back. "Of, of course not, course not," she stuttered. "Any time you feel threatened, back out."

"Would I have backup?" I asked. "In case I had to 'back out' of the rear seat of a car?"

"Let's just see how today goes," conceded Rowell. "Think about now."

Rowell wanted me to wait until they had spotted Fuzzi, "person of interest Henry Fuznekza," as they were calling him, enter Koffee Korner. "T." in the phone book must have been a parent. Theodore? Theresa? There would be a recording van, easy to hide, parked on busy, commercial Stella Street, and two teams of undercovers perched discreetly nearby. Neither Bozel nor Rowell would tell me exactly what that meant. "So I would not give myself away by looking at them," they said. Did that mean they'd be in Koffee Korner? I hoped not. You can spot cops easily. They try to fit in, like at frat parties, but usually they're just so obviously damned uncomfortable, and older.

"No," I said. "I want to be there waiting for him. Give him a little feeling I'm eager to meet him. Also, find a lonelier spot, if possible, to make him feel more comfortable talking."

"Oh, well, okay," said Bozel.

So there I was, quarter to two, nursing a large mocha frappuccino, or something like that, in Koffee Korner. I had actually gotten a little nervous and ordered "what you made her," while waiting in line at the counter, and now I was looking at a huge, cold strawberry-and-banana puree with coffee calorie bomb topped with whipped cream. I pushed a straw into it. Let it sit, the whipped cream melting and sliding to the edge of the tall, translucent KK beverage glass.

I had chosen a seat at a window table. It was colder there. No one else was in that row against the large plate glass, and only one other couple had just entered, a scrawny twentysomething and his nature-child girlfriend in an ugly, bright knit cap and scarf. No makeup. Toothy. Athletic, though.

"Hey, you KT?"

I looked up; there he was. Almost said, "Yeah, Henry," to Fuzzi standing opposite me.

Said, "Yeah, H—hi," and coughed a little, as if I had choked a bit on my monster drink.

"Fuzzi," he said, grinning. "Do ya like that? Is it good?" He sat down. Plop.

"Nah, too sweet. Was just curious."

"You the curious type?" asked Fuzzi. Damn, it didn't take him long to start grope-talking.

"Definitely," I said, smiling, taking the straw out of my drink and gently licking the cream off the end. "But I think I'd like a cappuccino, medium." I pointed to the drink with my straw and smiled at him. "Too cold. Too sweet." I giggled. "Way too large."

"Gotcha," he said, beaming at me and bending forward slightly. He took my hand in his and guided the straw back to his mouth. He lapped at it. Ewww. Weird boy! "You're right," he said. "I'll be right back." He placed my hand down on the table, rose, and almost ran over to the counter to order. I heard "Two medium cappuccinos." Hmmm. Same drink for him. Ingratiating, or just lack of imagination? He looked back at me. "Cinnamon?" he called out.

I shook my head. Waited. Watched. He seemed a little nervous for a casual meeting with a girl, since I assumed he had done this zillions of times before. Fuzzi kept leaning left, then leaning right, then talking toward the barista, who was answering him in one or two words, occupied with the coffee machine. His hands drummed on the counter. Meth? Was ol' Fuz-a-riffic cooking up more than roofies in his little home lab?

He jiggled the coffee cups as he carried them back to our table. As he brought mine in front of me, I took his hand softly and guided it and the drink gently down to the table. I looked up at him and laughed. "Careful, Fuzzi, I don't want to wear it! Late night?"

"Na, just meeting ya, ya know, introductions and stuff."

Oh, you lying troglodyte, I thought. You've had a hit already. I looked at him as he sat down. Yup, meth head. Skinny and pale. Acne. Hair, beautiful. Long red hair, neglected except for a quick comb through that left a bunch of knots. Green eyes that should have been accenting a ruddy face on this winter day on the close of the year, but instead are flickering over dark bags. Old blue fleece hoodie pilled with a small stain on the right chest pocket. No hat. No scarf.

How the hell was he still in school? Well, not my problem, now.

"So, uh," my little quarry began. Moment of silence. I jumped in.

"Just hangin' out until spring term starts. You?"

"Same." Oh, boy. Maybe he had two hits. I had to get him talking, without trapping him. This was becoming a challenge. Hmm, maybe get right to it? Make him feel like I was bored enough to want to play? Uck. With him? Uck, uck, uck. But this was for Margee.

"Kinda bored here. Not much to do. My BFF's in the hospital, gonna be there a while."

"Oh?" Oh? Got to work with that as a response? Oh? C'mon, man. Play with me. Damn, you started out fast; now you're just twitching in neutral.

"Yeah, she OD'd over at Lammi a while back. Been trollin' for a new BFF. Can't wait forever, ya know."

"How is she?" Uh-oh. What did he know? What was the word at the frat? Was this a test? Then, I looked at him. All the dishevelment. Those words at the student union: "before she went veggie."

"Yeah, well, a lot o' people hear she went veggie, say it too, but I visit her every day. Help feed her dinner."

"Yeah?" Fuz's eyes lit up. He grinned. Toothy. Yellow and crooked teeth. I had to look away briefly, out the window, as though I were interested in the traffic, or something.

"Yeah, but she's gonna need a shitload of rehab. Luv the girl, ya know, really did, but a girl's gotta have fun, and this'll be my senior spring."

"Loved her, huh? Had a thing?"

Oh, hot damn. An opening. Decided to see where this might go.

"Yeah, probably we were just LUGs, well, not just. Boys, too." That was awfully risky. But a meth head? The few synapses remaining might just light up and find one another across the deep space of an empty brain pan.

"So, whadda ya into now?" Bait taken.

"Got a new prospect for BFF. But she's a little uneasy. Just wants to spend time with me, and, well, I'm bi, and I'd like to introduce her to the other team."

"Loosen her up?" One more step. Time to drop back a little.

"Yeah, somehow. I'm so bored. How's the cappuccino?"

"Hot." Fuzzi took a small sip and looked up at me carefully with those darting eyes. "You're hot looking too," he said. Whoa, boy! Back in overdrive, huh? "What's your new BFF's name?"

"Annie Lee," I said.

"Asian?" Leapin' logic, meth man! Well, if that's gonna help you levitate the table. Oh, please don't ask me how I met her, because I'm not into any squirmy online chats and such.

"Yeah," I said. "Lives in the East Village."

Pause. Fuzzi caressed his coffee cup, smiling at it wistfully. Had to head off any sudden mental spasms from Fuzzi.

"She's comin' up later today. Metro North. Quiet little party at my place. Parents in Colorado. Just like to loosen her up a little."

"I could help," said Fuzzi, trying to be cool and leaning back in his chair, head cocked to the side, attempting a suave grin that looked more like the leer of an emaciated Jabba the Hutt.

"Really," I said. "She's lithe. Careful with her drinks. Health conscious."

"Well, if you invited me over, maybe we could work on her together." Careful, girl.

"How?" I asked.

"Alcohol's not the only way."

"Careful," I said. "Pills? My girl, Margee, got wonked with enough roofie to put her into deep space for the night."

"I didn't mean that, I swear," Fuzzi blurted out. "I thought she had only had a drink or two, and I just wanted to be sure she was, you know, relaxed. I only put two pills in her drink."

I pushed myself back from the table but stayed seated. Back far. That had to be enough. I stared at him. "You what? You did what?"

"I didn't mean it!"

"But you did it?"

"Yeah, I vegged her. Now, about Annie Lee."

"Margee," I said. "You roofied her?"

"Yeah, sorry. I roofied Margee."

Then, there at the edge of our table, stood the scrawny twentysomething and his nature-child girlfriend. She pulled me rapidly away from the table. Twentysomething had Fuzzi's head on the table. A cop in uniform was already scrambling through the door. Other customers were yelling and trying to get out.

"Henry Fuznekza," the twentysomething said, "You're under arrest for depraved indifference. You have the right to remain silent—"

Fuzzi started screaming. "What? What? You, you? Cunt! You fuckin' cunt! You set me up! Fuckin' bitch! Fuck you! Fuck you!" He lunged forward and head-butted the young undercover. Fuzzi was coming after me. I backed away, and his partner slipped in front of me. She dropped him with one kick. And then I saw it. A large, gleaming knife. A bowie knife. It slid across the floor and stopped at my feet.

The young woman picked up the screaming Fuzzi, now yelling about police brutality. "And also," she said calmly, "you're under arrest for assault on a police officer with a deadly weapon."

"I know my rights," screamed Fuzzi. "Entrapment. Entrapment."

"Even if it was," said the young man, rising slowly and holding his groin, "that knife will get you a home in Sing Sing."

Fuzzi shut up.

By then, there must have been at least six cops in the coffee shop, and more were arriving every second. Fuzzi got scrummed. I was taken out. Officer Bozel was there. "You did great," she said. "We got him good." She slapped me on the back.

Tears welled up in my eyes. Bozel looked at me anxiously. "Don't worry," I said. "I'm not gonna snot gob your uniform again."

We both laughed. Then I cried. Briefly.

KT

Friday, December 31, 2010. Very late.

I guess it's really New Year's. The town fire signal went off. A few fireworks. I probably won't sleep much tonight. I keep seeing that knife at my feet. Fools rush in, I guess, and I sure rushed in. But it was for Margee, and I'm proud of what I did. Would I do it again?

Yes, without hesitation. I suppose that makes me brave?

After debriefing at police headquarters, which took several hours, I left by a back door; there were some reporters and a TV truck with that silly dish on its roof out front. So what? I get my fifteen minutes of fame, or notoriety, early in life. No regrets.

But I had to get to Margee. I had to tell her, before it was too late. Before she slipped away from me, as I had told her it was okay to do. I don't remember the drive up Main Street to Route 7. I don't remember any of the familiar traffic lights along the way. Parsons Street. Keepman Avenue. St. Paul's Hill. Not parking in the visitors' lot at Hudson. Not the walk to Margee's room.

I just remember entering her room. Too late. Having slipped between an aide in pink and a nurse in white at her door, and seeing my Margee, my Margee's body, all wrapped up in a sheet, still and stiff like a mummy, I froze. There were others there. Medical types. I ignored them.

All the machines and IVs were gone. There was only the bed, the obscene DNR sign atilt atop the headboard and my Margee's shrouded body left in the room: pale, bright, and yellow-white in the light from the falling winter sun surging in coldly through the rattling window behind me.

Early reports from Fuzzi's arrest in town must have reached Hudson. No one in the room tried to escort me out. They shifted back as I walked up to the edge of her bed.

I stood there. I sniffled. A few tears rolled down my face. "Oh, Margee," I said. "I'm so going to miss you." I didn't care what the mass of pink, blue, green, and yellow uniforms thought as I continued. "I hope you were on that beach, girl, as you passed. Remembering after prom, Margee. Us down on the Jersey shore late afterward, giggling quietly as Billy and Jed called out our names frantically, thinking we were lost. Remember, Margee, our bare feet splashed by the lapping waves, damp as we lay in our wrinkled dresses on the beach. The moon was lying just at the edge of the sky over the ocean. Light from coming dawn slowly overwashing it. Holding hands.

"You've reached the edge of a new ocean, Margee," I said. "I don't know what it really is or where it brings us. We call it eternity, nirvana, death. But you know. It washed over you, Margee; you've joined it."

I leaned over and kissed the taut, slippery sheet. Just where her forehead must have been. Briefly. Tenderly. "I'm glad you let go," I said. "Good-bye."

KT

Saturday. January 1, 2011.

I spent much of the night thinking about many things. A lot unresolved. But I'm going to keep up this dairy. Also, I'm going to read Kati's to the end. I have to. So many questions. How many children do Kati and Gus have? Which one am I descended from? What about Cara's misplacement of the Tomkins Square riot? Her having Lillie Blake's daughter teaching at the wrong school? That forboding observation about Kati and Gus having their aspirations dashed! I so hope Cara is just embellishing Kati's story and not twisting or inventing parts of it.

Does Kati become a suffragette?

I'm going to find a paying career—how about Chief Cantori? The town's never had a woman as police chief. It's way past time. If Bozel doesn't beat me to it. More power to her!

I feel strong. I already feel placed beyond this HIV thing. Healthy and free, somehow. And even if I do test positive this January, February, March, or June, I can be treated. I will be productive. And I will sue the shit out of Ken.

I'm dedicating my diary to Margee. I'm going to write up our whole, silly, grand friendship as part of it. After all, that is how we live on, in how others remember us and how we spur others to act, isn't it. Duh! Some of us wake up late.

Thank you, Margee. Thank you so much! I hope someday to be as gutsy as Kati.

Poor Momz. She was just a bewildered mess yesterday evening. She insisted on getting me legal counsel. That's okay. They'll be my counsel, but counsel only. Decisions, as they arise out of this Fuzzi thing, will be mine.

To calm her down a bit, we began to open those six mystery boxes I had hauled down to the den. We got to box three. No original diary yet. Tomorrow we finish the job. If I do find Kati's original diary, I'm adding learning German to my list of to-dos. Sorry, Cara. Got to find out for myself. I also hope the photograph of Kati is there. The one Cara described in her introduction: an older Kati set in an oval frame. Facing right, gazing off calmly and proudly, with the hint of a smile, just a hint, keeping her face attractive. Her hair, auburn and stylishly set with a deep-yellow ribbon woven carefully through it behind her ears, with a modest forehead curl stopping about an inch above her eyebrows. A high-necked, ruffled blouse positioning itself staidly between the light-blue lapels of a coat of some sort. She would be wearing no earrings. Her blue eyes focused far away contently, but offered no hint as to what she was contemplating.

Guess what I found in the second one?! A fine, rectangular box, fairly deep and wide, carved on top, if primitively, with a wreath of slender, indeterminate leaves surrounding a large, fat-petaled rose. When I placed it on my lap, I looked up at Momz and said. "Gottlieb carved this for Pauline when she was fifteen." I gazed down at it, ran my fingers across the uneven depictions of the foliage, and said, "It was so, so long ago." In it I found a lovely star, small and fragile in gossamer thread of pure white. It was so light, I barely felt it resting against my skin. Pansies in yellow and lavender, small expressive faces centered among the petals in deep black. Four in number, bold and substantial, angling quickly to a firm, dark-brown stem. Soft, flattened baby booties tatted of marvelously crafted loops and frilled edges. A miniscule rose crafted of almost imperceptible scarlet strands at each toe.

Lastly, a supple butterfly in redolent blue-gold interweaving, exceptionally balanced in color, its broad wings ready to bear it happily into flight. Tiny stars and delicate, cavorting fillips filled its span. "This would have been Mary's," I said.

"What?" asked Momz.

"But what about Sofia? Where is Sofia's gift?"

Momz just shook her head. "You've lost me," she said.

"I'll explain later," I told her. "Let me pour you a glass of red!"

I'm so glad I'm such a lazy bitch that I dawdled on getting a new phone.

Kaitlyn Cantori

ABOUT THE AUTHOR

G. W. WAYNE IS A NATIVE New Yorker who recently moved to Virginia. The recent events in Charlottesville inspired the author to speak out against fascism and the world's many other evils. This new novel is based on the story of the writer's immigrant family and the rights we must work hard to win and keep.

MAR – – 2019

97201689R00126

Made in the USA
Columbia, SC
10 June 2018